FRESH FRUIT & AMMO
BOOK THREE OF
ABNER FORTIS, ISMC

P.A. Piatt

Theogony Books
Coinjock, NC

Chris Kennedy/ Theogony Books
1097 Waterlily Rd.
Coinjock, NC 27923
https://chriskennedypublishing.com/

Publisher's Note: This is a work of fiction. Names, characters, places, and incidents are a product of the author's imagination. Locales and public names are sometimes used for atmospheric purposes. Any resemblance to actual people, living or dead, or to businesses, companies, events, institutions, or locales is completely coincidental.

Cover Art and Design by Elartwyne Estole.

Ordering Information:
Quantity sales. Special discounts are available on quantity purchases by corporations, associations, and others. For details, contact the "Special Sales Department" at the address above.

Fresh Fruit & Ammo/P.A. Piatt -- 1st ed.
ISBN: 978-1648552267

"My center is giving way, my right is in retreat; situation excellent. I shall attack."

General Ferdinand Foch, French 9th Army

DINLI

DINLI has many meanings to a Space Marine. It is the unofficial motto of the International Space Marine Corps, and it stands for "Do It, Not Like It."

Every Space Marine recruit has DINLI drilled into their head from the moment they arrive at basic training. Whatever they're ordered to do, they don't have to like it, they just have to do it. Crawl through stinking tidal mud? DINLI. Run countless miles with heavy packs? DINLI. Endure brutal punishment for minor mistakes? DINLI.

DINLI also refers to the illicit hootch the Space Marines brew wherever they deploy. From jungle planets like Pada-Pada, to the water-covered planets of the Felder Reach, and even on the barren, boulder-strewn deserts of Balfan-48. It might be a violation of Fleet Regulations to brew it, but every Marine drinks DINLI, from the lowest private to the most senior general.

DINLI is also the name of the ISMC mascot, a scowling bulldog with a cigar clamped between its massive jaws.

Finally, DINLI is a general purpose expression about the grunt life. From announcing the birth of a new child to expressing disgust at receiving a freeze-dried ham and lima bean ration pack again, a Space Marine can expect one response from his comrades.

DINLI.

* * * * *

Prologue

United Nations of Terra (UNT) Fleet Frigate *Nelson* slipped out of warp space near the Redshift Jump Gate. *Nelson*'s captain, Commander Ruud de Haan, breathed a sigh of relief as the nausea passed, and he was able to unbuckle his harness. He'd been through the jump gates many times, but he never got used to it.

A voice crackled in his headphones.

"Captain, sensor three. Unidentified object bearing two niner zero, green thirty, range two zero zero and steady."

In a three-dimensional battlespace with no true compass heading, all contacts were reported using relative bearings. "Two niner zero" meant the contact was just forward of *Nelson*'s port beam. "Green thirty" told de Haan that it was thirty degrees above *Nelson*'s deck level. "Range two zero zero" meant the contact was two hundred kilometers distant, and "steady" meant the range and bearing were constant, so the contact was traveling parallel to *Nelson*.

Too close.

De Haan forgot his physical discomfort as he tapped the command screen to bring up the contact information.

"Visual?"

"Affirmative, sir. Sending it to the big screen."

The largest screen on the Command Display Array that covered the forward bulkhead of the operations center came to life. There was a collective gasp in the command space as the unidentified object came into view, and de Haan's mouth went dry.

It was a spacecraft, long and lean, with vaguely familiar lines. Enormous engines perched atop the fuselage and sleek weapons pods hung under the wings. The craft was matte gray and there were no identifying markings.

Stunned watch standers broke into conversation around the operations center.

"That's incredible!"

"I've never seen anything like it!"

"One of ours?" an anonymous voice asked over the internal circuit.

"No way. That's not a Fleet vessel. It's an alien craft!"

De Haan felt a surge of anger at the unprofessional reaction among his crew. "All stations, this is the captain. Maintain circuit discipline and mind your consoles. Sensor Operator, designate the contact as Unknown One. Initiate laser tracking."

The operations center watch snapped out of their shock and went into action to evaluate and identify the contact.

"Captain, Intel. The profile doesn't match any spacecraft in the database. Highest confidence ID is twenty-eight percent for a *Union*-class destroyer."

"I sailed on a *Union*-class. That's no *Union*," replied the captain. "Signals, are you getting anything?"

"Captain, Signals. Negative, no emissions detected on any spectrum."

"Comms?"

"No response on the standard hailing circuit, sir."

"Captain, Weapons. Do you want me to designate Unknown One for weapons engagement?"

"What? No! Negative! Unknown One has not displayed hostile intent. Weapons are tight, release on my command only. Self Defense, be ready to throw up shields and fire a full spread of countermeasures."

"Defense, aye."

De Haan's pulse pounded as he stared at the display screen while the two vessels cruised side-by-side through space. Unknown One hadn't reacted to their presence and he had a fleeting thought that the vessel might be some weird anomaly, perhaps a reflection of *Nelson*, created by their passage through the gate.

No, this thing is real. Maybe it's a derelict. But whose?

"Captain, Sensor Three. Unknown One is turning away, range two five zero."

He watched as Unknown One pivoted until it was pointed back the way they'd come.

"Unknown One is accelerating, sir."

Back toward the jump gate.

Unknown One became a streak of blue light as it reached jump speed, and then it was gone.

"Captain, Sensor Three. Lost contact on Unknown One. Estimate the contact passed through the Redshift Jump Gate."

"Very well. All stations, this is the captain. Preserve all records in accordance with my Standing Orders. Intel, collect everything and let's get started on a detailed report. Fleet Command will want everything we have."

"What do you think it was, Captain?" Ayoki Nakitomi, de Haan's executive officer, asked over the private command circuit.

De Haan breathed a sigh of relief and relaxed his grip on the arms of his chair. He realized his uniform tunic was damp with sweat. The Fleet protocols for what *Nelson* had just experienced suddenly seemed grossly inadequate.

Should I have engaged?

He fought to keep the nerves out of his voice.

"I don't know, XO, but if I had to guess, I'd say we just made first contact."

* * * * *

Chapter One

"It took us three thousand years to find an intelligent species among the stars and only three months to pick a fight with them."

The group of junior International Space Marine Corps (ISMC) officers gathered in the Second Battalion intelligence space chuckled. Major Anders, the battalion intelligence officer, shook his head.

"You guys can laugh, but that's what happened." He tapped his keyboard, and a large blue question mark holograph appeared over his desk. "As you're all aware, eighty-seven days ago, Fleet Frigate *Nelson* had a remarkable encounter with an unidentified vessel near the Redshift Jump Gate." Another tap on his keyboard, and an image of the alien vessel replaced the question mark.

"*Nelson* and Unknown One traveled on a parallel course for approximately five minutes before the unidentified vessel turned back toward the jump gate and disappeared.

"After the captain reported the encounter, *Nelson* continued on her mission to investigate a report by the Terran civilian vessel *Repose* that they were under attack by an unknown craft in vicinity of Balfan-48. When they caught up with the *Repose*, *Nelson* discovered the engines had been destroyed by precision weapons fire and the vessel had been abandoned. They observed damage to the hull around the main hatch that indicated a boarding pod had been attached.

"*Nelson* reported all of this and requested further orders. Then she vanished."

"Pirates, sir?" asked one of the gathered lieutenants.

"Pirates might have attacked *Repose*, but *Nelson*? Unlikely. Even well-armed pirates would have a hard time taking down a Fleet vessel like *Nelson*. It almost sounds like the *Imperio* incident all over again."

Imperio was the Fleet Academy training ship that disappeared without a trace a year earlier with the entire junior and senior classes aboard. Three thousand cadets and Fleet personnel, gone.

"Maybe they swarmed her."

Anders shrugged. "Sure, an unexpected swarm attack is possible, but we've never observed pirates operating that way. An attack on a Fleet frigate carries a lot of risk without much reward. We can speculate, but without additional information, it's all guesswork."

Second Lieutenant Abner Fortis raised his hand. "Major, why was *Repose* in that sector?"

"Good question. *Repose* was the flagship of the Science Church fleet, and she was loaded with pilgrims seeking out a planet to call their own. They must have discovered something in the Balfan Belt, but if they did, they didn't report it to us.

"The simple fact is, we don't know what happened to *Repose*, or to *Nelson* for that matter. Fleet deployed scout drones to the vicinity of where they reported their discovery of *Repose*, but nothing was found of either vessel. Any discussion of events after that is just speculation."

A tall first lieutenant seated in the back of the room stood up as if to challenge Anders. "Major, it's obvious that *Repose* and *Nelson* fell victim to Unknown One or other ships in its fleet."

"Let's not get too far ahead of ourselves, shall we?" Anders tapped his keyboard, and a bullet list replaced the image of Unknown One. "Here's the sum total of what we know so far. *Repose* reported an attack. *Nelson* deployed to investigate and encountered an unidentified spacecraft, after which she disappeared. Are those events related?

"The unidentified craft encountered by *Nelson* was piloted by a race we have since begun to call Maltaani for the Maltaan System, near where *Nelson* had their encounter. We have the information contained in *Nelson*'s report, from which we've inferred that the Maltaani have technological abilities similar to our own, at least in the field of space travel.

"We have since detected a fleet of unidentified spacecraft, presumably Maltaani, operating in the vicinity of Balfan-48. An intelligence probe sent back imagery of a military force on the surface before it stopped reporting. All subsequent missions have failed to report or return."

The first lieutenant wasn't deterred.

"This unprovoked aggression cannot go unanswered, Major. Our landing on Balfan-48 is entirely justified. If they want a fight, we'll give it to them."

Murmurs of agreement swept through the room.

"That's the opinion of the commanding general," replied Major Anders. "Move and countermove, and God help us if we're wrong. However, it's possible that we provoked them in some way which we don't yet understand. Perhaps *Repose* or *Nelson* did something to instigate a confrontation." He shrugged. "Whatever the reason, it seems we are bound to confront them ourselves. Based on *Nelson*'s report, the Maltaani are capable of using our jump gates, which makes them a significant threat to Terra Earth. Our mission is clear: prevent an unknown enemy from establishing a base near the Redshift Jump Gate. Like it or not, Ninth Division has the job."

"You're not afraid, are you, Major?" sneered the lieutenant.

Fortis expected the major to put his challenger in his place, but Major Anders only rubbed his chin thoughtfully.

"I'm not afraid, son. I'll be here while you're down there, fighting an enemy that we know almost nothing about."

The brief devolved into a series of theories, each more unlikely than the last. Fortis was relieved as the attendees trickled out of the room until he was alone with Major Anders.

Anders smiled as he logged out of the computer. "You're becoming popular, Fortis."

"I don't understand, sir."

Anders swept the vacant room with his arm. "You don't think all of these eager young officers crowded in here to listen to me, do you? They came for you."

"For me? I didn't bring anyone, Major. I saw your brief on the daily schedule and wanted to hear what you had to say. I was surprised to see all those guys here. I don't know most of them, to be honest."

"Fortis, before you reported to the battalion, I used to sit here all day alone with my thoughts. None of the junior officers, and damned few of the senior ones, cared about intelligence. Now that they've discovered *you* attend my briefs, *they* attend my briefs."

Anders saw the confusion on Fortis's face.

"Since your arrival to Ninth Division, you've won the *L'ordre de la Galanterie* for your actions on Pada-Pada, and you earned your kukri *and* the crimson handle." He laughed and threw up his hands. "Hell, most of the officers in the division haven't even earned a kukri, much less the crimson handle. You're practically a cherry, yet you walk around looking like a war hero."

ISMC custom dictated that only combat veterans could carry a kukri, and a Space Marine earned the crimson handle if he killed an enemy with it.

"I didn't ask for any of this—"

Anders cut Fortis off with a raised hand.

"Don't get defensive. I think it's great. I get to brief real audiences, and maybe some of the other officers will use their heads for something other than a place to carry their helmets. Frankly speaking, if not for your court martial, I believe you'd be a first lieutenant already."

Fortis winced at the mention of his court martial but remained silent.

"What I'm trying to say, Mr. Fortis, is that the other lieutenants emulate you in hopes of improving their own chances for recognition and promotion. By doing so, they risk accidently becoming better officers. Even that arrogant prick first lieutenant who is truly in need of a slap down. It doesn't matter whether you asked for it or not, they follow your lead."

The lieutenant shook his head and gingerly rubbed the pink skin of his newly healed scalp. "I'm a biodome engineer," he said with a wry smile. "I joined the ISMC to pay off my student loans."

The two men locked eyes. Anders snickered, Fortis snorted, and soon the two men were laughing together.

"DINLI, Fortis," Anders sputtered as he slapped the lieutenant on the shoulder. "Go get ready for your jump, and good luck."

* * *

ortis navigated his way out of the battalion spaces on his way to find Corporal Ystremski and Third Platoon. He was deep in thought and stopped just short of colliding with another Space Marine officer in the passageway.

"Uh, excuse me sir, er, ma'am. I apologize, my mind was elsewhere."

The other officer, a female captain, glared at him before she read the nametape sewn on his uniform.

"You're Fortis? Third Platoon, Foxtrot Two-One?"

"Yes, ma'am."

"My name is Captain Witzke. I'm the new commander of Foxtrot Company."

Fortis didn't know whether he should offer to shake her hand or not, so he remained silent. Her hostile demeanor puzzled him.

Witzke eyeballed him for a long second.

"I know what you did, Fortis."

He stared back in surprise. "What I did? What did I do?"

"Tim Reese is a friend of mine. We went to the Academy together. You fucked him."

"I didn't fuck him, ma'am. I wasn't even here when he left. You have the wrong guy."

Captain Reese had been the Foxtrot Company commander when Fortis reported aboard. He was reassigned to battalion administrative officer for his leadership failures when Fortis and two platoons were trapped on Pada-Pada.

As the battalion admin officer, the captain buried Fortis in an unending avalanche of paperwork. Most recently, Reese misrouted Third Platoon to Eros-28 out of spite while the rest of the fleet went to Eros-69 for liberty. When the battalion commander, Colonel

Sobieski, found out, he fired Reese on the spot. The colonel then initiated Reese's immediate transfer to a logistics job on Terra Earth.

Fortis had heard the stories when he returned to the flagship, but he wasn't sure what to believe. Reese was gone when he got back aboard the flagship, and he was glad the captain was off his back.

Until now.

"Captain, I had nothing to do with Captain Reese's transfer. I went where he ordered me to go, and, when I got back, he was gone."

Captain Witzke glowered at him. "You don't fool me, Fortis. You think you can get ahead by stabbing your superiors in the back, but I'm onto your game. I've seen it played a hundred times by far better officers."

She turned on her heel and strode up the passageway while Fortis stared after her, speechless.

* * * * *

Chapter Two

Fortis caught up with Corporal Ystremski in the Foxtrot Company spaces.

"Hey, LT, did you hear the news? We have a new company commander."

"Yeah, I just met her."

Ystremski smiled. "Pretty impressive, eh? For an angry warthog, I mean."

Fortis ushered the corporal into the company XO's office and closed the door. "Don't talk about a superior officer that way. You know better."

He told Ystremski about his encounter with Captain Witzke.

"For some reason she's already got it in for me, and I don't want to give her any excuses."

Ystremski shrugged. "I don't think it's going to matter for either one of us, LT. She brought her pet gunny with her, so while she's climbing up your ass, he'll be up mine. It's just a matter of time."

"What do you know about her?"

"She's been with the same mech company since she graduated from the Academy, and she got promoted to command the company. My buddy over there said she's a micromanager and a screamer, but she gets the job done so the chain of command lets it go. They sent her over here to get some experience with the infantry before they promote her up the battalion staff ladder, I guess."

"Her gunny, Clay Parker, was a sergeant with me back in the day. He was an ass kisser then, and I don't imagine he's changed much."

As if on cue, there were three sharp raps on the door and a slender Space Marine gunnery sergeant with a tight haircut and a bristly mustache entered the office. His utilities fit perfectly and the creases looked sharp enough to slice bread.

"Sorry, lieutenant. I'm looking for the XO's office."

"This is it, Gunny." Fortis gestured around the cramped space. "Standing room only. What can I do for you?"

Ystremski said. "Lieutenant Fortis, allow me to introduce Gunnery Sergeant Parker. Gunny Parker, LT Fortis."

The two men shook hands and then Parker turned to Ystresmki.

"Still a corporal, I see."

"Third time's the charm. Still a gunny, I see."

Parker puffed up as tall as he could and leaned toward Ystremski. "I'm *your* gunny. You might want to keep that in mind, *Corporal.*" He practically spat the last word.

Fortis got the sudden urge to step between the two men to prevent a fight, but at that moment, Captain Witzke stuck her head in the door.

"Ah, Gunny Parker, you found it. Hello, Fortis." She displayed none of the venom from their previous encounter. Her eyes landed on Ystremski.

"Do you have business here, Corporal?"

"No, ma'am, I just stopped by to see how Lieutenant Fortis's wounds were healing. We have a big drop in three days, and we're gonna need him."

"Hmm. Well, he looks fine to me, so carry on. Grab-ass on your own time."

"Aye, aye, ma'am." Ystremski executed a parade ground-perfect facing movement and squeezed past her into the passageway.

"Fortis, I told Gunny Parker to set up shop in here as the company gunnery sergeant," Witzke told Fortis.

"Sure thing. I'll move all my stuff to this desk here—"

"No. That's not what I meant. This is Gunny Parker's office now."

Fortis blinked in surprise. "Yes, ma'am. Where do you want me to move the XO's office?"

Witzke's face darkened, and her eyes narrowed.

"Are you stupid, Fortis? The XO's office stays here. The gunny is moving in."

Her response confused Fortis, and he felt his neck growing hot. Parker stifled a snort, and he had a faint smirk on his face.

"Ma'am, I'm sorry, but I don't understand—"

"For fuck's sake, Fortis! I don't need an XO to run an infantry company. If I need help, I have Gunny Parker. Go back and play Space Marine with Third Platoon. Get out!"

Lieutenant Fortis was angry and happy at the same time, and he fought to conceal his smile as he gathered his Third Platoon paperwork and left the XO's office.

No more acting XO!

The previous company CO had pressed Fortis into service as the acting XO. It was a job normally filled by a first lieutenant, but Fortis was the only other commissioned officer in the company, so he got the job. It had all the headaches and none of the pay of the higher rank, and it had exposed him to constant harassment by the battalion admin officer. It was a heavy load for a brand-new officer, and Fortis had worked hard to keep up.

Now, with one hasty decision, Captain Witzke had freed him from all that.

Fortis allowed himself to smile as he dropped his paperwork on the desk in his stateroom and checked his watch. Twenty-five minutes to evening chow.

Twenty-five minutes with absolutely nothing to do.

* * *

After an uncharacteristically leisurely meal, Lieutenant Fortis went to his stateroom to rest. His left arm ached from the deep antibiotic injections he'd received after the wounds he sustained on Eros-28 had become infected. The battalion surgeon insisted that Fortis use his arm as much as possible, so he left the sling in his stateroom and gritted his teeth.

The doctor was impressed by the work done by platoon medics Cowher and Durant to treat the dueling sword slashes on his cheeks. It had only been a few days since his fight with the mercenary leader on Eros-28, but the wounds were almost completely healed. The doctor assured him that dermal abrasion whenever Fortis returned to Terra Earth would make the scars almost invisible.

Fortis leaned back in his chair and closed his eyes. An image of the mercenary Mikel Chive flashed into his mind, sword overhead, lips peeled back in a snarl of rage. His memory replayed the finale in slow motion: the Kuiper Knight charged, Fortis ducked low and sidestepped, and then he delivered the crotch-to-throat killing blow with his kukri.

Fortis was no stranger to violent death. He'd seen plenty of it on Pada-Pada, but that was the impersonal killing of troops in enemy uniforms. The fight with Chive had been different; it was personal, and it was in the forefront of his thoughts by day and dreams by night. He could still feel the dead man's hot blood on his face and hands, and the smell of ruptured viscera clung to his nostrils.

"LT?"

Fortis blinked his eyes in surprise when Corporal Ystremski's voice snapped him back to consciousness.

"Hey, Corporal."

"Sorry, sir, I didn't mean to intrude on your nap."

"I wasn't—" A big yawn took Fortis by surprise, and he chuckled. "Okay, I might have been napping. What's up?"

"Good news. I just talked to Gunny Parker. Captain Witzke wants the entire company to rehearse drop ship landings first thing after muster tomorrow. Full battle rattle."

"DINLI."

"Yes, sir."

"I have some actual good news. Witzke decided she doesn't need a company XO, so I'm back to being just a platoon commander."

"Hey, that's great. Congratulations."

"She said if she needs help, she's got the gunny."

"That's not so great, but it sounds about right."

"What is it with you and Parker? Is there something I should know?"

Ystremski shook his head. "Old history. Like I told, you we were sergeants together. He was something of a headquarters commando. Always found a reason not to go in the field with the rest of us. I called him on it once, but nothing ever came of it. Did you see his creases?"

Fortis smiled. "I was quite impressed. You know, Witzke said she is close friends with Reese."

"Why doesn't that surprise me?"

"You probably shouldn't mention that you're a corporal now because you punched Reese when you were a gunny."

It was Ystremski's turn to smile. "I didn't just punch him, LT. I starched him standing. He was stiff before he hit the deck."

* * * * *

Chapter Three

Fourteen hours later, Foxtrot Company was sitting and sweating in their lightweight battle armor, LBA, on a stifling dropship the Fleet made available for training while Captain Witzke and Gunny Parker stalked the craft and berated and belittled them.

The morning had started off badly. When the troops mustered and platoon commanders reported they were ready for training, Witzke noticed that most of them didn't have their mouthguards. That prompted the first threat-laden tirade, and the grumbling began.

After the Space Marines were properly equipped, Captain Witzke ordered them to board the dropship. There was some momentary confusion as the cherries hesitated, unsure of their places in the troop compartment. The veterans took charge and sorted them out, but it was enough to earn another tongue lashing as Witzke and Parker directed them all to disembark and do it again.

When the company was reloaded, Parker ordered the ramp closed, and Captain Witzke read the standard assault procedures word for word from the ISMC tactical manual. The temperature in the dropship soared, and attention wandered as the captain droned on.

The Space Marines were loaded in a standard assault configuration. Third Platoon sat along the port bulkhead with Fortis, as the platoon commander, seated next to the ramp. Second Platoon was double stacked on the centerline with the heavy weapons and medical teams behind them. First Platoon sat on the starboard bulkhead.

When the ramp dropped, Fortis would lead his platoon down the ramp and angle to the right to establish the right flank. Warrant Officer Takahashi would simultaneously lead Second Platoon straight down the ramp to form the center of their position, while Warrant Officer Taylor led First Platoon off to the left and established the left flank.

After they were clear of the dropship, the Space Marines established their position in two stages. First, the troops ran approximately twenty meters and took cover to avoid the down blast from the dropship engines as it climbed away from the landing zone. As soon as the dropship was clear, the Marines would move another thirty meters or so to get clear of the LZ before the next dropship landed. A dropship on final approach had the flying characteristics of a falling safe, and a miscalculation by the pilot could be deadly to the troops on the ground.

After the entire force landed, First and Third Platoons would link up with Echo Company on the left and Golf Company on the right and the battalion position would be secured. It was simple but effective.

Finally, Captain Witzke concluded her lecture and gave the "stand by" signal. As the company commander, she and Gunny Parker were seated on the port side by the ramp, directly in front of Fortis and Third Platoon. The company tensed for action, the ramp dropped, and Witzke gave the go order.

First and Second Platoon exploded down the ramp into the vacant hangar and, in textbook fashion, fanned out twenty meters from the dropship. Third Platoon was far less organized.

Witzke and Parker were too slow coming up out of their seats, so Third Platoon slammed into them before they were clear of the ramp. Fortis did his best to divert the rush of bodies behind him, but the power of the herd overwhelmed him. The captain and gunny went down with Fortis on top. The rest of the platoon plowed over them, and a mass of bodies tumbled down the ramp to the hangar deck.

The Space Marines untangled themselves and ran for their positions. Captain Witzke climbed to her feet and sputtered with rage.

"Foxtrot Company, fall in!" she shouted over the company comm channel.

The company formed up at attention and counted off. When they were finished, the platoon commanders saluted and reported all present or accounted for. Meanwhile, Witzke paced in front of the formation.

"What was that? What was *that?*"

While the captain ranted from her place in front of the formation, Gunny Parker patrolled the edges. He poked and prodded at Marines whose focus wandered.

After a brief tirade, Witzke ordered the company back onto the dropship. When everyone was loaded and ready, she gave the go order again.

First and Second Platoons charged down into the hanger. Fortis and Third Platoon hesitated while Witzke and Parker navigated the ramp, and then launched themselves to their appointed positions and sprawled on the deck. After several seconds, the entire company rose and ran for the far side of the hanger.

"Too slow! Do it again."

Fortis could tell by their body language that the Space Marines were running out of patience. They were well-trained warriors, and even the rawest privates knew the problem wasn't them. When they climbed back aboard the dropship, their movements were slow and grudging.

To make matters worse, part of the cooling system in Fortis's LBA failed. Sweat ran down his body and collected in his boots, which was uncomfortable but better than when he sat on the drop-ship and it pooled in his crotch. Corporal Ystremski's voice crackled over the point-to-point circuit in his helmet.

"Why are you fidgeting, LT?"

Fortis looked up and found the corporal in the middle of the platoon.

"Fucking cooling loop failed, and I'm literally sweating my balls off," he replied. "Itches like hell."

The reaction of the entire company made Fortis look down at the comm panel on his forearm. To his horror, instead of the privacy circuit, he had hit the wrong button and announced his discomfort to the entire company. Including Captain Witzke.

"Do we need to pause training so you can scratch yourself, Fortis?" the captain demanded over the circuit.

"No, ma'am, I'm good."

"DINLI," remarked Ystremski.

"Let's try it again. Stand by!"

Witzke gave the go signal and the platoons surged down the ramp. Fortis narrowly avoided running over the captain and gunny, but Third Platoon was still behind First and Second. Even the heavy weapons teams got into their position first.

"Again!"

As the troops trudged back up the ramp, Fortis approached Captain Witzke and took off his helmet.

"What do you want, Fortis? Change your mind about scratching your balls?"

"Maybe he should focus on leading his platoon," injected Gunny Parker.

"Ma'am, with all due respect, Third Platoon can't get off the drop ship with you and the gunny on the ramp."

The captain's eyebrows shot up in surprise. "You're blaming your failure on me?"

Fortis shook his head. "No. I'm not blaming anyone." He pointed to her LBA. "I can tell your armor is brand new and so is his," he said gesturing at Gunny Parker. "It has to be broken in or it slows you down. Until you break it in, we need to find a workaround."

Witzke eyed him with suspicion. "What do you propose, Mr. Fortis?"

"My guys don't know any speed but full speed and I can't hold them back. How about on this next run, you and the gunny stay in your seats until Third Platoon is down the ramp. Then you follow us and the whole company will be in position."

"The tactical assault procedure calls for the company commander to be in the lead position, Lieutenant. Perhaps you should read it sometime."

"I've read the procedure manual, Captain. The first section talks about how the tactics are strongly recommended, but commanders are responsible for tailoring them to meet operational needs. As I see it, Third Platoon has an operational need to get down the ramp as fast as First and Second, but we can't because your armor won't allow you to move fast enough yet. So, our workaround is that you wait until we're off. There's nothing to see until we're clear of the LZ anyway, so you won't miss much."

Witzke's eyes flicked between Parker and Fortis, and for a second he thought she would shoot down his idea.

Captain Witzke gestured to Gunny Parker, who shrugged. "Makes sense to me."

"Let's try it one time, ma'am. If Third Platoon doesn't deploy as fast as the others, at least we can say we tried. If we succeed, then we know what to do and we can secure from training."

She nodded. "Okay. We'll try it your way, just once. If this is one of your tricks, Fortis, I'll have your ass."

The trio boarded the drop ship where Foxtrot Company waited.

"We're going to try something a little different this time," Captain Witzke announced. "Third Platoon, your platoon leader says you can get down the ramp faster than First or Second. This is your chance to prove it. Stand by!"

On "go," Fortis leapt from his seat and charged down the ramp in two long strides. He could feel the pressure of the platoon behind him as he dashed for the twenty-meter mark and dove flat on his stomach. Out of his peripheral vision he saw Space Marines sprawl on the deck alongside him. He jumped back to his feet and sped to the far end of the hangar where he dove flat again. When he rolled over and looked, he was satisfied to see that there were no Third Platoon stragglers. After the heavy weapons teams huffed and puffed to join the rest of the company, Captain Witzke ordered them to fall in by the dropship.

"Much improved," she announced to the formation. "Excellent idea, Mr. Fortis. Let this be a lesson to all of you. No matter who you are, your good ideas will be considered by myself and Gunny Parker. Gunny, dismiss the company. Platoon commanders, stand by."

After the Space Marines filed out of the hangar, Witzke addressed the two warrant officers and Fortis.

"In thirty-six hours, *Atlas* will arrive in orbit around Balfan-48 and the drop will commence shortly thereafter. You are responsible to execute the deployment checklist for your platoons. At this time tomorrow, I expect to have all of your completed checklists in my hand. If you become aware of a major issue before then, I want to know about it immediately. Any questions?"

The platoon commanders shook their heads, and Captain Witzke dismissed them.

Fortis headed for the battalion armorer to get his LBA cooling loop repaired and he was struck by the irony of his position. The amount of paperwork required to ensure the company was deployment-ready was daunting. Medical records, dental records, next-of-kin and emergency contact forms, life insurance, and last will and testaments all had to be accurate and up to date for every Space Marine.

When Fortis was the acting Foxtrot Company XO, Captain Reese had harassed him about the most minute administrative details, and the lieutenant had labored for many hours to meet his demands. All of the harassment meant Foxtrot Company was deployment-ready long before the warning order for the invasion was issued. And all because the former CO was an asshole.

Elsewhere on *Atlas*, frantic troop commanders and harried staff personnel scurried to complete the invasion preparations in time. All that remained for Third Platoon was to draw weapons and rations, which they would do just before they boarded their assigned dropship. Until then, the only thing Fortis and Third Platoon had to do was look busy.

* * * * *

Chapter Four

Fortis entered the battalion armory and found Sergeant Coughlin hard at work on a pile of LBAs.

"Hey Coughlin, how's it going?"

Coughlin looked up from his work bench. "It would be better if every swinging dick in the battalion didn't wait until the last minute to tune up their armor. How's it going with you, LT?"

Fortis started to unbuckle his LBA. "Cooling loop failed during training this morning. Can you squeeze it in?"

"I can do you better than that." Coughlin disappeared into the shelves on the back of the shop and returned a few seconds later with another LBA top and helmet. "Ystremski was already here. Dump your old ones in the bin with the rest, sir."

The lieutenant dropped his defective LBA into the bin and examined the replacement. It gratified him to see scuffs and dents from previous wearers. He didn't want to break in a brand-new LBA on the eve of a drop.

"What's all this?" he asked the sergeant as he pointed to the shoulders and the crown of the replacement helmet. The armor was coated with a shiny black composite.

"My latest invention, LT. Hypersensitive solar coating designed to provide a trickle charge to the LBA's atmospheric control system. As long as you're in the light of a primary star, your armor will charge, and there's a pad in the palm of your glove that fits the grip on your pulse rifle. Beats the shit out of lugging a bunch of replacement batteries."

Fortis ran his fingers over the helmet and nodded his approval.

"You made this, Coughlin? That's damn fine work."

"Well, I came up with the idea. When I couldn't make it work, I sent it over to the Science and Technology lab and they did the rest. Every set that comes in gets the treatment."

"I'm really impressed. Well done. And thanks for giving me a used set, too."

"Don't worry, LT. Ystremski told me not to give you the brand-new stuff."

Fortis chuckled as he slung the LBA top over his shoulder. "There's nothing better than a corporal with my best interests in mind."

"It's a tough job, but somebody has to keep you officers from hurting yourselves."

"Thanks, Coughlin. DINLI."

"DINLI, and have a nice drop, sir."

"You're not coming?"

Coughlin frowned and shook his head. "The gunner wants me to get all this armor fixed up and refurbished by the time you guys return." The gunner was the battalion armorer, a crusty warrant officer that Fortis had only ever heard rumors about.

"Well, if the gunner changes his mind, and you want to chew some dirt, come find Third Platoon, Foxtrot Company. You're always welcome."

* * *

After he showered and ate lunch, Fortis returned to his stateroom. He lived in a six-man unit, with racks stacked two-high on the three bulkheads and a cluster of workstations in the center. There were currently three other officers assigned to the compartment: two dropship pilots and a first lieutenant from logistics. The two pilots complained about the rigors of life as a Fleet officer until the day Fortis returned from Eros-28 with his hair burned off and his face swathed in bloody bandages. The logistics officer was a thin, sallow-faced man who said little and spent his time poring over spreadsheets and mooning over a holograph of the homely girl he left behind on Terra Earth.

For now, Fortis was alone in the space, and he was grateful for the solitude. The dropship pilots treated him like a barely tolerable peasant, and he made a point of leaving as much sweaty and smelly gear in their stateroom as he could. He'd also grown accustomed to the peace and quiet of the XO's office where he could work without distraction, even if he was buried under a mountain of paperwork while he was there. Even on a ship the size of *Atlas*, privacy was at a premium, and he relished the solitude.

Fortis picked up the platoon deployment checklist from his workstation and looked it over. Everything was marked as completed but two items: draw rations and draw weapons. Otherwise, Third Platoon was ready to deploy.

Just then, Corporal Ystremski rapped three times and poked his head in the door.

"You weren't napping again, were you?" asked the corporal with an amused tone.

"No, I wasn't napping, dickhead, I was looking over the checklist," Fortis said with feigned annoyance. "What's up?"

"I brought you some gifts." Ystremski hefted a large bag. "Pig squares and hydration packs."

The preferred rations of the Space Marines were dehydrated pork steaks, referred to as "pig squares." Pig squares didn't require cooking, they didn't taste too bad, and they were a lot lighter than the tinned alternatives. Logistics issued three days' worth to each Space Marine, but the veterans knew to carry several times that. Fleet resupply schedules were unreliable and rations were the lowest priority cargo, so it was wise to pack extra rations.

"Great, thanks. Why are you handing out food this early?"

"LT, the entire division will be chasing rations tonight. If we don't grab pig squares now, we'll have to hump cans of mystery meat and beans with the rest of the monkeys. If you don't want pig squares—"

"No, no. Pig squares are fine. I keep forgetting there are five thousand Space Marines getting ready to drop tomorrow."

Ystremski nodded. "It's been a long time since I've seen a drop this big, and that was an exercise on Terra Earth."

"How did it go?"

The corporal chuckled. "I was a PFC at the time, and it looked like a clusterfuck from where I stood. That was *my* cherry drop, and the first thing I saw when I hit the ramp was the smashed remains of some poor bastard who didn't clear the LZ in time."

"DINLI."

"You can bet your ass I run like hell now, so I guess the lesson was learned." Ystremski gestured to the checklist. "We missing anything?"

"No, we're good. Thanks to Captain Reese, we're good to go."

"Fuck Reese."

They laughed together and then lapsed into silence.

"LT, what do you make of all this? The Maltaani and the drop, I mean. There's nothing but rumors flying around the troop decks. What are we really doing?"

Fortis thought for a second. He completely trusted Corporal Ystremski, but he knew that what he said would become public knowledge, and he didn't want to feed the rumor mill.

"The Fleet Frigate *Nelson* had an encounter with an unidentified vessel and there have been a couple of recent ship disappearances in the sector, including *Nelson*. Intel detected an alien force that Fleet is calling the Maltaani. They seem to be establishing a base on a planet called Balfan-48, which is close to a jump gate back to Terra Earth. We can't allow that, so we're on our way to stop it."

"Who the fuck are the Maltaani?"

"We don't know much about them or what to expect, to be honest. The best thing we can do is make sure the lads are prepared to drop and fight like hell."

"First to go, last to know," replied Ystremski.

"DINLI."

"LT, I meant to tell you, I got some info on Captain Witzke from a mech driver buddy of mine, if you want to hear it."

"Is it rumors?"

"Not at all. Well, not all of it. She was only an assistant mech company commander before she got sent over here. Good with paper, not with the troops. This is her cherry drop."

"She's really a cherry? She's never dropped? Not even training?"

"Not once. Mech companies don't train like we do."

"I guess that explains why she was drilling us so hard in the hangar."

"She's good friends with Reese, too. Maybe more than friends."

"Witzke told me she knew him from Fleet Academy," Fortis replied. "What I don't understand is why she's so paranoid that I'm trying to screw her over. It's not like I have any influence around here."

"There's no telling what Reese told her about why he got relieved and sent home," said Ystremski. "He blamed you for the report from Pada-Pada that got him fired from the company."

When Fortis and two platoons of Space Marines were dropped on Pada-Pada for a training mission, it became a life-or-death struggle for survival. After repeated requests for guidance and assistance from Captain Reese went unanswered, Fortis transmitted a report detailing their situation directly to the battalion commander, which ultimately led to Reese being relieved as company commander.

"Yeah, I guess."

The corporal gestured to the door. "Sir, I'd love to hang around and shoot the shit like an officer, but I work for a living and there's a platoon of Space Marines that are without adult supervision right now. Do you have any preference for weapons tomorrow? You want a pistol?"

Every Marine carried a pulse rifle and a mixed bandolier of fragmentation, smoke, and concussion grenades. They also carried a standard bayonet and an entrenching tool that doubled as a wicked melee weapon.

In addition to the standard kit, Space Marines were free to carry personal weapons and most opted to carry a kukri—a curved, heavy-bladed weapon that they earned by serving in combat. Fortis had earned his kukri on Pada-Pada fighting cloned soldiers, and he'd earned the crimson paracord handle when he killed the mercenary leader Chive with it on Eros-28.

"Are you carrying one?"

"Nah. The pulse pistols look great in movies, but they don't have enough range for my liking."

"Okay then, I'll pass, too. And thanks for talking to Coughlin, he hooked me up with some good LBA."

"Gotta take care of all my Marines, LT. Even the officers."

* * * * *

Chapter Five

The worst day of Colonel Kivak Sobieski's twenty-four-year ISMC career began when his communications officer woke him way too early. The commo reported that the satcom constellation deployed over Balfan-48 had gone silent. The news didn't surprise Sobieski. Technology tended to fail at the worst possible moment. The loss of satellite communications wasn't a showstopper; their initial footprint on Balfan-48 would be so small that line-of-sight, LOS, frequencies would suffice. He thanked his commo and rolled over to get another hour of sleep, grateful that satcom wasn't his responsibility.

Twenty minutes later, the battalion intelligence officer roused him to report that Fleet Command had lost contact with the flight of intelligence drones deployed to conduct intelligence, surveillance, and reconnaissance, ISR, operations ahead of the invasion. That news troubled Sobieski, because, without the ISR birds, the division would be dropping in blind. Still, there had been no recent reports of enemy troops on the surface and the last contact Fleet Command had with the Maltaani was two days ago, when a squadron of scout ships chased off three enemy vessels as the fleet approached Balfan-48.

Colonel Sobieski gave up trying to sleep and got up. After a quick shower, he grabbed a cup of coffee from the staff wardroom and wandered into the division operations center.

That was a mistake.

Harried officers scurried back and forth with binders and papers clutched in their hands. A captain wearing the insignia of the logistics battalion brushed past Sobieski with tears streaming down his face.

General Gupta's voice boomed across the space. "Where the fuck is Colonel Upton? Someone find Colonel Upton!"

Sobieski had seen Dale Upton, the mech battalion commander, in the staff wardroom chatting with a shapely Fleet lieutenant commander, but he wasn't about to volunteer that information. He and Upton had attended the Fleet Academy together, where Upton had a well-earned reputation as a skirt chaser. Sobieski wanted no part of whatever trouble Upton got himself into.

Instead, he drifted around the periphery of the chaotic operations center and absorbed snatches of a half-dozen heated conversations. The finger-pointing over the comms satellites had begun, and the satellite technicians were pitted against the communications operators. Neither side would admit that the fault might lay within their purview, and there were even absurd accusations of deliberate sabotage. The failure of the ISR drones opened a whole new front in the internecine staff conflict, with the satellite technicians allying with the communications personnel against the ISR drone operators. It was a swirling, confused struggle, and all the while General Gupta sat at his command console and raged at anyone within earshot. As one of twelve infantry battalion commanders in the division, Sobieski was glad he had no part to play in it.

Upton rushed into the space. As soon as the general caught sight of him, he bellowed, "Upton, you idiot! What the fuck is going on with your battalion?"

Operations center personnel became intensely interested in anything besides the drama at the general's console. A public reprimand of a senior officer was a rare occurrence, and nobody wanted to become collateral damage.

From what Sobieski could make out, the mech battalion had conducted what was known as an administrative loadout and not an assault loadout onto their assigned drop ships. Instead of battle-ready mechs roaring down the ramps to provide fire support for the infantry, the crews had loaded their vehicles and gear as if they planned to unload at their home base. Everything was packed for efficiency and not immediate combat effectiveness. That worried Sobieski because the Space Marines relied on the mechs. An administrative offload would take hours, not minutes, and dropships sitting on the surface in the landing zone would present a tempting target to any enemies in the area.

Upton's answers didn't satisfy the general, and the division commander slammed his hand down on his keyboard and smashed it.

"Goddamn mech prima donnas! Upton, you're fired!"

Gupta jumped to his feet and was storming toward the exit when his eyes landed on Sobieski.

"You! Colonel Sobieski! You've got half a brain. Come here."

Sobieski did as he was ordered and joined the general.

"Unfuck the mechs, Colonel. Kick those pansy asses into shape in quick order."

The colonel wanted to protest that he had his own battalion to worry about, that the job rightfully belonged to a member of the general's own staff, but there was only one right answer to the general's order.

"Aye, aye, sir."

Gupta stomped out of the space, trailed by frightened division staff officers. Upton sidled up to his former classmate and colleague.

"Sorry, Kivak. I don't know what happened."

Sobieski shrugged. "DINLI. Who's the go-to guy in your battalion?"

"You've already got her in Foxtrot Company. Captain Witzke. I had to give her up and then everything went to shit."

"Well, I'm giving her back, at least until we get the mechs sorted out." He studied his old friend for a second. "You know, I'm starting to get a bad feeling about this one."

* * *

Fortis sat on the drop ship and watched the company fidget in their seats.

Hurry up and wait.

When Captain Witzke ordered Foxtrot Company to board the dropship, Fortis's adrenaline roared in his blood. There was a palpable sense of excitement in the troop compartment as the Space Marines checked packs and slings before they belted in.

And then time stood still.

Fortis listened in on the command circuit as their drop window was delayed, and then delayed again. There was a series of contradictory orders as tempers flared, and, at one point, an anonymous voice announced that the entire operation had been cancelled. That announcement was quickly superseded by General Gupta himself, but the seeds of doubt had taken root.

The lieutenant managed to glean some useful information from all the crosstalk. Fleet sensors detected unidentified spacecraft near Balfan-48, but they disappeared as *Atlas* and her escorts approached. The intelligence branch had deployed a variety of surveillance probes, and initial reports were that the surface of the planet was deserted. Next, the temporary constellation of communications satellites launched in support of the invasion suddenly failed and the intel probes stopped sending back reports. Comm technicians had attempted to restore contact with the probes, but they were unsuccessful so far.

In addition to equipment failures, another major screwup was caused by human error. All six mechanized companies, four heavy and two reconnaissance, had loaded their machines for an administrative transfer and not an assault. The vehicles and support equipment were packed into their assigned drop ships without consideration for immediate deployment.

The general decided to juggle the drop schedule and insert the mechs last to give them as much time as possible to get squared away, but it meant the infantry could not count on mounted reconnaissance or mech support during the first critical hours of the landing.

Taken together, the equipment and personnel failures caused over four hours delay while the Space Marines sweated in their dropships. Captain Witzke and Gunny Parker weren't in their seats next to him throughout the delays, and Fortis was grateful for their absence. It permitted him to close his eyes and achieve a state of restful consciousness; he wasn't asleep, but his mind rested as he listened to various reports on the circuit.

At least nobody is shooting at us.

* * * * *

Chapter Six

General Gupta spent the rest of the morning stalking from space to space like a human tornado. He told the assistant division commander that he did it to kickstart the staff, but it was obvious he was venting his anger and impatience on the unfortunates who crossed his path. It was inevitable that he would stop in at the divisional intelligence operations center, where he overheard a heated discussion between his staff intelligence officer, Lieutenant Colonel Roberts, and a major he didn't recognize.

"I think we're being jammed, Colonel!" insisted the major, whose nametape read Anders.

The general stepped up to the conversation.

"What do you mean, jammed, Major?"

Roberts cut in. "General, this is just hypothetical—"

Gupta cut off Roberts with the wave of his hand.

"I was talking to the major, Colonel. Major, continue. What do you mean, jammed?"

Anders cleared his throat. "General, what the colonel said is accurate. It is only a hypothesis, but based on everything we know this far, I believe we are being subjected to full-spectrum jamming from an unknown location."

"That's absurd! The—"

Gupta jabbed a stiff-fingered gesture known in the Corps as "knife hand," at Roberts.

"Colonel, if you interrupt the major again, I'll send you down to sit with the infantry in the dropship hangar. Is that clear?"

The color drained from Roberts' face, and her mouth opened and closed without a sound. The general looked back to Anders.

"Continue, Major."

"Sir, I don't have any hard evidence, but the loss of communications between the ships of the fleet, the failure of the satcom constellation around Balfan-48, and the surveillance probes going dark, all at about the same time, seem like pieces of the same puzzle to me."

Gupta eyed Anders carefully but said nothing.

"What I mean, General, is that any one of these failures could be the result of equipment malfunction or operator error. Stuff breaks and people make mistakes. But all three, right now, simultaneously?" He shook his head. "It feels deliberate to me."

"That's it, Major? You have a feeling, or maybe there's some special sense that you have?" Gupta spoke in a deliberate, slightly mocking tone. The major's theory wasn't the dumbest thing he'd heard all morning, but he wanted to test his sincerity.

"General, I don't claim to have special cognitive powers. Our situation may be the confluence of three remarkable pieces of bad luck that rendered the fleet deaf, dumb, and blind at the precise moment Ninth Division is set to begin a major orbit-to-surface movement. If that proves to be the case, I will happily admit my error. I believe it's somehow deliberate, and that possibility requires investigation."

"Okay, Major. How would you test your theory?"

"To start, we have to acknowledge that our assumptions are biased by our own knowledge. We're dealing with unfamiliar alien technology, but we have to start somewhere. Based on our technology, omnidirectional jamming techniques are only effective over a broad area at relatively short ranges. Directional jamming has a longer range, but the affected area is much narrower. If we can map the boundaries of the affected area, we can use that information to determine what type of jamming it is and, more importantly, where it's coming from.

"If we send out intel drones, two in opposite directions and one straight out into space, eventually they'll reach the boundaries of the jamming. When they return, we'll be able to plot the affected area, which should give us a fair idea where the jamming platform is located."

"What do you need to make that happen?"

"Permission to launch the drones."

"Permission granted, Major." Gupta turned to Roberts. "Give him whatever he wants. He might be the only intel officer on this ship that doesn't have his head up his ass."

* * *

The dropship ramp opened, and Fortis was instantly alert. Instead of Captain Witzke and Gunny Parker, a dropship loadmaster and a Space Marine in battle armor climbed into the vessel. The load master pointed at Fortis and the Space Marine waved his thanks as the ramp closed.

The new arrival removed his helmet, and Fortis recognized Sergeant Coughlin from the armory.

"Hey, Coughlin, what are you doing here?"

"I begged and pleaded and the gunner changed his mind. He said I could make the drop if I found a platoon to attach to, and I remembered your invitation, sir."

"Outstanding. Let me get Ystremski up here." He keyed up Ystremski. "Hey, Corporal, we've got a cherry dropping with us today. Can you find him a spot?"

Ystremski came to the front and thumped Coughlin on the shoulder. "Decided to see what real Space Marines do? C'mon, I've got a nice safe place for you in the back."

Fortis smiled as the pair picked their way through the crowded troop compartment. The ramp no sooner closed than it opened again, and Captain Witzke and Gunny Parker climbed aboard. They were accompanied by a woman in absurd blue body armor with PRESS written on the front. Witzke waved over Warrants Takahashi and Taylor for a pow-wow.

"Colonel Sobieski has ordered me to join the mech companies to help sort out their clusterfuck, so I will not be dropping with Foxtrot Company. Fortis, you're the senior officer, so you will assume temporary command until I join you on the ground. You know what to do. Get deployed, adjust your lines to conform to the battalion, and wait for my guidance. Questions?"

The lieutenant and warrant officers shook their heads.

Captain Witzke gestured to the person in blue armor. "Fortis, this is Liz Sherer of Terra News Network. The division public affairs office embedded her with Foxtrot Company for the initial assault. Do you think you can keep her safe until I'm done with the mechs?"

The news surprised Fortis, but he nodded. "Yes, ma'am, we'll take good care of her."

"Outstanding. Let's get it done."

Witzke and Parker descended the ramp, and it closed behind them.

Lieutenant Fortis pointed to the empty seats by the ramp. "Sit here, ma'am, and I'll go over the landing procedures. Can you run in that body armor?"

"Lieutenant, don't call me ma'am. My name is Liz or Sherer. I've been a TNN correspondent longer than you've been alive, and I don't need you to keep me safe or take care of me. I have authorization from the commanding general to go anywhere and report on anything, and I intend to do just that."

Fortis had no response for her aggressive response, so he sat back down. Sherer watched as he buckled up, then she took the seat next to him and did up her own straps. She fumbled with them, but the lieutenant watched in silence.

"Ma'am, uh, Liz, I didn't mean to imply that you need a babysitter. Have you made a combat drop before?"

Liz shook her head.

"When that ramp drops, the entire company is going to charge out into a blizzard of noise and dirt. You and I will be in front, and, if you move too slow, you'll get run over. You might even get someone hurt or killed. I don't care what you report on, but I won't allow you to put any Space Marines in danger. So, please, allow me to explain what's going to happen when this crate hits the surface."

Sherer opened her mouth to respond, then paused and nodded. "Okay, Lieutenant. We'll try it your way."

Fortis explained how the Space Marines were loaded and what was expected of them when the ramp dropped. He told her the importance of taking cover until the dropship took off, and clearing the LZ before the next one landed.

"It's quite simple, but it's easy to get lost when the engines are howling and blowing sand everywhere. I've been tasked with your safety, but my mission comes first, and my mission is to get Foxtrot Company on the ground safely and ready for combat."

Just then, an amber light above the ramp began to flash and a siren sounded throughout the compartment. The company whooped and cinched their harnesses a little tighter.

It was drop time!

Fortis pulled his mouthpiece out of his pack and put it in his mouth. He looked over at Sherer, who gave him a quizzical look. He took it out to speak.

"This is going to be a bump and dump. The pilots are going to come down fast and land hard, and I don't want to bite my tongue off or break any teeth. You don't have one?"

She shook her head.

"You have anything in your pack you can bite down on? A rag, maybe?"

Sherer dug in her pack and came up with a handkerchief.

Fortis nodded. "Perfect. Bite down on it until we're on the surface."

Sherer nodded and gave him a thumbs up, which he returned. Fortis tried hard to project the salty confidence of a seasoned veteran, but he didn't have the heart to tell her that this was only his second drop.

The intercom system in the dropship hanger crackled to life and General Gupta's unmistakable voice boomed.

"Space Marines of Ninth Division, this is your commanding general. In a few moments, we will begin a great crusade to protect Terra Earth against an alien enemy known as the Maltaani. The Maltaani must not be allowed to establish an operating base this close to a jump gate and threaten our homes. I expect every one of you to do your duty to the utmost of your ability. If you do that, victory will be ours. It will not be an easy fight, but I have every confidence that we will prevail."

The drop ship bounced when it was released from *Atlas*. In his mind's eye, Fortis saw the dropships form up in marshal stacks and trace giant circles in space as they waited for the rest of the flight. The inertial gravity of *Atlas* disappeared when they uncoupled from the flagship, and Fortis felt himself surge against his straps. All the confused chatter on the command circuit ceased when the support umbilical released as the dropship launched, and Fortis was glad to leave it behind.

He looked around the compartment and shook his head. Private Queen, Third Platoon jokester, was floating untethered above the seated Space Marines. His arms windmilled as he bounced along the overhead as though he was out of control, but Fortis knew he was putting on a show. He switched to the privacy circuit with Corporal Ystremski.

"Hey, Corporal, get that idiot down, would you?"

Ystremski double-clicked his mic in response and then Fortis heard him bawl over the platoon channel.

"Queen, get your ass strapped down and quit fucking around."

The rest of the platoon "helped" Queen float back to his seat with the butts of their pulse rifles, and the laughing private returned to his seat and cinched down.

The troopship bucked and rattled as it skipped along the ragged edge of the atmosphere surrounding Balfan-48. Sherer gave Fortis a wide-eyed look, and he nodded in return.

Everything's okay. I think.

The jerking and bouncing stopped as they penetrated the space-atmosphere boundary and began descending to the surface. All around Fortis, the other members of Third Platoon adjusted their helmets and checked equipment. The gravity of Balfan-48 asserted itself on the dropship, and the Space Marines prepared to release the straps holding them in their seats to charge down the ramp.

His pulse pounded in his ears as adrenaline flooded his bloodstream. Fortis checked the tactical display on his visor and noted the time.

Not bad. Only eight hours late.

For the hundredth time, he mentally rehearsed his moves for when the ramp dropped. His nerves were taut and time seemed to slow down.

The amber light above the ramp stopped flashing and a steady red lamp next to it lit up.

Final approach.

The drop ship shuddered as the pilots engaged full reverse thrust to slow their descent, and Fortis held his breath. If they mis-timed the maneuver, the dropship would either smash into the surface or end up in an uncontrollable hover and tumble to the ground.

All at once, the dropship bounced, the troop compartment lights went out, a green light took the place of the red, and the ramp slammed down. A whirlwind of sand and noise blasted into the hold as the pilots pushed the throttles to full power, necessary to get the ponderous craft airborne again.

In one smooth motion, Fortis unsnapped his harness and jumped to his feet. Beside him, Sherer struggled with her straps. The lieutenant punched her buckle and pulled her to her feet as the platoon piled up behind him. He yanked the reporter down the ramp and dragged her across the ground until they were clear of the drop ship. He shoved her to the ground and landed next to her as the dropship roared back into the air.

As soon as the drop ship was clear, he leapt to his feet and picked her up off the ground.

"Lieutenant, what the hell—"

All around them, the other Space Marines got up and rushed to clear the landing zone. Overhead, Fortis could hear the roaring engines of the next dropship on final approach, and he knew they only had a few seconds before they would be crushed.

Without a word, he grabbed Sherer around the waist and hoisted her over his shoulder. The lieutenant ran after the rest of the platoon as the reporter wriggled and kicked, but his strength enhancements held her secure. When they caught up to the rest of Third Platoon, Fortis knelt down and deposited Sherer on the ground. She jumped up, sputtering with anger, and yanked off her helmet.

"You had no right to assault me like that, Lieutenant! I'll see that you're brought up on charges—"

Fortis cut her off with the wave of his hand and pointed back toward the LZ. A dropship skidded to a stop where they'd been standing moments before, and the Space Marines of Golf Company poured out.

"I told you we needed to get clear, ma'am," he told the seething reporter. "You hesitated and you put both of us in danger."

Sherer stared at the LZ and then at Fortis.

"Thank you," she said in a small voice. "I panicked."

Fortis shook his head. "Don't worry about it. We got out, that's all that matters."

Corporal Ystremski appeared at his elbow.

"Sir, what the fuck's going on? We don't have comms with Echo or Golf Company. I can't even talk to you. You hear anything?"

Fortis checked his comm panel. He had the correct circuits dialed up, but when he tried to transmit, he was met with silence.

"Nothing. I guess the satellites are still down."

Ystremski snorted. "Typical lowest bidder government shit. What do we do now?"

"Take an azimuth, move out three and a half klicks, and conform to Echo Company on the left. Tell First and Second Platoon that we're moving and send someone to notify Golf Company to make sure they stay in contact with our right flank. We need to move fast; we're eight hours behind schedule and it's going to be dark soon."

"DINLI, sir."

"DINLI."

* * * * *

Chapter Seven

The Space Marines advanced at a steady pace, alert for signs of enemy activity. The sky on Balfan-48 had a weird texture to it, as though there was an opaque dome over the entire planet. The surface of the planet was featureless as far as Fortis could see, flat hard-packed dirt with few undulations and no vegetation. He began to wonder if the Maltaani had ever been on the planet.

Why the hell would anyone come here?

"Lieutenant Fortis!"

A Space Marine with the distinctive stripes of a headquarters messenger on his shoulders approached.

"Sir, General Gupta has ordered all infantry advances to halt in place and all officers and senior NCO's report to the command element ASAP."

Fortis gaped in astonishment. "A meeting? *Now?*"

The messenger shrugged. "The general is pretty pissed about this whole goat rope. I'm glad I'm just the messenger." He turned and jogged toward Golf Company.

"What do you think the meeting is about?" Liz Sherer had been so quiet since the LZ that Fortis had forgotten she was there.

"A whole lot of ass chewing," quipped Corporal Ystremski, who had come over as soon as he saw the runner.

Fortis looked around and saw officers and senior NCOs from Echo and Golf Company begin to head back to the headquarters.

"Shit."

He trotted over to where First and Second Platoons waited and joined Warrants Takahashi and Taylor.

"General Gupta ordered a halt to the advance. All officers and NCOs are to report to the command element."

The warrant officers shook their heads in disgust, and Takahashi spat into the dust. "What a clusterfuck."

"Sounds like the general wants to chew someone's ass in front of witnesses."

"It doesn't really matter. Leave someone in charge of your platoon and let's get moving."

Just then, a Space Marine approached the trio and waved.

"Lieutenant Fortis."

When he got closer, Fortis recognized Gunny Parker.

"What's up, Gunny? Did you get the word about the meeting?"

"That's why I'm here. Captain Witzke—"

A pair of hovercopters flashed low overhead, and the group flinched. The craft were the new tactical model, with swept-back wings loaded with fat pods of rockets and a lethal high-velocity cannon mounted under the nose.

"At least the flyboys are having fun," drawled Taylor.

"Captain Witzke sent me to tell you to remain with the company," said Parker. "She only wants the warrants to attend the meeting."

"Are you sure? I mean, the general outranks the captain."

"Yes, sir, I'm sure. She doesn't want to leave the company unsupervised, and she wants you to standby with the men."

Fortis looked at Takahashi and Tayler, but they were no help. He felt a curious stab of doubt, almost paranoia, at the directions from Gunny Parker. He couldn't think of a reason why Witzke would exclude him from the meeting, especially since it was ordered by the division commander himself. If it was some kind of trick, he would just have to wait and see how it played out.

"DINLI, I guess. I'll stay here and be ready to go in case something happens."

The warrant officers and gunny turned and jogged back toward the command element. Fortis turned to Corporal Ystremski.

"Pass the word to dig in. No telling how long we're going to be here."

* * *

Warrant Officer Bokerah "Bo" Brumley banked her hovercopter in a tight arc over the Space Marines deployed below and smiled as the centrifugal force pressed her into her seat. The simulators on the flagship could mimic actual flight, but there was nothing like the real thing. Live flight hours were hard to come by for hovercopter pilots, so she maximized every opportunity to put her craft through its paces. Bo had earned her reputation as a worm burner from her penchant for low-level flight, and today was no exception.

Balfan-48 whizzed past the amber nose bubble as Bo held the stick steady and controlled the turn with the foot pedals. She shifted the stick, switched feet positions, and the hovercopter banked hard the other way.

The voice of her crew chief, Staff Sergeant Marcus White, crackled in her ear. "Damn, Bo, give us a warning next time."

Bo grinned and wiggled the wings again.

"Is Bingo still there?"

Her wingman, Ben "Bingo" Goshawk, commanded the other hovercopter in the flight of two. The pilots complemented each other; Bo loved flying down and dirty, while Bingo maintained an overwatch position and covered her six. Even without voice communications, their many hours flying together meant he could anticipate Bo's maneuvers and stay right with her.

"Affirmative. Six o'clock high," Corporal Ballein, door gunner and cabin crewman, reported. "They're staying out of the weeds."

"Weary, can you talk to anybody yet?"

Bo's copilot, Warrant Officer Corey "Weary" McCleery, responded. "No joy on any circuit. I've got green lights, but nobody is talking."

White cut in, "Bright light at one o'clock, on the horizon. Anybody else see that?"

Bo leveled off and pointed the nose of her hovercraft at the light, which appeared to climb into the sky.

"Let's go check it out."

* * *

In the operations tent set up in the division headquarters area, Colonel Scott Tucker, the division operations officer, tried to explain to General Gupta why the landing operation had gotten derailed.

"Sir, we're experiencing full-spectrum jamming that started sometime this morning before the first dropships launched. The electronic intelligence folks have been working on it, but they haven't made any progress. They can't triangulate the source due to atmospherics, and we can't burn through it."

"Did the jamming cause the mech battalion to shove their heads up their asses?" demanded the general.

Tucker remained silent. It was a rhetorical question, and he'd already had enough ass chewing for one day.

Gupta sighed and pinched the bridge of his nose.

"What about the aviation element?"

"There is one flight of hovercopters airborne for recon right now and another flight prepping to launch. The other sixteen hovercopters are standing by for mission tasking. We don't have comms with them, but the aircrews were briefed to launch flares if they spot any hostiles." He paused and cleared his throat. "The, uh, the mechs that made the drop have begun to unload. We have nine available for mission tasking."

"Nine mechs to support the whole fucking division."

"There is some positive news, sir. The recon and logistics battalions are operational, as is the division headquarters staff."

Gupta grunted. "Okay, Ops. What's the status of the infantry?"

"The division is currently deployed in a circular formation around our position here." Tucker pointed to a chart on the tent wall. "As you can see, sir, there's no cover or significant terrain features for several kilometers in any direction, just a few low hummocks to the east and some to the north. I halted all advances until you've had the chance to address the officers and NCOs."

"And afterwards?"

"In the absence of an enemy force, I recommend we hold our current positions. At least until we get the comms situation sorted out."

The general's neck turned purple and his face a deep shade of red. "You just told me we're under electronic attack, Colonel. There's an enemy force out there somewhere that we need to find, fix, and destroy. My Marines don't maintain position when they're being attacked, *Colonel*. My Marines advance aggressively and take the fight to the enemy, *Colonel*. Is that clear, *Colonel?*"

Flecks of spittle sprayed every time the general punctuated his statements with "Colonel," and Tucker was taken aback by his reaction. Sending Space Marines to wander around in the desert with no intel or comms was a good way of getting them lost, or worse.

"Sir, I didn't—"

The tent flap flew up and Major Marc Heller, the general's adjutant, interrupted.

"General, sir, pardon the interruption, but you need to come out here." He motioned for General Gupta to follow him. "Now. Please."

The general gave the major a puzzled look but followed him outside. Captain C.J. Peterson, the division staff communications officer, caught up to Colonel Tucker.

"Damn, Scott. I'm sorry, dude. I thought the old man was going to tear your head off."

Tucker stared at the captain. "Don't apologize, Captain Peterson. Just get comms up, ASAP. We're almost a full day behind schedule. It would be nice to get back on track by tomorrow."

Peterson turned to walk away when Tucker stopped him. "One more thing, Captain. You might be married to my sister, but I am neither 'Scott' nor 'dude' to you. Not here, not at home, not anywhere. Is that clear?"

By then, General Gupta had joined the crowd of company commanders, senior enlisted men, and the rest of the command element gathered outside. They stared as a bright star on the horizon climbed high in the sky.

"What the hell is that thing?" Gupta asked. Nobody answered, and he looked around. "Anyone?"

"Some sort of weather satellite launch is my guess, General," Major Alicia Ibaretta, the staff meteorologist, answered. "It certainly looks like a weather rocket to me."

The general shot her an annoyed look, and several of the other staffers giggled and snorted as they turned away.

Major Ibaretta was a smart and sincere officer, but her view of the world was seen through the narrow prism of meteorology. Most of the staff thought she was along on the deployment because her husband was Colonel George Ibaretta, the division logistics officer. They were correct, but for the wrong reason. She didn't come on these deployments because her husband was a colonel, she came because she suspected her husband of dallying with the enlisted females on the staff.

"Hey, Matt, your guys are going to engage this thing, aren't they? It looks like it's heading straight for us," the general said.

The task force air defense officer, Major Matthew Wallace, fumbled for an answer. "Yes sir, I mean, the batteries should engage, sir. You see, it's the comms, sir, and the jamming. Not really our fault. The radars…" His voice faded under the general's withering glare.

"So you're not going to engage. Is that what you're telling me?"

Major Wallace looked sad. "No, sir. I mean, yes, sir. I mean—"

General Gupta took off at a run for the crude landing zone where rows of hovercopters stood ready for mission tasking.

"Major Stodden, get one of those damn surveillance birds down here on the double! I need to get out of here."

Major Karl Stodden, the division air operations officer, followed the general at a trot. His eyes searched the sky for the hovercopters that had been buzzing the deployment area since the force inserted. The only thing visible in the sky was the rocket, which had tipped over and was headed directly for the division headquarters. Without a radio to call them in, the hovercopters might as well have been back on Terra Earth.

Colonel Tucker watched the general run toward the landing zone with several staffers in tow.

"What the fuck's going on, Scott?"

Tucker turned as Kivak Sobieski stopped beside him. Tucker shrugged. "I have no idea, but I think it has something to do with that thing." He pointed at the incoming rocket.

The crowd of Space Marines gathered outside the HQ tent drifted away by ones and twos until they saw the general run for the hovercopters. After that, it became a stampede. Some of them ran to hide in their tents, while others took off running for the barren desert. Tucker heard the word "nuke" and he knew that running just meant he would die tired.

He could hear it now, the roar of a rocket engine and static electricity. The weapon was just a blur as it dove toward the division headquarters, and then it vanished in a brilliant flash of white light.

* * * * *

Chapter Eight

Thirty minutes after Gunny Parker disappeared for the rear, Fortis had become a little anxious. Whatever grand strategy the command element had come up with couldn't require much explanation, because without communications the Marines were limited to basic maneuvers. He considered a trip to the command element himself but changed his mind. Maybe—

Someone flopped down next to him and startled Fortis from his reverie. It was Liz Sherer.

"Are you guys always this disorganized. Lieutenant?"

Fortis shook his head. "Landing a force of five thousand Space Marines and all our equipment is a complex evolution that requires flexibility to improvise, adapt, and overcome obstacles as they present themselves. That's why we train so often and so hard."

Sherer laughed. "If I wanted the book answer, I would have read the book. C'mon. No quotes, just deep background. What's really going on?"

Fortis thought for a second. "I've been a Space Marine for less than a year. Maybe that's a question for someone with more experience. Why aren't you back at headquarters for the big pow-wow?"

"There's another TNN correspondent embedded with the staff. I'd rather be out here with the grunts."

Corporal Ystremski approached and took a knee next to Fortis. "Hey, LT, any word?"

"I was going to ask you the same thing. I'm still waiting to hear what the meeting was all about. Do you know?"

Ystremski made the "okay" sign with his thumb and forefinger and then poked his nose in and out of the hole.

"What does that mean?"

"Fuck nose, sir. As in, fuck knows what's going on at HQ. Buncha officers and sergeants drinking coffee and comparing dicks, I expect."

Fortis rolled his eyes, and Sherer chuckled.

Ystremski pointed at the distant horizon. "Hey, what's that?"

A bright streak climbed skyward, a trail of white against the pale blue backdrop of the upper atmosphere.

"Looks like a rocket," said Private Parrello from a nearby position. "Long-range rocket artillery, maybe."

Parrello was a Foxtrot Company cherry, a graduate school washout who took a ton of shit from the other Space Marines because he seemed to know something about everything. A scout sniper, he had also earned an early reputation among the other scout snipers as a long-range, stone-cold shooter.

"Why only one?" Fortis asked.

The rocket continued high into the sky before it nosed over and turned down toward the Space Marines. It passed overhead at about five hundred meters, and the sound it made was a rumbling buzz.

"Oh shit!" cried Parrello. "Oh, holy shit!"

"What? What is it?"

"Take cover! I think it's a nuke!"

* * *

"**W**hoa!"

A brilliant flash of light from the direction of division headquarters was followed by a powerful shock wave that buffeted Bo's hovercopter and threw it perilously toward the desert floor. The internal communications circuit exploded in confused chatter.

"What was that?"

"My eyes!"

"Are we going down?"

"Shut up!" shouted Bo as she fought to get control of the hovercopter. She got the nose pointed up and climbed away from the danger. "Where's Bingo?"

"I don't see him," replied Weary.

"Crap. Okay, who's hurt?"

"Ballein is down," reported Staff Sergeant White. "He was looking back when the blast went off and it blinded him."

Ping! Ping! Ping!

"We're taking fire!"

Bo banked left and right to escape the ground fire. The hovercopter felt sluggish, and she knew they had taken damage to the flight controls. The pilot grunted as she hauled back on the stick to climb up above the enemy fire, and she felt two *thunks* as Weary launched flares to indicate the location of hostiles to the Space Marines below.

"There are enemy troops everywhere down there," said White. "Are we going to engage?"

"Negative," Bo replied through gritted teeth. "Leave them for the ground pounders. We need to find out where that rocket came from and destroy the launcher."

* * *

The Space Marines hit the ground at Parrello's warning. Fortis grabbed Sherer, threw her down into his fighting position, and dove on top of her. An instant later, a blinding flash ripped across the sky, followed by the hammer blow of a shockwave and a searing blast of wind. Fortis got his helmet on a split second before the blast, and his visor whited out as a million grains of sand scoured the surface. When the wind subsided, he pulled the helmet off and looked in the direction of the explosion.

The force of the blast had produced a mushroom cloud of sand, rocks, and dirt two thousand meters high. All around him, Space Marines struggled to their feet. Liz Sherer groaned when Fortis grabbed her arm.

"I'm okay. See to the others."

Fortis staggered to check on the nearest Space Marines and discovered that most were merely stunned by the huge detonation.

"That wasn't much of a nuke, LT." Parrello emerged from under a pile of sand and rock. "Their technology must suck, because if we fired a nuke that big it would have fried us all at this range."

"Lieutenant Fortis!" Ystremski waved from a small depression where he had taken cover. "Take a look at this!"

Fortis got down next to the corporal and accepted his binoculars.

"There."

Fortis looked in the direction Ystremski indicated. He saw two hovercopter flares drifting down over what looked like a mass of soldiers in the distance.

"I guess those are Maltaani, sir?

"Yeah." An icy fist squeezed Fortis's heart.

There are millions of them.

* * *

"There it is. Two o'clock low."

Bo looked where Weary indicated and saw two large trailers and a few smaller support vehicles arrayed on the desert floor. One of the trailers had an empty launch rail in the bed, and the other had a large rocket angled at forty-five degrees. She slowed the hovercopter until they were almost in a hover to get a better look at the situation on the ground.

"Looks like they're getting ready to launch that other one."

Soldiers scrambled for cover at the approach of the hovercopter.

"What are we doing, Bo?"

"Any sign of Bingo?"

"No, ma'am."

"Then we're going to attack on our own. We can't let them fire that other rocket."

By then, the Maltaani launcher crew had finished raising the second rocket to the vertical.

"Let's do it."

The hovercopter vibrated as Weary activated the visor sighting system for the guns and rocket pods mounted under the craft.

"You okay back there, White?"

"Yeah, we're good. Let's get this over with."

Just then, Bingo roared by in his hovercopter, diving toward the launchers.

"Hey! Where did they come from?"

"Who cares? Hang on!"

The engines whined and the hovercopter surged forward in pursuit of Bingo. As Bo and Weary watched, Bingo fired a full spread of rockets. Ground fire chewed at the hovercopter, and Bingo's craft lurched as pieces of the rotor and fuselage spun off in all directions.

The damaged hovercopter lurched out of control, rolled sideways, and exploded in a fiery ball of aviation fuel when it impacted the desert floor. Bingo's rockets had peppered the ground around the launchers, but the vehicles appeared undamaged.

Bo aimed her hovercopter straight at the target and dove at max power. The airframe shook as rocket salvos left their pods and streaked toward the launchers. Enemy fire ripped into the hovercopter and the windscreen became a spiderweb of cracks. A round punched through the glass, tore off Weary's head, and blood sprayed all over the cockpit. The machinegun turret under the nose of the craft slewed wildly as the copilot's helmet tumbled around the cockpit with the visor sighting system still activated.

Despite Bo's close-range attack, the Maltaani rocket launcher still stood and white smoke began to billow from the bottom of the weapon. With all her rockets expended and no way to control the gun system, Bo knew what she had to do.

"DINLI!"

The aircraft slammed into the launcher just before the rocket lifted off. Both launchers were destroyed by the resulting explosion and the weapon roared off on a crazy horizontal flight before it exploded harmlessly in the empty desert.

* * * * *

Chapter Nine

The Space Marines shook off the effects of the massive blast and prepared to meet the Maltaani assault. Fortis watched the Maltaani soldiers grow larger as they closed in on the Space Marines. They looked human, although somewhat taller, with elongated arms and legs.

Fortis heard a wobbly blaring sound—*a bugle?*—that seemed to urge the attacking troops forward. The enemy advanced, shoulder to shoulder at a fast walk. Fat bolts of blueish plasma streaked out from the Space Marine positions as heavy weapons crews opened up at long range. Gaps appeared in the Maltaani ranks, but other troops filled in and their advance continued without pause.

"It's a slaughter!" shouted Sherer. She got to her feet to get a better view and aimed her camera down the line.

"Get down!" Fortis pulled her down to the ground. "You'll draw fire."

On cue, the low earthwork in front of Fortis's hole exploded in a spray of dirt. Fortis rolled over and peeked up at the enemy. The heavy weapons fire was continuous now, and he saw bright red flashes as the scout snipers engaged individual targets. The lieutenant couldn't discern any badges of rank among the Maltaani, but he knew the shooters would concentrate their fire on anyone who looked like a leader. Still, the enemy advance seemed inexorable.

The Maltaani began to return fire in earnest and Fortis ducked as heavy caliber rounds snapped past overhead. The projectiles bounced across the ground when they landed behind the Space Marine lines and Fortis saw two Marines go down with ricochet wounds.

He charged his pulse rifle and aimed at the approaching Maltaani. The surging mass was well within range and the Space Marines ruthlessly mowed them down. When the enemy was about fifty meters out, the front rank knelt and leveled their weapons while the rank behind them prepared to deliver a standing volley.

The salvo tore into the Space Marines. A platoon from Golf Company vanished in a cloud of dirt, rocks, and body parts, and the Maltaani charged toward the gap.

The Space Marines increased their rate of fire when they recognized the danger they were in. The Maltaani stumbled over the bodies of their comrades as the corpses stacked up, slowing their assault. Fortis fired and reloaded as fast as he could at the mass of attackers. The charging system wasn't keeping up with his rate of fire, and he reached for a battery magazine to discover he only had one left.

Aimed fire, dammit.

On his right, a heavy weapons crew set up and began to hammer the attackers at point-blank range. Privates Jim Yount and Jim McCoy, "the Jimmies" as they were known around the company, fired their automatic pulse cannon with devastating effect. The high-power pulses shredded row after row of enemy soldiers and the assault stalled. Fortis watched as the Maltaani tried to respond with another mass salvo, but their troops milled around in stunned confusion at the ferocity of the Space Marine defense. Slowly but surely, they started to fall back from the Space Marines.

"They're falling back!" an anonymous Space Marine called out. "We won!"

"Shut up and keep shooting," shouted Ystremski in reply. "They're not finished by a long shot."

A company-sized group of Maltaani broke away from the main force and charged forward. They reached the first line of hastily dug fighting holes, and the fighting became a swirling hand-to-hand mass of humans and aliens bent on the destruction of the other.

Fortis watched a Space Marine jam his bayonet deep into a Maltaani soldier and struggle to jerk it loose. He pulled the trigger and got his weapon free, only to be shot in the back by another Maltaani. Two Space Marines avenged their fallen comrade with the butts of their pulse rifles as they bludgeoned the Maltaani to death.

Grenades landed beyond the advancing enemy troops and blasted gaping holes in their ranks. The Space Marines surrounded the surviving Maltaani and killed them with grim precision.

The Maltaani withdrawal continued, and they were soon out of pulse rifle range. The scout snipers kept finding marks and the heavy weapons chewed at the ranks of the retreating enemy as they fell back. A leaden silence blanketed the battlefield as the firing dwindled away. For now, the battle was over.

Fortis rose to a low crouch and surveyed the scene around him. Corpsmen were moving along the lines, and it shocked the lieutenant to see how many Space Marines had fallen. He'd been so focused on reloading and firing that he hadn't realize the Space Marines had even taken casualties. Corporal Ystremski skidded to a halt and dove down next to the lieutenant.

"What's our status, LT?"

"I was going to ask you the same thing."

"You're in charge. I'm just a corporal."

Liz Sherer emerged from the hole she had taken cover in amid the fury of the Maltaani assault and shook off the sand and dirt that caked her LBA.

"Do you two ever stop fucking around?"

Fortis and Ystremski exchanged glances.

"Gallows humor, Liz."

"It's going to be dark soon," called Parrello from his firing position.

"How the fuck do you know that?" demanded the corporal.

Parrello rose up on his knees and pointed at the horizon. "The sky over there—argh!" Parrello pitched over backwards before Fortis heard the crack of the shot.

"Sniper!"

The Jimmies opened up on the tangled mass of Maltaani corpses that marked the high tide of their advance. Gore and body parts flew up into the air as the pulse cannon obliterated the enemy dead. A single Maltaani soldier rose up from his hiding spot among the piles of bodies and stumbled toward his own lines, but he couldn't outrun the Jimmies. One pulse sent his head spinning one way while another blew his body in half, throwing it in the other direction. The Jimmies continued to fire long after their target was dead, and the resulting carnage sickened Fortis.

"Cease fire! Cease fire!"

Corporal Ystremski waved his arm to get their attention and the pulse cannon fell silent.

"Watch the pile in case there are more of them playing possum."

Fortis scrambled to where a corpsman named Nugent was hovering over Private Parrello.

The wounded man writhed in pain and gurgled as blood bubbled from his mouth and nose. "Mama. I want my mama," he pleaded.

There was a large hole in his body armor just above his waist. The corpsman looked up at Fortis and shook his head.

"I want to go home…Mama…"

"You're gonna be okay," Nugent lied smoothly. "Just relax, buddy, we'll get you home." He pulled a syrette out of his medical kit and jabbed it into Parrello's exposed neck. "Just a second."

The wounded Space Marine stopped moving as the powerful narcotic took over, but he continued to moan.

"Mama… Mama…"

The corpsman motioned Fortis to one side so they could speak out of earshot.

"I can't fix this, LT," he said in a grim whisper. "I stuck my hand inside his LBA and there's nothing intact to work with. I can't believe he's still alive."

Parrello's agony had attracted the attention of other nearby Space Marines, and they drifted closer to stare in horrified fascination.

Corporal Ystremski approached Fortis and Nugent. "Doc, you gotta do something. The other troops are starting to panic."

The corpsman threw his hands up as tears of frustration spilled down his cheeks. "I can't. He's too fucked up."

"Then give him something for the pain."

"I already did."

"Mama…"

Ystremski leaned into the corpsman's face. "I mean, *give him something for the pain.*"

Nugent looked at Fortis. The enormity of what Ystremski wanted the corpsman to do hit the young officer like a gut punch and he felt light-headed.

"Sir?"

A lump in the back of his throat stopped Fortis from speaking, all he could do was nod.

When the trio returned to Parrello, they saw Liz Sherer on her knees next to the wounded man.

"Mama's here, baby," she murmured as she held his hand and stroked his forehead. "Mama's here."

Parrello's cries had faded to a soft mewling as he drifted in and out of the narcotic-induced unconsciousness. Nugent kneeled next to him and pulled out another syrette. He looked up at Fortis, who squeezed his eyes shut and nodded again.

"Come home to Mama," crooned Liz as the drug took effect.

Finally, Parrello lay still.

"What the fuck are you looking at?" Corporal Ystremski demanded of the Space Marines who had gathered around the scene. "Get back to your posts and keep digging." He turned to Fortis. "A moment, LT?"

The troops scrambled back to their holes as Ystremski led Fortis a short distance away.

"We gotta keep these guys busy, sir. If that's the last thing they see before the sun goes down, they'll think about it all night."

"Makes sense."

"The other thing we need to do—that *you* need to do—is find out what the hell is going on with the rest of the division. It looks like the Maltaani have given up for now, so this is a good time to unfuck ourselves."

Fortis looked back in the direction of division headquarters. "That was a helluva blast. What about radiation?"

"I didn't bring a Geiger counter. Did you?"

Fortis shook his head.

"Then don't worry about it, LT. The Fleet hospital ship can cure cancer, but they can't cure bullet holes. I'll keep these guys focused here. You go find somebody in charge and figure out what the hell is going on."

* * * * *

Chapter Ten

It was well after dark by the time Fortis returned to Foxtrot Company. He found Ystremski and slumped down next to him.

"There's a giant crater where division headquarters used to be," he said. "I found a captain from logistics. He was missing an arm and half his chest and I don't think he's going to make it. I also came across two dropship pilots holding hands and crying. They were naked because the blast shredded their flight suits. Neither one of them registered that I was talking to them. Other than them, I didn't find a single living officer."

"I guess you're in command, LT. DINLI."

"Yeah, thanks."

"What about the perimeter? Did you get a chance to check it out?"

"I started to walk the perimeter, but I stopped when it got dark. I almost wandered out into the desert through a gap in the line between Hotel and India Companies."

Ystremski snorted. "Hotel and India are in the same battalion. How the fuck are they not linked up?"

"Golf got hit pretty hard during the attack, so Hotel shifted left to hold the flank. India didn't follow, and that opened the gap. I found a sergeant from India and told him to square it away. I'll inspect the rest at first light. Too many nervous Space Marines ready to shoot anything that moves in the dark. From what I can tell they only hit us from one direction, so most of the division is still fresh. What's been happening here? All quiet?"

"Digging in. Haven't seen any Maltaani."

"Did you get casualty numbers?"

"Foxtrot Company had four KIA, nine wounded. Golf had thirty-six KIA, unknown wounded."

"Could have been worse."

"There's a helluva lot of those fuckers. Good thing they don't understand tactics."

"A lot of kukris were earned today."

"More tomorrow, I reckon."

The two men sat in silence for a moment before the corporal spoke.

"Any word from Fleet, LT?"

"I don't know if we have comms with them. I think all the radio gear got nuked."

"Figures. Never around when we need them. Oh hey, that reporter lady was looking for you."

"Damn, I forgot all about her. Is she still around?"

"I don't know. Maybe. She's pretty freaked out, to tell you the truth."

Fortis sighed. "Makes two of us."

Ystremski pushed something into the lieutenant's hands.

"Have a pig square, sir. It'll make you feel better."

"Thanks."

Fortis munched his pig square and stared at the stars suspended in the dark sky over Balfan-48. His thoughts turned to *Atlas* and the rest of the fleet, and he wondered if they were aware of the events on the surface.

High overhead, a bright streak burned white toward the horizon and disappeared in a flash. Fortis imagined he heard a loud *boom*.

"You see that, sir?"

"Yeah, it looked like something burning into the atmosphere."

"I hope it wasn't *Atlas*."

Fortis groaned. "Why would you even *say* something like that, dickhead?"

"Lieutenant Fortis? Does anyone know where I can find Lieutenant Fortis?" Liz Sherer's voice carried a long way in the night air.

"Keep your damn voice down," hissed Corporal Ystremski.

The reporter flopped down next to the corporal. "Have you seen Lieutenant Fortis?"

"I'm right here, Liz."

"Sorry, I didn't see you. What's our status? When is Fleet coming back?"

Before Fortis could answer, Ystremski chimed in. "This is what we call being in the shit, ma'am. Just another day in the Corps."

"What the esteemed corporal means is, our status is unchanged since the Maltaani withdrew. I went to see what was left of division HQ and found a huge crater. As for Fleet, I don't know if they even know we've been attacked because we don't have comms."

"In the shit," Liz intoned.

"Here, Liz. Have a pig square. It'll make you feel better."

Fortis pulled out his ringed notebook and a pencil stub. The notebook cover had a small built-in light, and he began to write.

"What's he doing?" Liz asked between bites of pig square.

"He's writing his next citation for bravery," Ystremski replied.

Fortis looked up from his work and smiled. "Shut up, dickhead. I'm making notes about today's events, Liz. It helps me keep track of what's happened so I can submit an accurate report when we get back to *Atlas*. I do it every night."

* * *

*M*ama... Mama...

    Liz woke with a start. It took her several seconds to remember where she was. A few stars glimmered high overhead, but they didn't shed enough light to illuminate the surface. She squeezed her eyes shut, but she couldn't wipe away the image that had haunted her dreams and woken her so abruptly.

Parrello.

Liz was a well-traveled reporter who had spent her career in dangerous places pursuing stories no other reporter had the courage to cover. She'd been a pool reporter on bug hunts with the Space Marines, and she had accompanied bounty hunters into deep space in pursuit of slavers and resource pirates. She'd seen the aftermath of battle before, but nothing had prepared her for the shocking level of violence she'd witnessed during the Maltaani attack. The agonizing death throes of Private Parrello had ripped a hole in her heart, and the memory was seared into her soul.

"You okay, Liz?" Fortis whispered from his hole next to hers.

The reporter was embarrassed to discover her cheeks were wet with tears, and she didn't respond.

"It's okay to cry, you know. It was a helluva a day."

When she thought she could trust her voice, Liz spoke. "How do you do it?"

"Do what?"

"The fighting. These guys. Most of them are just boys. How do you stand it?"

"DINLI."

Liz propped herself up on one elbow and stared at the darkness in Fortis's direction.

"Don't give me that macho nonsense. This stuff has to affect you."

"I never said it doesn't affect me."

They sat in dark silence for a long moment. Liz thought Fortis had fallen back to sleep.

"Liz, I'm responsible for the men under my command. All of them. If I hesitate to issue an order because some of them might die, it could get us all killed. If we pause to mourn every time someone dies, it could get us all killed. Every mistake, every misstep, and someone dies. Death is at our elbow every step of the way in this life, and, if you want to stay sane, you have to make peace with it.

"DINLI might sound like macho nonsense to you, but it's emotional insulation that gets me through days like today. I know that every single Space Marine that dies is my responsibility, but I can't afford to stop and feel it every time it happens. DINLI helps me push it away. Later, when it's quiet and I have time to think, that's when it gets to me. That's how I know it's okay to cry."

They lapsed into silence. After a few minutes, Liz heard the lieutenant begin to snore lightly. She rolled over and hugged herself as silent tears spilled from her eyes, and she waited for dawn.

* * * * *

Chapter Eleven

"Wake up, LT! We've got company."

"Wha-what?"

Fortis shook his head to clear his sleep-addled brain and sat up. The night sky had retreated, and the gray light of dawn settled over the Space Marines. Off in the distance, he heard the tinny wail of bugles.

"The bastards are back." Corporal Ystremski squatted next to the hole where the lieutenant had fallen asleep the night before. He cupped his hand behind his ear and rotated his head. "Third Regiment, is my guess."

Fortis grabbed his pulse rifle and got to his feet. "Anything on this side?"

The corporal pulled him back down to the ground.

"Nothing yet, sir. No point giving them a target, though."

The bugling continued, and Fortis heard automatic pulse cannons open up on the far side of their position. His mind raced.

"Okay. Pass the word, stand to fighting holes and prepare for attack. I'll go see what's happening over there."

Fortis ran in a low crouch toward the sounds of firing. Pulse rifle salvos joined the cacophony and the lieutenant picked up his pace. Hissing lumps of rock skipped across the ground in front of him, and it took him a moment to realize they were Maltaani rounds that passed over the Space Marines and ricocheted behind the lines.

The sounds of battle guided him to the fighting in front of Third Regiment. Dead and wounded Marines littered the ground and knots of Space Marines were hammering at the ranks of advancing enemy. Fortis almost tripped over a dead Maltaani soldier. It alarmed him to see how far they had penetrated through the lines. More enemy soldiers surged forward, and Fortis knew that the Space Marines couldn't hold much longer.

Two scout snipers were firing from a position behind a pile of dirt and rocks. Fortis dove into position next to them. Scores of Maltaani soldiers fell to their well-aimed fire, but the press of enemy bodies was inexorable.

"If we don't get reinforcements in here most riki-tik, they're going to break through," he shouted over the din.

"No shit." One of the scout snipers glanced sideways at the lieutenant as he reloaded. "Sir."

Fortis scrambled over to a pair of Space Marines who had taken cover behind a low pile of rocks and dirt. He thumped one of them on the shoulder and pointed to the left.

"Take off that way. Every company you find, tell them to send a platoon this way, on the double." He slapped the other Marine and pointed to the right. "You go that way. Tell every company to send a platoon."

Before the Marines took off, Fortis grabbed them. "Don't delay or we'll be overrun. Now, go!"

Fortis fired and reloaded and fired again, but the Maltaani continued to advance. He watched in horror as the enemy surged forward and engulfed a group of Space Marines on the edge of the formation. The hand-to-hand fighting started and the Maltaani only fell back when another group of Marines charged into the fray, firing from the hip.

A series of sharp explosions peppered the Space Marine lines and shrapnel tore through their ranks, killing and wounding them by the score. Fortis searched the mass of enemy for the source of the fire and located a squad of soldiers armed with what looked like stubby grenade launchers. He fired a long burst from his pulse rifle and noted the dead and dying with grim satisfaction.

Meanwhile, the main body of the attack surged up to the Space Marine lines. The combatants mixed together as the Space Marines rose from their fighting holes to meet the charge. Rifle butts, fists, and boots became deadly weapons as the two sides collided.

Someone slammed Fortis on the shoulder and he whirled, his rifle ready to fire.

"Friendly!" shouted the sergeant who grabbed him. "Echo Company, Second Battalion. Where do you want us?"

"There!" Fortis pointed to a growing gap in the Marine lines. "Fill that hole."

The sergeant ran forward, followed by his company. The arrival of fresh troops blunted the Maltaani attack, and they began to give ground.

Another sergeant approached Fortis.

"Hey LT, First Battalion, Alpha and Charlie Companies, reporting as ordered."

"Who sent you?"

"I don't know, sir. A runner came by and said an officer wanted every other company to get over here, pronto. You're the only officer we've seen since yesterday."

Fortis pointed to the left, where the right flank of the Maltaani attack threatened to overwhelm the Space Marine defenders.

"Reinforce the left flank, and don't let them roll up that side of the line."

"Aye, aye, sir." The sergeant gestured to his men. "Follow me!"

Fortis no sooner turned his attention back to the battle when he heard a familiar voice behind him.

"Hey, LT, where do you want us?"

The Jimmies were behind him, straining under the weight of their automatic pulse cannon.

"What the fuck are you doing here?"

"Corporal Ystremski sent us, said you might need the help."

"Set up right here and put some fire on their second and third ranks. We've been holding them, but they are building momentum."

Yount and McCoy had their weapon in action in seconds, and the high-velocity pulses tore gaping holes in the Maltaani formation. Enemy soldiers ran in every direction to escape the onslaught, and Fortis sensed a shift in the momentum of the battle. The moment was fleeting; there were still too many Maltaani for one pulse cannon to repel. It didn't take long for the Maltaani to zero in on the Jimmies.

The ground around the Jimmies exploded as incoming rounds peppered the ground. Yount jerked and twitched as shrapnel tore into his body, and his helmet somersaulted high in the air when the top of his head exploded in a reddish-gray spray.

"Jimmy, no!" McCoy screamed. He concentrated his fire on the spot where the enemy gunner had fired from and the enemy shooter disappeared in a flash of pulse energy.

Suddenly, an impromptu duel developed between McCoy and another enemy position. The fighting paused as combatants on both sides stopped and watched in stunned silence as the gunners stood to their weapons and traded shot for shot. It became one of those weird moments in combat when the world around the duelists ceased to exist and their entire beings were focused on killing the other.

Finally, the enemy gunner scored a hit on McCoy's pulse cannon. While the Space Marine struggled to fix his weapon, an explosive round struck him in the abdomen and tore him in half. His head and arms flipped one way and his legs the other, and horrific gore tinged the air red. The Maltaani victory was short-lived because a hundred Space Marine pulse rifles fired as one and the enemy soldier was shredded by high energy bolts.

Meanwhile, the attackers surged closer to the Space Marine battleline. They didn't seek cover or maneuver to avoid Marine fire, they marched forward and died. There were still so many that even the withering fire of the Marines couldn't stop them, and Fortis felt a stab of fear as the distance between the lines narrowed.

Too many.

"Get the fuck out of the way!"

Fortis watched in amazement as a Space Marine with a cigar clenched between his teeth and an FGU, a flame generation unit, on his back charged forward. The Space Marines typically used FGUs to clear bug holes, but the Marine sprayed fire on the attacking Maltaani horde. Oily black smoke rose above the battlefield as hundreds of Maltaani were set aflame. Their screams of agony and fear were drowned out by the horrifying *whoosh* of the weapon.

The Marine stalked forward through the burning hellscape he created, sweeping the tongue of fire back and forth as he advanced. Despite the enemy fire aimed at him, he remained on his feet until a Maltaani round hit the FGU. The unit exploded in a spray of fire and he managed three more steps toward the enemy before he fell facedown among the smoking dead.

The astonishing heroics of the fire-wielding Space Marine broke the back of the Maltaani assault. Fortis watched as thousands of enemy soldiers scrambled back the way they'd come, and the Marines began to press their own attack.

Corporal Ystremski appeared at Fortis's elbow.

"We gotta stop them, LT. We can't chase 'em, we'll get chopped to pieces if they turn on us."

The two men ran after the ranks of the Space Marines pursuing to fleeing enemy. After a great deal of shouting and pointing, the men relented and fell back to their positions.

The sheer savagery of the battle stunned Fortis. Unidentifiable pieces of bodies littered the battlefield, and the stink of burning flesh added a horrific tang to the pungent odors of burned ozone and torn-open bodies. The carnage of the first day had been severe, but it paled in comparison to what he'd just witnessed. Fortis shuddered when he thought how close they'd come to being overrun.

The Space Marines picked their way through the fallen. Wounded and dead Marines were recovered from the battlefield and wounded enemies were dispatched with a bayonet thrust. Two of the Marines grabbed the charred remains of the cigar-smoking Marine and dragged him back behind the lines.

"Who was he?" Fortis asked.

"Carrasco," one of them replied.

"Lance Corporal Carlos Carrasco," the other one added. "Alpha Company, Two-One. Got out of the brig just in time to make the drop."

"DINLI."

"Fuck yeah, DINLI."

"Hey, LT, we've got a problem." Ystremski gestured at the Space Marines around them. "There must be eight different companies here, and nobody knows what the hell is going on. We need to get organized, quick, before they come back."

"What do you recommend?"

"Fall back."

"Fall back?"

"Yes, sir. Consolidate our position and set up a reserve force. We can't have a thousand Marines leave their posts to respond to every attack on the other side of the perimeter. Eventually those fuckers will figure out how to attack from two different directions at once."

"Hmm. Okay. How far back?"

"Half. Maybe more. Right now, the formation is seven klicks side-to-side. Let's cut it to three."

"What if they have another nuke?"

"Then we die sooner than we thought, sir." Ystremski kicked at a clod of dirt. "The Maltaani lost a helluva lot of troops in the past couple days. If they had another nuke, I think they would have used it by now."

Fortis nodded. "That makes sense."

"If we cut the perimeter in half, that would free up enough Marines for a ready reserve and get some of the other stuff we need done."

"What other stuff?"

"We need a casualty collection point, somewhere to move the wounded away from the line so the docs can work on them. Somewhere to collect the KIAs, too."

"Okay, Gunny. Where do we start?"

"Gunny?"

The lieutenant dug into his equipment belt, pulled out a set of gunnery sergeant chevrons, and handed them to Ystremski. "I took these off a dead Space Marine I found near the crater yesterday. He doesn't need them anymore, and I need a gunny to help me sort things out. Battlefield promotion."

The newly minted gunnery sergeant rubbed his grizzled chin. "I'm gonna regret this."

"DINLI."

* * * * *

Chapter Twelve

Back on the flagship *Atlas*, Major Kiti Niskala entered the FOC, the Flag Operations Center, and paused by the rear hatch to allow her eyes to adjust to the dim lighting. Three rows of consoles faced a trio of large blank screens that covered the forward bulkhead, while smaller screens dotted the side walls.

A chief petty officer approached. Major Niskala indicated the forward row of consoles where Fleet Admiral Kinshaw and his primary staffers were stationed.

"Major Niskala, Ninth Division Drop Coordinator, here to see Admiral Kinshaw."

The chief nodded and waved Niskala through

"Excuse me, sir?"

Admiral Kinshaw swiveled around.

"What is it?"

The major struggled to control her nerves. Burle "Ooze" Kinshaw had earned his callsign during his days flying atmospheric light bombers. He was even-tempered with a keen eye for detail, and he had a reputation of being unflappable in the most stressful situations. Kinshaw was the perfect counterpoint to the mercurial General Gupta, but he was not known to suffer fools lightly.

"Sir, I'm Major Niskala, the Ninth Division Drop Coordinator. General Gupta tasked me with coordinating follow-on drops for the mechanized battalion."

"Have you sorted out the mech issues?"

"Yes, sir, we have. Three companies; thirty-six battle mechs and three command mechs in all, loaded and ready to drop. We just need authorization."

Admiral Kinshaw laughed at Niskala and nearby staffers chuckled, and her cheeks burned with embarrassment and confusion.

"Where exactly do you want to drop them, Major?"

"I don't understand."

He pointed to the blank screens. "Those monitors represent the totality of our situational awareness of what's happening on the surface. We've had no contact with the landing force since the comms umbilicals were unplugged, and the dropships launched. The entire Ninth Division dropped onto Balfan-48 and disappeared."

The news stunned Niskala. "Sir, I... uh—I didn't know. I've been so busy with the mechs that I haven't been tracking the situation on the surface."

"The intel shop believes the Maltaani have aimed some kind of super jammer at us. They're still working out how to defeat it. Until then, there's not much we can do to support the invasion."

"Drop us where the division landed—"

"Major, did you not hear what I said? We have no comms and we have no sensors. There's nothing we can do right now. Go back to your mechs and stay ready to drop at a moment's notice. Got it?"

"Yes, sir."

Niskala walked to the hatch on wooden legs and stepped into the passageway leading to the dropship hangar.

"Major!"

She turned and saw another Space Marine flagging her down. When he got close, she saw he was a fellow major.

"Hi. Nils Anders." He offered his hand, and they shook. "Second Battalion Intel."

"Kiti Niskala, Division Drop Coordinator."

"I overheard you talking to the admiral. Your mechs, they're ready to go?"

"All dressed up and nowhere to go, apparently."

"Yeah, well, we're working on that. What the admiral didn't tell you was that we have infrared coverage of the surface, but the atmosphere diffuses the heat signatures. All we can see are hot spots with no definition."

"Five thousand Space Marines should make a pretty big heat smear, right?"

"They should, but shortly after the division landed, we detected an intense hot spot that might have been a nuke. For all we know, the entire division is gone. We won't know for sure until we get the jamming sorted out, but it's a possibility. That's why you can't drop where the division landed."

"Damn."

"I've got a pair of autonomous drones ready to surveille the landing zone when the surface cools down after dark. We won't be able to analyze their data until we recover them. There are no guarantees about what that data may show, but it's the best thing we've got going right now."

"How long until you know?"

"We're scheduled to recover the drones in twelve hours. If the imagery is good, we'll know within an hour after that."

Niskala checked her watch.

"The mech battalion will be manned and ready to launch in twelve hours, Major Anders. Just point us in the right direction."

Anders smiled and nodded.

"Will do."

* * *

Fortis spent the rest of the morning touring the perimeter. He talked with countless Space Marines, commended them for their stubborn defense, and let them know that there was a plan in the works to reduce and secure the perimeter. Most seemed relieved that there was still a command structure in place, albeit a second lieutenant. He was frank about their position, and he did his best to quell the rumors circulating among the men.

The two most common complaints were about ammo and water. The diffuse light on Balfan-48 didn't generate enough energy for the LBA solar panels to quickly charge their pulse rifle batteries, and the hardest hit companies were running low. He promised to look into the battery situation, but all he could do about the water was encourage the Space Marines to conserve what they had.

"I don't know when the Fleet will be back," he repeated countless times. "I'm sure they know what's happening down here."

The first part was the truth, but the second was guess work. The Maltaani jamming had proven so effective that he didn't know if Fleet was capable of following the situation on the surface.

After he finished his tour of the perimeter, Fortis went in search of Ystremski. He found the gunny and Liz hunched over a diagram scratched into the dirt.

"The lieutenant ordered us to fall back into a more defensible position. When we contract our lines, it will free up a lot of Marines to serve as a reserve force to reinforce our lines when needed without weakening our defenses elsewhere. We can also use that manpower to replace the support troops that died with the headquarters staff."

"How can I help?" the reporter asked.

"As soon as the lieutenant gives me the order, we're going to fall back to the new lines. Anywhere you pitch in will be a big help. Maybe you can help with the wounded." He saw Fortis approaching and straightened up. "Speaking of the lieutenant."

"What's this about a plan?" Fortis asked with a grin. "How did that happen?"

"I was explaining your tactical brilliance to this esteemed member of the press, sir."

Liz snorted and shook her head.

"I just finished walking the perimeter. There's a lot of confusion about what's going on. They're not scared, but the uncertainty is creating a lot of very anxious Space Marines."

"While you were wandering around, I've been hard at work implementing your plan, sir. I collected musters, and we've got about twenty-eight hundred able-bodied Space Marines and another three hundred walking wounded."

Fortis gasped. "Twenty-eight hundred? That can't be right. There were five thousand of us when we landed yesterday."

"The nuke killed about fifteen hundred guys, sir. The entire staff, the air combat element, the support battalion, medical. Hell, the only HQ types we didn't lose was the mech battalion and that's because most of them are still on *Atlas*. Add to that the two attacks... We might have pushed them back, but they killed a lot of our guys before they withdrew."

"Did you see how many of them there are?" Liz blurted. "You'll never kill them all."

Gunny Ystremski nodded. "If we keep fighting their way, you're probably right. However, we're not going to do that anymore. First things first; while I was collecting musters I marked our fall back positions. As soon as you give the order, every other company will withdraw. When they're set, the rest will follow."

"WIAs and KIAs?"

"We've been sending them back all morning, LT. The corpsmen set up a casualty collection point near the crater and every company has litter bearers assigned." He nodded to Liz. "That might be a good place for you to help out, ma'am. If the offer is still open, that is."

"Of course. I'm not much of a nurse, but I'll do my best. Where is it?"

Ystremski pointed in the direction of the crater. "Go that way until you find the big hole and then look for the wounded guys, I guess. I haven't been there myself."

The reporter set off in search of the field hospital while Fortis considered the diagram Ystremski had scratched in the dirt.

"You know something, Gunny? The longer I look at it, the more I think our position looks like a noose."

Ystremski scuffed over the diagram with his boot. "You think too much, sir. We have 'em right where we want 'em."

"Yeah. All right, fall back."

* * * * *

Chapter Thirteen

Four hours later, the Space Marines completed their withdrawal to the new positions. Some of them grumbled about having to dig new holes, but from what Fortis saw, it was a smooth evolution. The compact lines were more defensible, and organized reinforcements would be critical if the Maltaani continued their mass attacks. If the Space Marines had had their usual complement of air and mechanized support, he would never have concentrated the troops. Given what they'd seen of the Maltaani, they would be forced to match strength with strength. So far it looked like the enemy was the stronger force, but if they could continue to take advantage of interior lines, the Space Marines might be able to thwart Maltaani attacks.

Fortis and Ystremski came across Sergeant Coughlin with Foxtrot Company in their new positions. The armorer squatted next to several Maltaani weapons spread out on the dirt in front of him. When he saw the pair approach, he straightened and saluted.

"Stop saluting, numb nuts. Are you trying to get the lieutenant sniped?"

Coughlin blinked in surprise when he saw Ystremski's gunnery sergeant chevrons. "Sorry, Gunny. Um, anyway, these Maltaani weapons are shit." He poked at them with his boot. "I mean, they shoot, but the tolerances are too high. They're practically falling apart. How do they expect to hit anything?"

Fortis shook his head. "Don't worry about that junk, Coughlin. We've got a bigger problem." He gestured overhead. "The ambient light conditions aren't strong enough to charge pulse rifle batteries, and some of the men are running out of ammo. You invented the solar charging system, any ideas on how to make it work better?"

"Hmm." Coughlin thought for a long second. "We could wire up the cells in series and see if that works. I'd start with four sets and go from there."

"Don't just stand there, make it happen," growled Ystremski.

"Where am I going to get four sets of LBA, Gunny? The guys aren't going to give up their armor."

"There are seven hundred dead Marines lined up at the casualty collection point. They won't be needing theirs anymore."

"Aw, Gunny," Coughlin's eyes flicked between Ystremski and Fortis. "I don't know, I mean—"

"Sergeant Coughlin, if you can't solve our ammunition problem, there are going to be a lot more dead Marines stacked up over there. I'm certain that if any of them could speak, they'd give us permission to use their armor. DINLI."

Coughlin sighed. "Okay, sir, I'll get started. Can I use some of these guys to help me?"

Ystremski gave Coughlin a platoon to assist with his grisly task and then turned to Fortis.

"I've got two companies of the reserve force policing around the crater. I heard a report—"

"Lieutenant Fortis? Lieutenant Fortis!"

A runner trotted through the formation calling for the lieutenant.

"I'm over here."

"Sir, you gotta come quick. They need you over at Second Regiment."

The runner led Fortis and Ystremski back to the perimeter defended by Second Regiment.

"I don't know exactly what's going on, LT," the breathless runner explained as they ran. "We fell back like we were supposed to, but some of the guys stayed."

When the trio arrived at the lines, Fortis saw a group of Space Marines far out in front of the new positions.

"What's going on here?" Fortis demanded.

A corporal named Branch stepped forward. "Sir, we got the order to fall back, so we did. Then the lieutenant came to and ordered Bravo Company to stay put and keep digging in."

"Lieutenant? There's an officer out there with Bravo?"

"Yes sir. Lieutenant Campanile. He came back the night after the HQ got nuked, passed out in his hole, and hasn't moved until this afternoon. We thought he was dead."

"Why did he order the company to remain out there?"

The corporal shrugged. "Beats me, LT. We started to pack up and fall back when he got up and started shouting that the orders from division were to dig in."

"And the company stayed? What a bunch of apes." Ystremski's voice was heavy with anger.

"Hey, Gunny, he's an officer. *Our* officer, and he gave us an order. What the hell were we supposed to do, tie him up and drag him back here?"

"You're supposed to use your heads for something more than a place to carry your helmets, Marine. This lieutenant is crazy if he doesn't see the danger he put the company in, and crazy people don't get to give orders in the Corps."

Fortis stepped between the men. "We can argue about it later. Right now, we have to bring those men back here. We can't leave them out there."

Fortis and Ystremski took Corporal Branch with them when they trotted out to the Bravo Company forward position. Fortis grew more nervous with every step. He felt dangerously exposed and he kept his eyes focused on the horizon for any sign of Maltaani troops.

When they got close, Corporal Branch called out.

"Lieutenant Campanile. Lieutenant Fortis to see you."

A tall Space Marine rose from the ground and Fortis recognized him as the first lieutenant who had challenged Major Anders during the intelligence brief on *Atlas* four days earlier.

Only four days? It feels like forever.

"What do you want?" Campanile was brusque and he had a wide-eyed expression that looked like panic.

"Abner Fortis." Fortis stepped forward and offered his hand, but Campanile didn't return the gesture. "I've come to talk about our tactical disposition."

Campanile motioned around him. "This is Bravo Company's position. Our orders are to maintain our position, so that's what we're doing."

"You understand those orders were issued two days ago, before the Maltaani attacked?"

"Of course I do. I'm not stupid."

"I'm not suggesting that you are. I simply want to make sure you understand that since those orders were issued we've lost half our force, including the entire command element that issued those orders. We were nearly overrun this morning. I ordered everyone to fall back to a smaller, more defensible position."

Campanile's eyes were glassy and didn't focus on the same spot for more than a second.

"Who are you to give such an order? You're not the division commander."

"The division commander is dead. All of the staff are dead. As far as I know, you and I are the only Space Marine officers still alive.

Since you outrank me, that makes you the division commander, Lieutenant."

"Then I order the division to resume their original positions."

Gunny Ystremski stepped forward until he was nose to nose with the stricken officer.

"Listen, you crazy fucker! There are a million Maltaani out there waiting to destroy us, and you're babbling like a madman." He poked Campanile in the chest. "Order your men to grab their shit and fall back, or I'm going to knock your ass out and carry you back there myself."

A dozen Bravo Company Space Marines mobbed Fortis and Ystremski and pushed them away from Campanile.

"Whoa! Whoa! Take it easy," shouted Fortis. He grabbed Ystremski and held him back. "There's no need for this. We're on the same side."

"Fuck off and take that asshole with you," replied one of the Marines. "We don't take orders from you."

Fortis started to argue, but several were holding pulse rifles held at the low ready and he knew one wrong word would ignite a fight that none of them would survive.

"Okay, all right. We'll leave. C'mon, Gunny." He took several steps toward the lines with Ystremski in tow. "I don't need to tell you men how much danger you're in, you can see it for yourselves. It's your choice; if you change your minds, we could use you."

Thirty meters from Bravo Company, Ystremski exploded.

"What the fuck are you doing, LT? That's a mutiny!"

"Yeah, it is. A company of armed mutineers led by a lunatic against us. You want to die out here, too?"

"They weren't going to do shit."

"That's not a chance I'm willing to take, Gunny." He cast a look over his shoulder at the Space Marines standing and watching them.

"We have enough to worry about without adding a firefight with fellow Marines to the list. Besides, I don't think they're going to stay out there for long. Did you see the looks they were giving each other? They're already trying to figure out how to fall back without violating their orders."

"What are you going to tell the rest of the men?"

"The truth. Those Marines decided to stay out there, and I'm not going to start a shooting match to get them back. If anybody wants to join them, they're welcome to go. If not, we will send their fellow First Battalion Marines to go out and bring them in later tonight."

Ystremski stopped midstride and stared at Fortis. "You're as crazy as that lieutenant."

Fortis laughed. "I thought it was a pretty clever way to solve the problem." He broke into a sprint. "Let's go, old timer. We've got work to do."

* * * * *

Chapter Fourteen

When Lieutenant Fortis and Gunny Ystremski returned to their lines, Sergeant Coughlin was hard at work on a solution to the problem of the looming ammunition shortage.

"I think I've got it right," he told them. "I made a charger out of bits and pieces of stuff I found lying around. The wires melted and the battery overheated when I wired up six sets of LBA so I cut back to four. So far, the battery I'm testing it with is accepting the charge. I've got a couple guys looking for damaged pulse rifles so I can salvage the meters to measure the charge."

"How long to charge one battery?"

Coughlin shrugged. "With full daylight, a little less than an hour. Some of these batteries are in rough shape and charge slower. Some of them won't take a charge at all. Trial and error."

"How many chargers can you make?"

"Now that I know what I'm doing, if I can get four hundred sets of usable LBA, I can make a hundred chargers. Some guys collected full batteries from our casualties and I sent them out to trade the full ones for dead ones with the companies who fought this morning. When they get back, we'll get started charging them as fast as we can."

"Outstanding work, Coughlin. We're going to need every round."

"Thank you, sir. After I get this going, I'll take a look at recharging the pulse cannons. That's going to be a much tougher nut to crack because the batteries don't come out. I might be able to come up with a mobile charger, but I won't know until I can fool around with it. I'm a pulse rifle and LBA tech, I didn't go to pulse cannon school."

"When we get out of here, you can go to any damn school you want," said Gunny Ystremski.

A series of explosions on the far side of the perimeter got their attention. The explosions became a continuous rumble, like the thunder of a distant storm. Fortis started for the sound, but Ystremski stopped him.

"That sounds like incoming artillery, LT. Let's hook up with the reserve force and check it out when the barrage lifts."

The reserve force was assembled and ready to move when the two leaders arrived at the rally point.

"Anybody know what's going on?"

"The first report we got said the Maltaani are shelling the positions we fought them from this morning, Gunny," a grim-faced corporal reported with scorch marks across his chest and a bloody bandage on one hand. "I guess they didn't notice that we pulled back."

Several nearby Space Marines chuckled, and Ystremski glared at them. "Laugh it up, meatheads. When they realize we're gone, they'll start dropping rounds on us for real."

Fortis and Ystremski set off for the front line to see for themselves. The reports turned out to be true: their former positions were shrouded in dust and smoke as round after round slammed into the ground around now-empty holes.

All along the new line, Space Marines dug in with renewed vigor. A few inches deeper might mean the difference between life and death under an artillery barrage, and none of them wanted to die because they hadn't dug deep enough.

The firing died off and the dirt clouds drifted away. Through his rifle scope, Fortis made out Maltaani troops, but it didn't look like they were massing to attack the new Space Marine positions.

"You think they're coming, Gunny?"

"I don't know, sir. I gave up trying to figure those bastards out."

"It looks like they learned their lesson about just charging forward."

"Yeah. Too bad we didn't charge them more for the education." He looked at the Marines hacking and scraping at the rocky soil. "School will be back in session when they bring those guns up."

"Hmm."

They remained at the front lines for another thirty minutes, but the Maltaani assault never materialized. It gratified Fortis to see runners moving among the troops exchanging fresh pulse rifle batteries for drained ones.

Coughlin, hard at work.

"C'mon, LT, we ought to get moving, unless you want to sleep out here. It's getting close to sundown. I want to check on First Battalion and see if that maniac from Bravo Company has come to his senses yet."

"While you do that, I'll check in on the casualty collection point and see if the docs need anything. I'll hook up with you at Foxtrot's new position."

"Okay, sir, and don't worry, I had the lads dig you a nice comfy hole to sleep in tonight."

"You're going to make some Space Marine a good wife someday, Gunny."

"Fuck off. *Sir.*"

The pair laughed and set off for the far side of the perimeter.

* * *

Fortis met Liz Sherer at the casualty collection point, deep in conversation with a portly, white-haired man in bloody surgical scrubs.

"Lieutenant Fortis, this is Nils Loeblein of the Fleet Medical Corps. The boys call him Pops. Pops, this is Lieutenant Fortis."

Pops clicked his heels and gave a slight bow before he and Fortis shook hands.

"The pleasure is mine, *Leutnant.* Your exploits are well known."

Fortis couldn't keep the confusion from his face. "Fleet Medical Corps? Did I miss a landing?"

"Ach, no *Leutnant,* I dropped in with the division medical staff. Two Space Marines from Third Regiment were injured in the drop, so I went to tend to them and was not present at the headquarters when the nuke landed."

Fortis chuckled and clapped the other man on the shoulder. "You're a doctor?"

"*Ja, ja.* I am an ophthalmologist on Terra Earth." He held up his bloody gloves. "On Balfan-48, I am a trauma surgeon."

"It was a little chaotic here earlier, Abner," said Liz. "The wounded showed up in waves, but there was no organized triage. Then Pops showed up and got things sorted. Come on, I'll show you." She led Fortis to a group of makeshift tents.

"This is the triage area where the litter bearers bring the wounded. Corpsmen evaluate them and assign them a priority, then they're directed to the proper area to be treated by other corpsmen. Or Pops."

"We do the best we can, *Leutnant*. Sadly, it's not always enough."

"Anything you can do for our wounded is greatly appreciated, Doctor. Er, Pops."

A Space Marine sprawled out on a litter with a bloody bandage wrapped around his shoulder waved at Fortis.

"How are you doing, Marine?"

"LT, sir, please. You gotta get me out of here. I need to get back with my platoon."

"This is Lance Corporal Thibodeaux," said Liz. "He lost a good chunk of his arm in the attack this morning."

"I can fight, sir," Thibodeaux pleaded. He held up his good arm and mimicked pulling a trigger. "I'm a better shot one-handed than most of these monkeys are with two."

Fortis looked at Pops and Liz, both shook their heads.

"If it was up to me, Thibodeaux, I'd carry you out there on my back. Unfortunately, the doctors say different."

The wounded Marine slumped back on his litter and scowled. "I gotta get back into the fight, LT. I want to kill more of those bastards."

"Don't worry, you'll get your chance. There will be plenty to kill when the docs say you're ready."

Fortis thanked Pops and Liz for the work they were doing and started back to Foxtrot Company as the light over Balfan-48 faded. While he walked, he couldn't shake the image of Thibodeaux, grievously wounded and desperate to get back into the fight.

I hope we don't need guys like him to win this battle.

* * *

Fortis met up with Ystremski near Foxtrot Company's new position.

"I've got somebody you need to meet, sir."

Ystremski waved over a grim-faced sergeant who took a knee next to Fortis.

"LT, this is Sergeant Ward."

Ward and Fortis shook hands.

"What can I do for you, Sergeant?"

"I watched the artillery barrage earlier and it occurred to me that those shells were light stuff, somewhere in the 80mm to 90mm range. Definitely nothing over 100mm."

"How does that help us?"

"Well, sir, I was artillery before the Corps took away our guns and made us recon infantry. Anyway, those are lightweight guns. They don't have the power to shoot long range. I'm guessing they can't shoot more than eight or ten klicks."

"Which means what, exactly?"

"Look here." Ward scratched a circle in the dirt. Outside the circle, in the eleven o'clock position, he made a question mark.

"This circle is our position. The question mark is the position of the guns."

"If you knew where they're at, why didn't you say so?" asked Ystremski.

Ward gave the gunny an incredulous look.

"Are you fucking with me, Gunny?"

Fortis put a hand on Ward's shoulder. "Yes, he's fucking with you, Sergeant. I'm sorry, it's been a helluva couple days, and I think we're all losing our minds."

Ward shook his head and then continued.

"Sir, I don't think the Maltaani have us completely surrounded. The guns are located behind their lines somewhere up in this area." The sergeant scratched a line straight out at nine o'clock. "I want to take my team out in this direction, find their right flank, and work around it until we're behind them. When we get there, we can locate the guns and destroy them."

Ystremski gave a low whistle and Fortis cleared his throat.

"That's a helluva risk, Sergeant. We don't have any way to support a mission like that."

Ward nodded. "I understand, sir, but we have to do something about those guns. If we don't, they can just sit back and blast us at their leisure."

"Without comms, you'll be all alone out there. If you get in trouble, we probably won't be able to help you."

"LT, we're recon Marines. We don't get into trouble that we can't fight our way out of. And if we do—" Ward shrugged, "—DINLI."

Fortis and Ystremski exchanged glances and the gunny cocked an eyebrow. Fortis rubbed his chin and considered the drawing.

"How many men are we talking about? What will you use to destroy the guns?"

"Six Marines, plus me. Everyone has maxed out strength and speed enhancements, so we can move fast and carry a shitload of grenades. I'll take an FGU in case we find something worth burning."

"When do you want to jump off?"

"We'll move out as soon as it's dark. That will give us seven hours of dark to find their flank and move around it. If we can't get through, we'll make our way back here and hope we don't get shot coming back in."

"What if you can't find the guns before sunrise?"

"We'll hunker down and keep searching tomorrow night."

"It's a bold plan, Sergeant. Can you give us a minute?"

Ward walked out of earshot and the lieutenant and gunny put their heads together.

"What do you think, Gunny? Will it work?"

"We don't have a lot of options, sir. Ward is right, we don't have an answer for artillery. He said those were small guns, but I sure as shit don't want to be hiding in a hole when they shoot them at us. If he succeeds, it's a huge win."

"And if he fails?"

"It's cold-blooded, but it's only seven guys. If they fail, we come up with another plan."

"Okay then. I'll let him go."

Ystremski waved Ward over.

"Mission approved, Sergeant Ward. Draw whatever supplies you need. Gunny Ystremski will hook you up with our armorer, Sergeant Coughlin. He can give you all the ammo you'll need."

"Yeah, sounds good. That new solar charging system is a piece of shit."

Fortis and Ystremski laughed.

"That was Coughlin's invention," said Ystremski. "C'mon, let's go find him. You can thank him yourself."

* * *

It was almost dark when the lieutenant and the gunny got time to sit down to munch on pig squares and exchange news. Fortis told Ystremski about Liz, Pops, and the field hospital, and the veteran Marine nodded his approval.

"These Space Marines will fight all day and night if they know their brothers are being taken care of. We're going to have to bury our dead, though. In another day or two, they're going to smell."

"Ugh. What about the Maltaani? Should we bury them?"

"Fuck, no. They can rot, or their guys can come get 'em, and we'll kill some more."

"Huh." Fortis thought for a second. "What did you find out about Lieutenant Campanile?"

"The Marines I talked to said Corporal Branch has most of the company ready to fall back at first light tomorrow."

"Most?"

"The lieutenant won't budge and he's got four or five guys convinced to stay as well."

"It's suicide."

"You should have let me knock him out and drag him back."

Fortis chuckled. "They would have shot us both and then where would we be?"

"Still in the shit."

"DINLI."

* * *

Thirty minutes after darkness settled over Balfan-48, seven shadowy figures slipped out from the Space Marine lines. The point man, Corporal Gomez, moved with confidence; he had one of three helmets with functional low-light optics worn by the team. Only eighteen helmets in the entire division had functional low-light capability, but between the EMP from the nuke and the resulting sandblast, almost every helmet had been rendered inoperative.

The team guided on a distant star to stay on course as they moved out into the trackless desert. The stars threw off enough light to navigate the broken terrain, and the only sound was the muffled crunch of sand under their feet. The second Space Marine in line maintained the official pace count for the group to track the distance traveled, but from long experience, they all kept their own count. When they had traveled five klicks, Sergeant Ward called a halt. To their right, he could see the glow of lights on the horizon and he heard faint noises carried on the night breeze.

Gomez and Private Sewell, another of the Space Marines with functioning optics, crept forward and scouted for Maltaani positions. It was a nerve wracking task and their progress was painfully slow. They were highly trained special operators unused to groping in the dark for an enemy they knew virtually nothing about, so nerves were taut.

The absence of troops in the area didn't mean the Maltaani had no visibility there. Remote sensors were common, as were aerial surveillance platforms, and even satellites. The Space Marines also didn't know if the Maltaani had their own night vision capabilities. They could easily walk into an ambush under the mistaken belief they were hidden by the darkness.

The pair advanced another kilometer without raising an alarm. Gomez stopped and pointed back the way they'd come. He made the "Move up" sign and Sewell gave him an "Okay" before he started back to Ward and the rest of the team.

When Ward caught up to Gomez, he pulled the team leader close so he could put his lips close to Ward's ear.

"Six klicks. I think we're through."

"Three more and then we'll turn," Ward whispered.

He moved among the men and repeated what he told Gomez. As one, the recon team stood up and moved out in search of the Maltaani artillery.

* * * * *

Chapter Fifteen

Major Anders pulled up the infrared drone footage on his computer and projected it over the pre-invasion imagery Fleet intelligence collected of Balfan-48. The drone operators had programmed their craft to fly a basic collection pattern based on time and distance since the navigation system on the drone was jammed, so the alignment between the two intel sources wasn't perfect. Still, it was better than nothing, and Anders was determined to use everything at his disposal to support the Space Marines on the surface.

The results disappointed the intelligence officer. Even after dark, when the surface of the planet was at its coolest, the atmosphere diffused the heat signatures and did not permit clear infrared imagery.

Anders scanned the footage as it played, pausing periodically to collect individual screenshots for enhancement. He recognized the heat signatures of a large concentration of troops in a rough circle, almost completely surrounded by a much larger force. It was impossible to tell friend from foe, but he guessed the smaller force was Ninth Division. He made a rough comparison of the signatures based on a nominal division size of five thousand Space Marines, and estimated the size of the Maltaani army at twenty-five thousand.

Five to one.

A bright spot appeared on the edge of the screen, well behind the Maltaani lines, but the drone turned to follow the pre-programmed flight path before Anders could get a good look at it. It frustrated him to watch the spot disappear; the focused infrared signature suggested a concentrated heat source like a fire or an eruption, but there had been no indications of volcanic activity or magma events.

After he finished with the video, Anders sorted through the screenshots to find the ones that gave the best overall perspective on the situation on the ground. He applied a series of techniques to enhance and sharpen the images, and when he was done, he had a collection of images that reflected the situation on the surface, if his assumptions were correct.

If.

Despite his confidence in the analysis, Anders knew he didn't have enough to prompt Admiral Kinshaw to deploy the mechs. Guessing troop strength and position based on the relative size of unidentifiable heat signatures wasn't the stuff of sound military decision-making. If he was wrong, the mechs might land in the middle of the Maltaani.

There were three sharp raps on his door and Staff Sergeant Thein from the drone detachment entered Anders' office.

"How's it looking, Major? Having any luck?"

"Not a lot. Here, take a look."

The pair examined the enhanced images. Anders explained his theories, and the enlisted analyst nodded.

"You're more of an optimist that I am, sir. I washed this stuff through every filter we have, but I couldn't make anything out of it. Are you planning any more missions?"

"If I can justify it. I'm not going to send another mission until I know we can gather better intel than this."

"Okay, sir, if we come up with anything, I'll let you know. Right now I need to get back to the hangar; one of the heat shields got dinged up on recovery and we need to replace it before we send it back out."

Thein opened the door and almost collided with Major Niskala who had her hand up in mid-knock. He stepped back and held the door open.

"Pardon me, ma'am."

"Major Niskala, please come in," said Anders. Niskala entered, and Thein stepped out, pulling the door shut behind him.

"I'm sorry, I couldn't wait any longer. I'm not interrupting anything, am I?"

"Not at all. I was just reviewing the drone footage with Sargent Thein."

"Any luck?"

Anders frowned and shook his head. "I'm sorry, Kiti, but there's just not much here."

He showed Niskala the images and walked her through his analysis, careful to stress that it was based on assumptions which might be faulty.

"I believe these are Ninth Division positions, surrounded by the Maltaani, but I can't confirm it."

"Why don't you send a drone with cameras?"

"Unfortunately, our photo birds don't have onboard storage. They're designed to collect high resolution imagery and link it back real-time. The IR birds store data because they're actually civilian technology used by survey crews to scout locations for resources to exploit. The companies don't have the money to set up satellite constellations to receive real-time info just for a survey. They have the time to collect the IR data and wash it through a bunch of processors, and they don't need the level of resolution we do."

"What's next, then?"

"I can't do much more until the other drones come back, and we know what the boundaries of the jamming are."

"Too bad we don't have any pigeons."

"What?"

"Ah, nothing. One of the military history classes I took at the Fleet Academy talked about how old-time soldiers used homing pigeons to send messages, is all."

"I've never seen a space pigeon."

The majors shared a laugh, but Anders suddenly fell silent and stared at Niskala. She stared back, nervously.

"What?"

"Your space pigeons just gave me an idea."

"I don't understand."

"I don't have pigeons to carry messages, but I have birds."

* * *

Ystremski roused Fortis before dawn, and the pair headed for the line where they thought the Maltaani would attack. They found the Space Marines awake and ready in their holes. The gunny nodded with satisfaction when he saw how deep they had dug in.

"When you think your foxhole is deep enough, keep digging," he told Fortis. "C'mon, sir, let's fall back before we get our asses shot off. There's nothing we can do to help these guys except make sure the reserve force is ready."

The reserve force set up two hundred meters behind the line and waited for dawn. As soon as the sky lightened, the first shells landed in front of the Space Marine positions.

"Looks like Ward failed," observed Fortis.

"It was always a long shot."

The gunfire increased, faltered, and then built to a crescendo. The Space Marine positions disappeared in a cloud of dust and dirt as the Maltaani showered the line with high explosives. When the barrage lifted, Maltaani troops appeared, marching forward through the dust. Space Marine scout snipers and crew-served weapons fired on the mass of approaching enemy soldiers and opened holes in the ranks, but the Maltaani pressed their attack. Fortis heard the *whoomp* of a grenade launcher, and moments later a string of explosions shredded a hundred Maltaani soldiers. Bolts of plasma added to the carnage as the Space Marines began to find their range. The Maltaani attack began to sputter.

"Send the reserves in," Fortis ordered Ystremski. "Let's crush these bastards."

The reserve force charged forward from their positions in the crater and added the weight of their rifles to the defense. The withering fire cut down hundreds more Maltaani, and still they came forward.

"What the hell are they doing?"

"I don't know, LT, but never help the enemy when they're making a mistake."

A rumble of fire to the left took them by surprise. Fortis realized the Maltaani artillery had begun to engage another section of their perimeter. The barrage was joined by the cracks of a thousand

Maltaani rifles as a mass of enemy soldiers rose up from the desert floor where they were concealed and raced forward.

"Damn it, the attack was a feint!" Ystremski shouted as he took off running for the front with the lieutenant right behind him. "We've got to turn the reserve force!"

Fortis changed direction and sprinted toward the new attack. The Space Marines had to hold until reinforcements could arrive, or the entire perimeter might collapse.

He was too late.

The front ranks of the Maltaani broke over the Space Marine trenches like a rogue wave and spread out in all directions. Small pockets of Marines withstood the initial surge, but the fighting soon became a desperate hand-to-hand battle.

A flame generation unit *whooshed* and dozens of Maltaani scattered in panic as their uniforms ignited. Moments later, the FGU exploded and rained fire down on friend and foe. Fortis watched as a Marine clubbed one attacker after another until he went down, shot in the back by a wounded Maltaani. A grenade exploded near a pair of Space Marines who were fighting back-to-back in the middle of the rush and their legless bodies somersaulted high into the air.

Fortis took up a firing position twenty-five meters from the breach in the lines and shot enemy after enemy. Space Marines from other positions joined him and they poured unrelenting fire into the Maltaani tide.

The attack slowed as the shock of the sudden action wore off, and Space Marine resistance stiffened. The attackers seemed momentarily confused by the stubbornness of the defenders and they began to withdraw beyond the trenches.

Artillery fire began to land deep in the Space Marine perimeter as the Maltaani retreated and the Space Marines reclaimed their trench line. Fortis advanced with the rest of the men, firing and moving as he picked his way through the thick layer of bodies that carpeted the ground. By the time he got into a fighting hole the firing had dwindled, and the enemy faded into the distance.

All around him, wounded men groaned and cried out for relief. Litter bearers moved among the fallen, collected the injured, and headed for the field hospital. The foul stench of ruptured viscera clotted the air, and Fortis had an acrid twinge of scorched flesh on his tongue. He dug out a hydration pack—his last—and rinsed out his mouth.

Angry shouts grabbed his attention. He spotted a group of Space Marines struggling to subdue another man.

"Kill that fucker!"

Fortis jumped from his hole and jogged over, and he realized the "man" the Marines were struggling with wasn't a man at all, but a Maltaani soldier. One of the Space Marines was straddled across the prisoner's chest and was hammering him with powerful punches. Another Marine stood by with his bayonet in hand.

"Knock it off!" Fortis shouted as he waded through the crowd. "Stop it!"

He shoved the Marine off the now-unconscious Maltaani.

"What the fuck?" The Space Marine leapt to his feet and advanced on Fortis, his lips curled back and his fists clenched, but he stopped short when he saw Fortis's rank insignia.

"This piece of shit killed our brothers, Lieutenant."

"And now he's our prisoner," Fortis responded.

"Fuck that! He needs to die."

Gunny Ystremski shoved his way into the circle and stepped in front of the angry Space Marine.

"What's the problem here, troop?"

"I'm going to kill that prick, and this fucking cherry officer is getting in my way, Gunny."

"This officer here?" Ystremski pointed at Fortis. "That's no cherry, Private. That's your commanding officer, and if he says the prisoner lives, then the prisoner lives."

"Gunny Ystremski, have the prisoner taken to the crater and post a guard on him. The rest of you, get back to your posts before the Maltaani artillery spotters see you."

On cue, a shell exploded nearby. Fortis turned and walked away without waiting for acknowledgement of his orders. Ystremski could handle the Space Marines with murder on their minds. Fortis knew they would respond to the gunny.

He struggled with his emotions as he picked his way through the mangled bodies of Space Marines and Maltaani alike. The fighting had been ferocious all along the line and the sight of so many dead Space Marines was gut-wrenching. It was easy to understand why the others wanted to exact a measure of revenge on the Maltaani prisoner.

"Abner!"

Fortis looked up and saw Liz Sherer waving at him.

"I came to supervise transportation for the wounded and heard we took a prisoner."

"Yeah, Gunny Ystremski is moving him into the crater."

"Is he wounded?"

"I don't know. He was unconscious when I got there. I had to stop some of the men from killing him."

"I saw. Tough call."

"We're not animals, Liz."

"Still, those guys might have killed you, too, for getting in the way."

"That's why I let Gunny Ystremski handle it."

The pair turned toward the crater and the field hospital.

"You think they'll attack again today?"

Fortis shrugged. "I don't know. We killed a bunch of them today, but we lost a lot, too. If they decide their losses are worth it, they'll come back."

They ducked as two artillery rounds exploded harmlessly nearby.

"I think they'll keep up the harassing fire while they lick their wounds and figure out what to try next. They're learning, you know."

"What do you mean, 'learning'?"

"Their tactics. The Maltaani are changing, evolving. Learning. Their first attack, right after the nuke, was a headlong assault and we butchered them. Their next attack was more of the same, but when they withdrew they tried to lure us into following. That didn't work, so they brought up their guns. This morning, they crept up in the dark and tried a feint to break our lines, and they almost succeeded. If they figure out how to coordinate all of that, we're going to be in real trouble."

Fortis looked up and realized Liz had stopped with a look of disbelief on her face.

"What?"

"That's a pretty grim assessment of our situation, Abner."

"You've seen the casualties. Would you believe me if I told you everything was fine?"

"Well, no, but it's unnerving to hear the bad news from the commanding officer."

"It's not bad news. It's just news. The Maltaani aren't the only ones who have learned a few lessons in the last couple days." He grinned. "When I get a chance to talk to Gunny Ystremski, I'll find out what they are."

Liz shook her head. "Always with the jokes."

"Graveyard humor, Liz."

They parted ways, and Fortis started for Foxtrot Company.

* * * * *

Chapter Sixteen

Ward called a halt when the sky began to lighten. The team gathered around the sergeant in a tight circle facing outward and he spoke in a low voice.

"I think we're close, but it's going to be daylight soon. We're going to lay up and wait for dark. There's a little ridge over there, so we'll head that way to pair up and find holes. If you need to piss, do it now, because once we're settled in there's no moving around."

Gomez led the way to the ridge and the recon team found two-man positions to hide out in and wait for dark to continue their search.

Ward had just finished checking on the men and settled into his own hole when the opalescent light of the primary star lit the surface. He took a couple sips from a hydration pack and tucked it away before he allowed himself to settle into a relaxed state of wakefulness. His senses remained alert for any sign of the enemy, but he felt a pleasant tingling as the tension in his muscles drained away.

BOOM! BOOM! BOOM! BOOM!

Explosions jolted Ward wide awake. He scrambled to his knees and looked around but saw nothing.

BOOM! BOOM! BOOM! BOOM!

The explosions were coming from somewhere behind him, on the other side of the low ridge. Ward waved the other Space Marines to stay hidden and crawled up so he could see over the edge...and froze.

There were four Maltaani self-propelled field guns deployed in a line facing the Space Marine positions, and crews were scrambling to load and fire the weapons as rapidly as they could.

BOOM! BOOM! BOOM! BOOM!

Shell after shell whizzed off into the distance. Ward saw no troops deployed as security; all the Maltaani he saw were engaged in working the guns. Each gun had a large truck parked nearby, and Ward watched as ammo handlers retrieved shells from the trucks and stacked them near the guns. Were it not for their weirdly shaped heads and elongated limbs, he could have been watching a Space Marine gun crew in action. He took a quick head count and then ducked down to rejoin his team.

"Four guns in a line like this." He scratched a rough diagram in the dirt. "Ammo trucks parked behind them, here. It looks like fifteen crewmen per gun. None of them were armed and I didn't see any weapons. I guess they're not expecting company."

BOOM! BOOM! BOOM! BOOM!

Ward made marks in the dirt. "One shooter per gun, here, here, and here." He pointed to three of his team. "Jocko, Sewell, Welch. Kill 'em if you can, and if you can't, keep their heads down. The rest of us will hit the first gun and roll up their flank, one gun at a time. Speed is the key, ladies. We can't afford to give them time to call for help."

BOOM! BOOM! BOOM! BOOM!

"We go on the next salvo." He looked at the faces of his men and saw their eyes shining with excitement. "Let's do the deed."

The Space Marines spread out and waited for the Maltaani to fire the next salvo. Ward knew from his experience as an artilleryman that most of the crew would be preoccupied immediately after a round was fired. The blast would leave those closest to the gun momentarily numb to the sound of gunfire. He gripped his pulse rifle and braced himself.

BOOM! BOOM! BOOM! BOOM!

Ward surged over the ridge and advanced on the first ammo truck with his rifle on his shoulder as he searched for targets. His companions instinctively spread out to his right to cover the gun.

As expected, the sudden appearance of the Space Marines shocked the gun crews into inaction. Ward shot two Maltaani from the back of the truck before they could react, and three more ammo handlers fell before they recognized the approaching danger.

Pulse rifle bolts chased Maltaani soldiers as they scrambled to grab weapons or just escape the sudden violence. Ward and his men pressed the attack and soon secured the first gun.

Bodies dotted the ground around the second gun. Ward saw enemy soldiers crouched behind the gun and truck as Welch poured rapid and accurate sniper fire down on them. The element of surprise was gone, and Ward knew they would lose the initiative if they didn't press their attack. The team advanced steadily, his teammates providing suppressing fire as Ward moved, then he did the same for them from his new position.

Two Maltaani jumped up from their hiding place and ran for the truck. A pulse rifle bolt decapitated the first one in midstride and a burst of fire from Ward's team chopped down the second. Just as Ward rose to move forward he heard a *zing* and searing pain burned along his left arm. Another round slammed into his LBA. He spun around and sat down. The dirt around him exploded and he threw himself flat.

Ward heard several sharp *cracks* as Space Marine grenades exploded, and when he looked up, the Maltaani gun was on its side and his men were rushing forward. He forced himself to his feet and followed them.

The Space Marines opened up on the Maltaani soldiers defending the third gun. The ammo truck caught fire and thick, black smoke billowed into the sky. Suddenly, the defenders broke and ran for the fourth gun. Ward noted with grim satisfaction that none of them made it. But their panic was contagious and the remaining Maltaani abandoned their positions and raced into the open desert. The recon force picked them off one at a time, two of the Marines following the trail of bodies to deliver headshots to the fallen enemy.

"Hey, Sergeant, you're hit."

Ward looked down at his arm and saw a scorched and bloody hole in his armor. The pain he had pushed away to complete the attack flooded back, and he slumped to the ground.

Doc Welch, the team medic, stripped the armor from his arm and examined the wound. The Maltaani round had hit him where the glove met the gauntlet and ripped an ugly furrow along the flesh of his forearm before it passed through his bicep. When Ward flexed his fingers, he could see the muscles in his forearm move.

"No worries, Ward. I'll get you wrapped up and ready for action in no time."

Welch poured anti-bacterial powder over the wound and wrapped it with a roll of thick adhesive. In seconds, it formed a soft cast from wrist to elbow. He curled up pieces of gauze and stuck them into the hole in Ward's bicep before he wrapped it as well.

"If I stitch you up, you'll just tear 'em out," Welch told the wounded sergeant as he repacked his aid kit. "The soft casts will keep the wounds closed and protect them until we get back home."

"Hey, Doc! Come quick, it's Sewell."

The Space Marines gathered around the position Sewell had been firing from. He was face down in the dirt, brains and gore oozing onto the chewed-up dirt around his head.

"They must have seen him and hit him with a lucky shot," said Donk. "Bastards."

Ward realized they were a man short. "Where's Koloff?"

After a quick search, the team located the stocky Russian propped up against the second gun. He had been hit high on the left leg, and the bandages he had pressed over the wound were soaked with blood.

"Shot in the ass," he muttered. "Fuckers shot me in the ass."

Doc Welch pulled the bandage away to assess the wound and crimson gushed out.

"Shit!" Welch clamped his hands down on the wound. "Somebody, grab a large compress out of my pack."

Gomez tore open the bandage and held it out.

Welch nodded at Ward and the other Space Marines. "Grab his legs and hold them tight. This is going to hurt, and if he kicks his legs, he's going to make it worse."

Ward nodded and joined the rest of the Marines holding Koloff's legs.

"Put that thing right over my hands," instructed Welch. "As soon as I move them, slap it on and put as much pressure on it as you can, okay?"

Gomez nodded.

"Okay, here we go." Welch pulled his hands back, and Gomez leaned on the wound. Koloff cried out and tried to wriggle, but his teammates held him firm. Gomez held the compress in place while Welch bound it tightly with a long green bandage. The medic didn't realize his patient had passed out until he finished wrapping the wound.

"Whaddya think, Doc?"

Welch sat back and squeezed some water from a hydration pack to rinse his hands.

"The round tore out a big chunk of flesh. There aren't any major blood vessels in that area, but it probably hurts like hell."

"Can he walk?"

"It's hard to know for sure, Sergeant. I can give him something to numb it up, but there's a risk he could tear it open and not know it."

"Listen!" Donk pointed off in the distance. The sound was faint but unmistakable.

Boom! Boom! Boom! Boom!

"There's another battery out that way."

Ward gestured to the burning truck and the soaring tower of smoke.

"If the rounds on that truck start cooking off, we're fucked. Someone is going to get curious and investigate why this battery stopped firing. We need to be long gone when they do."

The Space Marines gathered with him nodded.

"Sewell's dead, and Koloff can't walk, so making a run for it is not an option. Besides, we need to hit that other battery. DINLI."

Boom! Boom! Boom! Boom!

The Maltaani artillery battery punctuated his sentence. Ward's statement wasn't an invitation for discussion and the others knew it.

Welch spoke up. "What's the plan, Ward?"

"We're gonna play a little Trojan Artillery Piece with these pricks. Donk, jump up in that other truck and see if you can figure out how to drive it. Gomez, check the gun. Jocko, grab some high ground and watch for Maltaani. The rest of you, collect some of the Maltaani weapons and get Koloff and Sewell away from that fire."

The Space Marines scrambled to complete their tasks. The ammo truck roared to life, jerked forward, and stalled. Donk let out a string of curses and tried again, this time the ponderous vehicle lurched into motion.

"Hey, Ward! It's working!"

The Space Marines raced to load Koloff and Sewell's body into the back of the truck, along with their stack of captured rifles. Gomez got the gun engine started, and he rolled up next to the waiting truck. Ward mounted the running board of the gun.

"Spike those guns with grenades and we'll head off that way to find the other battery. When we get close, park that truck close by and you guys start passing me shells. We'll blast them with their own gun. Let's go!"

Welch dropped grenades down the barrels of the two remaining artillery pieces. The explosions mangled the barrels with muffled *thumps*. Jocko ran down from his overwatch perch and climbed aboard the ammo truck as Gomez steered the self-propelled gun in the direction of the distant fire.

Boom! Boom! Boom! Boom!

* * * * *

Chapter Seventeen

"**L**ieutenant Fortis!"

Fortis saw a group of Space Marines waving to get his attention.

"We need you over here, now!"

He sprinted to the far side of their perimeter and recognized Corporal Branch.

"What's going on?"

"Sir, you need to see this."

Branch led the way to an elevated observation post built from piled up dirt. He pointed toward their abandoned fighting holes.

Fortis raised his pulse rifle and scoped the scene. He saw a group of Maltaani, easily identified by their strange body shape, gathered around the former Space Marine position. One Maltaani, a head taller than the others, was brandishing a large sword. Fortis noted that four other Maltaani soldiers had large, four-legged animals on leashes. He couldn't make out a lot of detail, but they looked similar to Terran canines.

Suddenly, a group of Maltaani dragged a person out and forced him to his feet; Fortis recognized Space Marine utilities.

"They've got one of ours."

"Yes, sir. That's Private Vera," Branch told him. "He stayed out there with Lieutenant Campanile and two other guys."

The sword-wielding Maltaani paced in front of his men and brandished the weapon toward Fortis and the Space Marines. The others reacted by waving their weapons and mouthing soundless shouts.

Gunny Ystremski scrambled up next to Fortis. "Looks like a pep rally to me."

The Maltaani seized Vera by his wrists and stretched his arms out. The sword flashed, and the swordsman chopped Vera's arms off at the elbow. Crimson spurted as the Maltaani shoved the wounded man toward the Space Marine lines. The dog handlers released their hounds. Fortis watched in horror as the animals knocked Vera down from behind and savaged him. All around Fortis, the Space Marines reacted.

"What the fuck!"

"Oh my God!"

"Bastards!"

One of the scout snipers opened up with his rifle, but the plasma bolts fell short.

The tall Maltaani waved his bloody weapon over his head as the dog handlers dragged their beasts away from the shredded remains of Private Vera. Another Space Marine was dragged out in front of the Maltaani and forced to his knees.

"Oh shit, that's De Jesus."

"We've got to stop this!" Fortis exclaimed.

The Space Marines growled their agreement and started to surge forward.

"Stand fast!" shouted Gunny Ystremski. "Stand fast and hold the line!" He turned to the lieutenant. "Those motherfuckers aren't alone, sir. Look behind them."

Fortis peered again through his scope and saw Ystremski was right. There was a mass of Maltaani soldiers deployed in ranks, braced for the Space Marines to attack.

"They want us to charge over there, LT."

Fortis squeezed his eyes shut and clenched his teeth. The casual brutality of the Maltaani shocked him, but the gunny was right.

It's what they want.

"The gunny's right," he announced in a loud voice. "If we charge over there, we'll be slaughtered."

Fortis raised his rifle and looked back out at the Maltaani. De Jesus kneeled with his head down while the swordsman held his bloody blade high and exhorted his men.

Fortis saw movement in his peripheral vision. When he looked up over his rifle, he saw two Space Marines advancing toward the Maltaani position. They were bent over and moving from cover to cover. He recognized the scout sniper who had attempted to shoot the Maltaani at long range.

"What are they doing?"

"Looks like they're closing the range to do a little shooting."

Fortis turned his attention back to the captive Space Marine in time to see the sword flash down across his neck. The Maltaani threw the decapitated body down and unleashed their dogs before the dead Marine's head came to a rest on the rocky ground.

"Fuck this." Fortis scrambled to his feet. "You men stay here, and no matter what do not advance."

He jumped over the trenchworks and began to walk toward the Maltaani with his rifle held over his head.

"Lieutenant, what are you doing? Get back here!" shouted Ystremski.

Fortis ignored the shouts and continued across the broken ground. To his left, he saw the scout sniper and spotter set up behind an outcropping of boulders.

"I hope you can make the shot," he muttered under his breath.

Before him, the Maltaani dragged Lieutenant Campanile to his feet. The Space Marine officer lashed out with his fists and boots, but he went down under a crush of attackers. Fortis watched, helpless, while the Maltaani beat Campanile into submission. The swordsman jerked the lieutenant upright and waved his weapon overhead and stepped forward.

A blue-white pulse rifle bolt hit the swordsman in the face and his body somersaulted backwards as the impact blew off the top of his head. Lieutenant Campanile jerked free and ran toward the Space Marine lines as the Maltaani scrambled for cover while more bolts of energy ripped through the crowd.

Fortis dove for cover as the enemy returned fire. He watched as Campanile stumbled across the rocky ground. Suddenly, the Maltaani dogs charged into view, intent on running down the fleeing human. Fortis shouldered his weapon and tried to draw a bead on the animals, but they bounded in and out of his scope. He let off a long burst where he thought they would reappear, careful to avoid firing too close to Campanile.

Campanile was close enough that Fortis could make out the fear in his face as he lurched toward the Space Marine lines. One of the dogs appeared two meters behind him, and before Fortis could get off a shot, the beast attacked.

Fortis heard Campanile scream as the other dogs caught up and tore into him. Fortis jumped to his feet and ran to help his fellow

Space Marine. Maltaani rounds cracked through the air around him and he dropped to one knee to draw a bead on the dogs.

Click.

Fortis pulled the trigger again, and again.

Click. Click.

He punched out the empty magazine and reached for a fresh one, but a Maltaani round had torn a ragged hole across the bottom of his ammo pouch and his spare mags had fallen out. One of the dogs looked up from the bloody remains of Lieutenant Campanile and barked, the other three raised their heads and stared at him.

Holy shit!

Fortis scrambled to his feet and sprinted back toward the Space Marine lines. The Maltaani dogs gave chase. Their howls raised the hairs on his neck and spurred him to run faster. Rounds cracked overhead as he ran for safety, and it became a race between a Maltaani bullet and the Maltaani dogs. Fortis threw a look over his shoulder and saw the largest beast was only a few meters behind him.

"Down! Down!"

Gunny Ystremski waved and shouted from atop the Space Marine earthworks, and it took the lieutenant a second to process what Ystremski wanted. Fortis spotted a small rock outcropping and threw himself behind it. The air was instantly filled with blue-white plasma bolts. The Maltaani dogs shrieked and whined as they were ripped to shreds. The weapons fire seemed to go on forever.

Suddenly, Fortis heard a loud snarl behind him and a wave of hot fetid breath washed over his neck. He rolled over and threw his arms up to protect his head as the beast attacked. Powerful jaws clamped onto his left forearm and squeezed. He gasped in pain as a fang punctured his armor.

The murderous canine squatted and whipped its gigantic head back and forth, and it was all the lieutenant could do not to be flung around like a rag doll. The monster's power shocked him, and he felt a fresh surge of fear and adrenaline as he started to lose the tug of war for his arm.

He jerked his kukri from its sheath and swung at the massive head with the flat of the blade to force the jaws open. The force of the impact vibrated his right arm from wrist to shoulder, but the dog growled and bit harder. In desperation, Fortis rose up as high as he could and aimed the weapon at the animal's neck.

Fortis missed the neck and the blade sank deep into a muscular shoulder. The dog shrieked in pain and let go of his forearm. When it jumped up it pulled the kukri from his grasp.

A stream of plasma bolts tore into the wounded animal and drove it back. It writhed in pain as it tumbled across the ground. Finally, the beast lay still. Gunny Ystremski ran up and crouched next to the officer.

"Let's go, LT."

Fortis looked up and took Ystremski's hand. His head reeled when he stood, and the gunny threw an arm around his shoulder.

"Let's get you back to our lines."

Fortis pulled away and staggered toward the dead dog.

"My kukri." He grabbed the handle and wrenched the weapon free before he threw an arm across Ystremski's shoulders. "Okay, now we can go."

* * * * *

Chapter Eighteen

Sergeant Ward caught sight of the second Maltaani artillery battery shortly after they pulled out. He heard a series of explosions, the ammunition cooking off in the burning truck they'd left behind. Angry screeches blared from a speaker on the dashboard, but Ward didn't have to speak the language to know what was being said.

He directed Gomez to stop and waved the ammo truck up close.

"This ought to do it. Get Koloff set up to provide covering fire and let's get this gun into action."

The Space Marines were almost giddy as they prepared to fire on the Maltaani battery.

Boom! Boom! Boom! Boom!

"Hey, Ward, we've got company coming," called Koloff from his perch atop the truck. A sort-of motorcycle with a sidecar was approaching from the battery. "You want me to engage?"

"Negative. Not yet. We're not ready to fire."

Ward fumbled with the controls of the Maltaani artillery piece. The breech levers and firing mechanism were similar to the guns he had worked with in the ISMC, but the sights were an incomprehensible jumble of scopes and meters. He opened the breech, and Welch gave the first shell a kiss before he shoved it in.

"C'mon, baby, do your magic."

Ward motioned the other Marines back. "Stand clear! I don't know what the fuck's going to happen," he warned them. He spun the barrel elevation handwheel until the barrel was aimed at the other battery.

"Ward, hurry up! What do we do?" shouted Koloff.

The sergeant looked up and saw the motorcycle had stopped fifty meters away and the riders were staring at the Space Marines. One of them held a microphone up to his face, and Ward knew their subterfuge was over.

"Kill 'em!"

Koloff's pulse rifle spat bolts of blue-white energy at the motorcycle, and the Maltaani went down in a heap. In the distance, the gun crews saw what happened and scrambled to respond.

Ward pulled the lanyard on the gun, but nothing happened. He pulled it again, but the weapon still didn't fire.

"Ward, what the fuck? They're aiming their guns at us!"

"I don't know, goddammit! Something's wrong."

He examined the firing mechanism, but it appeared to be ready to fire. He noticed a lever protected by a guard on the side of the breech.

"I think I found a safety—"

Ward squeezed the lever.

KABOOM!

The recoil tossed Ward backward and he landed on his ass with a *whoof!* The shell screamed along the ground and impacted forty meters short of the other battery.

Gomez picked Ward off the ground as he shook his head to clear the ringing in his ears.

"Your range is short," Gomez told him.

Ward scrambled back to the gun and spun the elevation handwheel four times.

"Gimme another round."

Welch shoved another round home and Ward slammed the breech. He squeezed the safety and pulled the lanyard.

KABOOM!

The shell whizzed through the Maltaani battery at head-height and exploded ten meters behind it.

Ward cursed and gave the elevation handwheel half a turn and Gomez fed the gun.

"This is it!"

KABOOM!

The shell exploded in the middle of the enemy guns, and the crews scrambled for cover.

"Whooee! Gimme another shell, boys!"

Welch and Gomez fed Ward shell after shell as he pounded the Maltaani gunners. Jocko and Donk moved up to outflank the enemy and kept up a steady rain of sniper fire on the panicked troops.

Ward worked the gun like a machine. Open the breech, eject the spent shell, insert a fresh round, slam the breech closed, squeeze the safety, yank the lanyard.

KABOOM!

The fumes from the gun scorched his throat and burned his eyes, and he was deafened by the constant roar of the gun. Nevertheless, he kept up a steady rate of fire until Welch grabbed him by the shoulder.

"Ward, cease fire! Cease fire!"

Ward looked up at Welch, uncomprehending.

"They're all dead, man. You blew them to shit!"

Welch sounded like he was shouting underwater. The silence was a shock to Ward's ears.

"Dead?"

Welch and Gomez laughed. "Hell yeah, dead. Look."

A heavy pall of smoke hung over the former artillery battery. He could make out the twisted barrels of two guns, and a third was on its side. Ward tried to laugh, but he only managed a painful croak. Welch pressed a hydration pack into his hands. Ward groaned with relief as the water washed down his raw throat.

"Those bastards never had a chance!" whooped Donk as the trio rejoined Ward and the others. "That was some fine shooting, Sergeant."

"We need to stop grab-assing and get the hell out of here," said Jocko. "A couple of them got away and when they come back they're not gonna be riding motorcycles."

Ward spat a globule of black goo that rolled up into a sandy mess. "Yeah. Jocko's right, we need to scoot. Where's Koloff?"

A quick search revealed the Space Marine dead on the ground beside the truck. An explosive round had cracked his helmet and torn off his left arm at the shoulder.

"Damn. I don't remember them shooting back."

Ward gestured to the truck. "Wrap him up and load him next to Sewell. We need to get moving."

"Not before I take a look at that arm, Sergeant." Welch pointed to the blood dripping from Ward's hand. "You tore open your wound."

The blood surprised Ward. He hadn't felt a thing during the battle, but his arm immediately began to throb.

Ward fidgeted while the medic worked on his arm, and the others prepared to move out.

"The ammo truck is half-full," reported Donk. "Are we taking both vehicles?"

"We might as well. There's no telling what we'll run into."

"What direction, boss?"

"I don't think we'll be able to surprise too many more artillery batteries up that way, and I'm having too much fun to go home, so we'll head further out into the desert. Maybe we can outflank them again."

The two-vehicle convoy drove through the smoldering ruins of the Maltaani battery. Jocko and Welch grabbed several fuel cans from the surviving ammo truck before tossing an incendiary grenade inside and clambering back into their vehicle. The grenade exploded in a shower of white smoke and flames and the truck was fully engulfed before the Space Marines were out of sight.

The trucks left faint tracks on the hard-packed desert floor, though Ward wasn't concerned about pursuers. His biggest worry was aerial surveillance, but they hadn't seen any Maltaani air assets thus far. The sky began to dim, and Ward felt fatigue tug on his eyelids. They hadn't slept before their current mission started, and they'd been running and fighting for almost twenty-four hours since they left their lines. He guided Gomez to a stop in a shallow depression and waved the truck alongside.

"It's getting dark," he told the squad as they climbed from the vehicles and stretched their sore muscles. "I don't think anyone is following us. We'll lay up here and rest for a couple hours."

Gomez and Jocko went on a short foot patrol to explore the surrounding terrain while the rest of the men relaxed. Welch checked Ward's bandaged arm and nodded.

"Looks like you'll live, Sergeant. Or at least, it won't be that arm that kills you."

"Great news, Doc. Thanks."

Gomez and Jocko returned and kneeled down next to Ward.

"Nothing to see out there. Dirt and more dirt, with some rocks thrown in for fun."

"No Maltaani?"

"Not even a dust cloud on the horizon. We either lost them or they're sneaking up on us and we're fucked."

Ward sighed. "Lads, we've got one more task before we can rest." He motioned to the ammo truck. "Koloff and Sewell; we have to bury them."

Gomez dropped his chin to his chest and stared at the ground while Donk and Jocko exchanged glances and scowled.

"'No Space Marine left behind' is a nice idea, and if our circumstances were different I wouldn't even consider this. But the fact is, we're operating behind enemy lines in stolen vehicles that we barely know how to drive, with no idea when or how this mission ends. We might never get a better chance than right now."

Welch scuffed the dirt with his boot. "Ward's right. Let's get it done."

They hacked and scraped with their kukris and some Maltaani tools they found in the ammo truck, but the rocky ground resisted their efforts. After an hour, it was almost dark, and they had only managed two shallow depressions.

"I don't know, fellas," panted Welch. "It's like digging through concrete."

Ward nodded his agreement. "There are enough rocks around here to build a cairn. What do you guys think?"

The Space Marines gathered rocks and mounded them over the bodies of their comrades. They finished their grim task by starlight and gathered around the graves.

"I'm not one for praying, but if there is a higher power out there, and I sure as hell hope there is, I think it will recognize that Koloff and Sewell died for something greater than themselves, and they'll be rewarded for it. They were good Space Marines, and they deserve better than an unmarked grave on a planet far from home. DINLI."

The other Space Marines replied in unison:

"DINLI."

* * * *

Chapter Nineteen

Major Anders entered the FOC and waited until Admiral Kinshaw waved him over to the flag console.

"Tell me some good news, Major," the admiral said as he massaged the bridge of his nose between thumb and forefinger.

"I've got my analysis of the latest infrared reconnaissance."

Anders waited while Kinshaw pulled up the file and paged through it on his monitor.

"What exactly am I looking at?"

"Sir, I laid the IR imagery over the division drop zone map. It's rough, but it looks like Ninth Division is here and the enemy has taken up positions around here."

Kinshaw shook his head. "I don't see anything but colored blobs. How do you know those are our troops?"

"I admit it's conjecture, Admiral, and not enough to make tactical decisions, but it's a start. I have a plan to confirm this data."

"Let's hear it."

"I want to strip the camera gear from an imagery drone, load some written instructions inside the body of the drone, and program it to land where I believe Ninth Division is at."

"What instructions?"

"Mark their position so our IR drones can detect it."

"What if you're wrong and it lands on the Maltaani?"

Anders shrugged. "Then we gave them a drone. Without the camera gear, our drones are pretty low-tech. If they did take it apart and find the message, it's unlikely that they can read our language anyway."

"Hmm. Seems like an expensive way to send a single message. How do they signal back to us?"

"By marking their positions. That will enable us to insert the mechs, make a logistics drop, and maybe support them with orbital bombing."

"Whoa, hold on, Major. Let's not get ahead of ourselves. It would be good to know where their positions are, but I'm not sending troops anywhere without knowing more about the situation on the ground. What's the status of the jamming?"

"The high orbit drones should finish their circumnavigation and be back within the next four hours. The deep space drone won't return until it maps the edge of the jamming lobe. Since neither high orbit drone returned early, I believe the jamming is omnidirectional and the source is probably located on Balfan-48."

"More conjecture."

"It is, Admiral, but it's based on how we programmed the drones. They're supposed to return to *Atlas* as soon as their passive sensors detected no more jamming. Neither one has returned, er-go—"

Kinshaw cut him off with the wave of a hand.

"I see your point, Major, but this isn't an intelligence puzzle we're trying to solve. A lot of lives depend on the decisions we make based on a lot of fragmentary information and educated guesses."

"Sir, we'll continue to work on the jamming issue. It's my highest priority, but until our drones return, I can't make any more progress.

In the meantime, I'd like to try and establish communications with Ninth Division by any means at our disposal."

Admiral Kinshaw pursed his lips and considered Major Anders for a long second before he nodded.

"Okay, Major. Send your messenger drone and see what happens." He raised a cautionary finger. "Don't let this interfere with your efforts on the jamming."

"No, sir. Thank you, sir."

Anders ran out of the FOC before Kinshaw could change his mind.

* * *

Two hours later, Anders and Niskala watched as Staff Sergeant Thein and his crew made final launch preparations on the stripped-down imagery drone mounted in the launch cradle.

"Are you sure about this, Major?" Thein asked for the tenth time.

"Positive, Sergeant. Are we ready?"

Thein gave the drone a final once-over and reviewed his launch checklist.

"Prelaunch checks are complete. The drone is ready for launch."

"Perfect."

The drone techs rolled the craft into the launch air lock and latched the door behind it. Anders, Niskala, and the drone techs evacuated the hangar and assembled in the drone operations center, where they observed the hangar via closed circuit cameras.

"All doors are green," reported the launch operator. "Standing by for launch."

"Equalize pressure," ordered Thein.

An amber warning light flashed, and Anders heard a soft hiss as tiny jets allowed the last bit of pressure inside the air lock to bleed off into space before the outer hatch was opened. The amber light went out.

"Pressure is equalized."

"Open outer doors," said Thein.

"Outer doors are open."

"Launch the drone."

The deck-mounted catapult rail propelled the drone out the outer door, and it sailed into space.

"Close outer doors and equalize pressure."

The doors slid shut and Anders heard the soft hiss as air replaced the vacuum inside the air lock.

"Outer doors are closed, pressure equalized. All doors are green."

"Secure from launch. Well done, guys." Thein turned to Anders. "I sure hope this works, Major."

"It'll work," Anders replied. "I feel pretty good about it. The intel types on the ground will understand what we're asking and why. We'll be able to get a better idea of what's going on after they mark their positions. Anyway, the high orbit drones should be back soon, so let's get ready for recovery. I have a good feeling about them, too."

* * *

"What happened to him?" asked Liz Sherer when Ystremski dragged Fortis into the triage area of the field hospital.

"Maltaani dog bit him on the arm."

"A *dog*? The Maltaani have dogs?"

"Something like a dog. I don't know, some kind of toothy bastard. Bit him on the arm."

Pops bustled in and shooed Ystremski out of the way. Fortis groaned when they peeled the armor off his arm and exposed the bite mark.

The wound had already turned purplish red and yellowish pus was leaking down his arm. Pops swore under his breath as he probed the margins of the puncture.

"It almost looks like fast-acting venom. It was a dog, you say?"

Ystremski shrugged. "Yeah, it looked like a dog. Mighta been a wolf."

"Hmm."

"It's starting to burn," Fortis complained.

Pops dug into his field medic kit and came up with a long syringe.

"Lieutenant, I'm going to give you a deep antibiotic injection. You might feel a slight pinch."

Fortis laughed as Pops swam in and out of focus. "My fucking arm hurts so much I won't feel—*Ow!*"

The world went black.

* * *

"Hey, Red, did you ever think you'd be an intergalactic garbage collector?"

Corporal O'Reilly, nicknamed Red for his shock of brilliant red hair, shook his head in annoyance.

"Get some new material, Placer. We've been at this for an hour, and you've asked everyone in the platoon the same fucking question."

"I'll take that as a no, then."

Red's platoon was part of a company tasked to police up the area around the crater where divisional headquarters had been. When they started it was fun, like a scavenger hunt. After an hour, all they'd found were pieces of twisted metal and a large chunk of plastic melted into a vaguely phallic shape, which prompted Placer to gallop around with it dangling between his legs. Then the endless stupid questions began and Red's nerves began to fray.

He turned to curse at Placer just in time to see the platoon comedian disappear with a shout. He ran over to see what happened to the missing Marine and discovered Placer had fallen through a dome of fused sand caused by the heat of the explosion.

"Hey, Red, get me outta here!"

"Yeah, hold on. You okay? Can you walk?"

"I think so. I hit this fucking thing on the way down, but I'm all right."

Red waved the platoon back from the rim of the hole and they probed the sand for the edge of the dome. When they punched through, Placer scrambled out.

"There are trucks down there," he told Red. "Big ones."

The platoon leader eyed Placer with suspicion. He'd been the target of Placer's jokes before, and the constant shenanigans made him wary.

"I'm serious, Red. Aliens buried some trucks down there." Placer gestured for Red to follow him down into the hole. "C'mon, I'll show you."

He climbed down behind the prankster. Once his eyes adjusted to the dim light underground, he discovered there were indeed trucks buried inside the dome of sand, but they weren't alien. He brushed off the door of the nearest vehicle.

"Placer, look here." He pointed at the writing painted on the door.

1st ISMC Air Wing
7th CAS Sqdn

"They're ours."

* * * * *

Chapter Twenty

When Fortis regained consciousness, Ystremski, Liz, and Pops were huddled together out of earshot. He looked around and saw Lance Corporal Thibodeaux smiling at him from the next cot.

"Whaddya say, LT? Let's bust out of here and go kill some Maltaani."

Fortis chuckled and swung his feet onto the ground.

"You're a stone-cold killer, Thibodeaux. How's the arm?"

"I'm good to go, sir. Same question back at you."

"It's just a scratch," Fortis lied smoothly as his arm began to throb.

"They said you got bit by a dog."

"Ah, Lieutenant, you're awake," Pops interjected. "How do you feel?"

"A little sore, but otherwise I feel great. What's the prognosis?"

"Hmm. I believe we got to the infection before it could spread. What I thought was venom was probably saliva. As soon as I flushed the wound with an astringent, the pus cleared up. Your arm is badly bruised, so I think a day or two of limited use would be best. Of course—" Pops gestured around him, "—just do your best."

Ystremski offered his hand and Fortis groaned as he stood up. His joints ached from his wrestling match with the enemy animal, and when he rolled his head his neck cracked.

Liz smiled and gave him a hug.

"Every patient gets a hug before they leave," she said.

"My turn," declared Thibodeaux as he stood up. "Gimme a hug, too."

Pops looked at Fortis, who shrugged.

"Liz, please hug this man so he can get back to his unit. He's beginning to drive me crazy."

Fortis and Ystremski walked away from the field hospital. When they were fifteen meters away, Ystremski's demeanor changed.

"What the fuck were you doing back there, sir?"

"What, there? Getting treated by Pops and Liz."

"No, I'm not talking about that bullshit and you know it. I'm talking about out there on the perimeter. Why the hell did you go out there like that?"

"I was trying to distract them while I came up with a plan. The Maltaani were butchering our guys, and we had to do something."

Ystremski grabbed Fortis by the shoulder. "Sir, if there's some suicidal shit that needs done tell me, and I'll get it done. That's how it works. Gunny Hawkins taught you that back on Pada-Pada. In case you haven't noticed, we're a little short on officers right now."

"You're right. I should have ordered you to your death."

Ystremski stared at Fortis for a long second until the officer cracked a smile.

"I know, I know. You're right. I lost my cool, and I almost lost my life. I appreciate you coming out for me; that dog was a monster."

"While we're on the subject of monsters, I put Foxtrot Company in charge of the prisoner while you were out. I trust every one of these Space Marines to do their duty, but some of them might get excited and forget themselves, especially after what we just witnessed. I'd rather see familiar faces on guard duty."

"Hey, look!" A private pointed into the sky. Fortis shielded his eyes and looked in the direction the private indicated. An aircraft was circling high above their position, and he recognized the familiar shape of an ISMC drone. Plasma bolts arced up into the sky as some of the Space Marines fired on the unexpected aircraft.

"Cease fire! Cease fire!" Fortis shouted. "It's one of ours."

The drone spiraled downward until it was just a few meters above the surface. The engines shut off and it glided until it touched down. The landing gear collapsed, the right wingtip dug into the dirt, and the drone cartwheeled. Both wings and the rear stabilizer snapped off, and the drone came to a stop in a cloud of dust and mangled parts.

"I hope the Corps still has the warranty card for that thing," Ystremski quipped as he jogged toward the wreckage with Fortis.

Space Marines gathered around and stared at the demolished drone. Several of them heaved the upside down craft over and examined the fuselage.

"Hey, LT, there's something not right about this bird." A corporal approached Fortis and Ystremski. "There are no sensors on it at all. No camera pods, no radomes, nothing. Why would Fleet send a drone like that?"

"Good question, Corporal. Who are you?"

"Sergeant Freivald, forward air controller with the Ninth Division Air Combat Element." He patted his rank insignia and gave a self-conscious chuckle. "I *was* Sergeant Freivald, until Eros-69. Now I'm *Corporal* Freivald. Controlling drones is my job."

"Hey, Freivald, look at this." One of the other Space Marines pointed at the craft. "Someone scratched the word 'Open' into the side."

"Grab a wrench and open her up."

The Space Marines made quick work of the bolts. When they got the access panel open, one of them reached inside and pulled out an envelope.

"It's addressed to 'Commanding General ISMC Ninth Division,'" he said. He handed the envelope to Freivald, who passed it to Fortis.

"I guess that's you, sir."

Fortis tore open the envelope.

From: Second Battalion Intelligence
To: Commanding General ISMC Ninth Division

Enemy jamming has prevented Fleet from reinforcing Ninth Division. Infrared is currently the only sensor available. If practical, request Ninth Division mark positions with heat sources to facilitate support. IR drones will conduct surveillance missions nightly.

/Anders sends

He passed the message to Ystremski. "It's good to know that Major Anders is on the job, Gunny."

"Hmm. 'Heat sources.'"

"Yeah, I saw that. Do we have anything that will burn?"

"We've got some incendiary grenades and FGUs. Let's pile up some Maltaani bodies and have a barbecue."

Freivald pointed to the wrecked drone. "Hey, LT, you mind if I keep this thing?"

Fortis looked at Ystremski, who shrugged.

"Sure. Go ahead, Corporal."

An explosion on the far side of the perimeter made everyone flinch.

"Incoming!"

Artillery rounds rained down inside the perimeter as Space Marines scrambled for cover. Maltaani spotters must have observed the activity around the drone, because the fire was concentrated in that area. Fortis and Ystremski took cover in a vacant hole, then watched as Freivald and two other Space Marines dragged the drone to the edge of the crater and tossed it in.

"What are they doing? They're going to get killed!"

"There's a lot of that going on lately, sir."

Fortis snorted and they slid to the bottom of the hole and laughed like maniacs as the Maltaani shells continued to fall.

* * *

When the shelling stopped, Gunny Ystremski set out for the perimeter to organize fires for the infrared drones. It was a grisly task, but the Space Marines soon had four head-high stacks of bodies positioned at the corners of a rough square around their perimeter. He decided to head for the crater to see if the reserve troops assigned to police up the area had recovered anything that would burn.

"Hey, Gunny! Hey!"

A red-headed Space Marine corporal he vaguely recognized ran toward him and gestured toward the crater.

"What's up, Marine?"

"In the crater. You gotta see what we dug up."

Ystremski followed, and he saw a group of Space Marines gathered around a hole in the ground.

"What is it?"

"Trucks, Gunny. *Our* trucks."

Ystremski sent runners to locate Lieutenant Fortis and when he arrived Ystremski was in the hole with Red, Placer, and a half dozen other Marines.

"What's up, Gunny? The runner said we found some trucks?"

"Not just trucks, sir, Tankers. Water tankers."

"How did you find them?"

Corporal O'Reilly waved at Fortis.

"Sir, my platoon was assigned to police up the area. Private Placer, here, fell through the crust and landed on these trucks. They must have been buried by the nuke."

"How many are there?"

"Six in all, LT," replied Ystremski. "Two of them are on their sides and they're empty. The other four are upright, and, when we tapped on them, they sounded full."

"Is the water potable?"

"I don't know, sir. Maybe Pops can test it."

Fortis thought for a second. "Okay. Send a couple samples over to Pops and get the two empty trucks dug out and upright."

"You want us to get them out of this hole?"

"No, they're safer underground. If we bring them up here, they'll give the Maltaani artillery something to shoot at."

* * *

A short distance from the tanker excavation, Fortis saw Corporal Freivald and two other Space Marines had the crashed drone dismantled and the pieces laid out on the sand.

"Having fun, Corporal?"

"Yes, sir. Well, not exactly fun, but we're making progress."

Fortis examined the drone.

"What kind of progress?"

"There were no sensor pods on this drone, but all the internals are still here. These things are basically a flying radio, you know. Everything the sensors collect is transmitted back to the control node. I might be able to use these parts to make a transmitter so we can send messages back to *Atlas*."

"What about the jamming?"

Freivald shrugged. "They can't jam us forever. Fleet will figure it out, and when they do, we'll have a transmitter ready to talk to them. I met a guy who's been charging pulse rifle batteries, and he said he could give me a solar system to power it. I hope it works."

"It'll work, Freivald. Keep it up; we're all counting on you. Carry on and keep me posted."

Fortis continued his tour and came upon two litter bearers struggling with the wounded Space Marine they were carrying.

"Take me back!" the injured man demanded.

"What's going on here?"

"Hey, LT."

Fortis looked at the bloodied Space Marine and saw a familiar face.

"What happened to you, Thibodeaux?"

"Goddamn artillery. Lucky shot."

"You need to be more careful. We need you out on the line."

"That's what I've been telling these pricks, sir, but they won't listen."

"He's got shrapnel in about a hundred places and a wound in his shoulder that's going to need surgery," one of the litter bearers told Fortis. He looked back at Thibodeaux. "And a severe head injury, I think. That or he's crazy."

"I just want to fight. What's crazy about that?"

Fortis snorted. "Thibodeaux, go with these guys and get your leaks patched up. I'll make sure there are plenty of Maltaani left to kill when you get back out there."

"Thank you, sir." Thibodeaux laid back on the litter. "To the hospital, boys. I need a hug and then it's back to battle!"

The litter bearers nodded their gratitude to Fortis and headed toward the field hospital. Fortis shook his head and continued his tour.

* * * * *

Chapter Twenty-One

Major Anders stood in front of Admiral Kinshaw's desk while the admiral clicked through several pages on his monitor. Finally, he leaned back and fixed Anders with a steady gaze.

"Where are your drones, Major?"

Anders' face flushed as his pulse pounded.

"There's been—" His voice was a croak, and he cleared his throat. "There's been no word, Admiral. The high orbit drones are now two hours overdue. They may have—"

Kinshaw cut him off with the wave of his hand.

"No more guesswork, Major. Where are they?"

"I don't know, sir."

"Did your messenger drone make it to the surface?"

"We can't be sure until we recover the next IR mission. If they mark their positions as directed, then we'll know."

"Our situation here is becoming more tenuous by the hour, Major. The Maltaani force Ninth Division encountered on Balfan-48 came from somewhere, which means they have support from a fleet located nearby. A fleet that I presently cannot detect or engage."

"I just need a little more time, Admiral. When the jamming drones get back, I'll have a better understanding of the jamming and how to counter it."

"*If* the drones get back."

"Yes, sir, if."

"That's all, Major."

* * *

Lieutenant Fortis caught up with Gunny Ystremski on the perimeter as the NCO was watching the Space Marines stack up Maltaani bodies to burn.

"That's a pretty big pile. Will it burn?"

"The lads got the two empty tankers upright and discovered the fuel tanks were full, so these will burn long and hot."

"More good news." Fortis scratched his head. "It worries me when we get good news."

Ystremski chuckled. "Don't worry, LT, there's another disaster right around the corner, I'm sure."

"Do we have numbers from the fighting this morning?"

"I haven't got all the numbers yet, but so far they're not good. My guess is six hundred KIA/WIA."

"Damn."

"Sneaking up in the dark was pretty slick. So was their feint. I gotta give them credit, those fuckers are starting to figure all of this out."

"Do you have any ideas how to stop them from getting so close? Without night vision we're pretty limited. Can we dig listening posts?"

"I don't know about listening posts, LT. After what we saw them do to those prisoners, it's going to be hard to order these guys to sit in a hole out there in the dark. How about we lay some booby traps instead? Tripwires and grenades a couple hundred meters out should give us enough notice; it might slow them down, too."

"Better than nothing, I guess."

They heard the whistle of more incoming artillery rounds and ducked into a nearby fighting hole. The rounds exploded harmlessly in the perimeter behind them. When they emerged from cover, they heard Space Marines grumbling as they resumed the gruesome task of stacking enemy bodies.

"The boys are getting tired of all this hiding. It's beginning to wear on morale."

"What do you suggest? Fix bayonets and charge?"

"C'mon, LT, we're a long way from suicide, but it would be good for morale if we fought back."

"I'm listening."

"Let me think about it for a little bit. I need to talk to some of the lads and see what their devious minds can come up with."

* * *

The flames from the burning bodies soared high into the air while Fortis strained his ears to catch the buzz of drone engines in the dark sky above or enemy fire from the no-mans-land beyond their lines. He heard neither and focused on his daily log entry.

Gunny Ystremski had sent a squad of Space Marines into the desert beyond the perimeter. When they were about a hundred meters out, they stopped and unloaded their packs. Using the faint orange light from the distant fires, the squad laid a series of simple snares with wire and grenades. The booby traps weren't intended to kill the enemy as much as warn the Space Marines of anyone approaching their perimeter.

The plan was simple. Lay a belt of live traps as an early warning system backed up by a mix of real and fake traps to slow them down.

Since the Maltaani had previously advanced headlong into the Space Marine defenses, slowing them down was a long shot, but it might give the defenders a few critical seconds to meet their attackers.

He turned his attention back to his notebook.

"Lieutenant Fortis?" whispered Liz Sherer from the darkness behind him.

"Here. Over this way."

A dark shape materialized next to him and flopped down.

"How's it going, Liz?"

"I'm fine. How's the arm? I haven't seen you since you got bit and thought I should check up on you."

"It's fine. There's no more pain, but it throbs sometimes."

"Please make some time tomorrow to come and get the bandage changed," she said. "I'd hate to see an infection take hold."

"I learned my lesson from Kilfoy."

"What? What's a Kilfoy?"

"Kilfoy's not a what, she's a who. Kilfoy was a Space Marine who was on Pada-Pada with me. She stepped in a bug hole and got bit. The docs couldn't stop the infection, and she died."

"Ah, sheesh, I'm sorry."

Fortis shrugged in the darkness. "DINLI."

"DINLI."

The smell of burning flesh drifted over them, and Liz gagged.

"You think this will work?" she asked through gritted teeth.

"We were all out of firewood," quipped Fortis.

Somewhere in the sky above, he heard a low buzz.

"Drone."

He scanned the night sky, but there was nothing to see. The drone made several long passes over the Space Marine position before the sound faded.

"Hey, LT. You awake?" Ystremski hissed from somewhere off to the left.

"Yeah, I'm up. Did you hear that drone?"

The gunny knelt down beside Fortis. "Yes, sir, I did."

"You think they saw us?"

"Hell, I don't know."

"They better have, because I don't think I can take much more of that smell," said Liz.

Fortis and Ystremski laughed.

"Sorry, LT, I didn't realize you had company."

Fortis groaned, but Ystremski's insinuation went unnoticed by the reporter.

"It could be Maltaani, reconnoitering our position."

"I don't know, sir. Our position isn't exactly a secret. We're here, they're all around us, and they have a hell of a lot more guys than we do."

"How did things go with the tripwires?"

"They all made it back safe, and there's a ring of traps out there now. All we can do is wait."

Fortis yawned and settled back down into his hole. "Whatever it is, it will be there in the morning."

"Sit up, sir. I have some good news and some bad news for you."

"Bad news first."

"I got final muster reports together. As near as I can tell, we have nineteen hundred and four able-bodied Space Marines and another three hundred wounded."

Fortis gasped.

"It was an expensive day, LT."

"We have to fall back again. There's no way we can hold them off with nineteen hundred men."

"The boys won't be happy."

"DINLI."

"Indeed."

"How far back? The crater?"

"Yeah, I guess. We can't go much further. At least we can defend it."

"Why not retreat?" Liz asked. Fortis and Ystremski had forgotten Liz was with them in the darkness. "We're not surrounded, right?"

"Two men per litter to carry the wounded is a third of our combat strength," Fortis said. "We'd be marching away from our water, and there's no real cover out there. We'd be fighting in the open against an enemy who doesn't seem to care about casualties."

"I'm sorry. I'm not a tactical expert."

"Neither are we," quipped Ystremski, and Liz giggled.

"What's the good news, Gunny?"

Ystremski pressed a canteen into Fortis's hands and the officer took a sniff. Sharp fumes scorched his nostrils and brought tears to his eyes.

"Holy shit, what is this?"

Ystremski chuckled. "DINLI, sir. Straight from the tap. Balfan-48's finest."

"How the hell did you manage this?"

"A couple of the boys stripped some parts from the tankers and got a brew going."

Fortis sniffed it again. Underneath the fiery raw alcohol he caught a whiff of a deep, unpleasant stench and his stomach lurched.

"Gah! That smells like stale farts. What did you brew it from, dirty skivvies?"

"Ha! No, LT. Not skivvies. Lima beans."

Fortis choked back the sudden thickness that climbed into his throat. "Lima beans?"

"It's all we have. Pig squares and lima beans, and we can't brew with pig squares. C'mon, drink up."

Fortis sighed and tipped out a splash in tribute to fallen Space Marines. "DINLI."

He took a deep breath and tipped some into his mouth and tried to swallow without tasting. The DINLI scalded his tongue and throat, and he gasped in pain. He inhaled a few drops of the incendiary liquid and exploded into a coughing jag that tore at his lungs and left him fighting to breathe.

Corporal Ystremski pushed a hydration pack into his hands and Fortis sucked greedily on the spout. He fell back into his hole and struggled to get his breath back.

"Smooth," he rasped, and Ystremski laughed aloud.

"What is that?" asked Liz.

"It's DINLI. Good stuff. Care for some?"

After a long moment, Fortis cleared his throat and spat into the darkness.

"Careful, Liz, that stuff will put hair on your chest, or burn it off."

"Here you go. Just splash a little out and then take a sip. You can't be a Space Marine if you don't drink DINLI."

Liz coughed. "This stuff smells like rocket fuel."

"That's why only Space Marines drink it. C'mon, I thought you deployed with Space Marines before. You're not scared, are you?"

Fortis heard a splatter and then a sipping sound. Immediately, Liz choked and gasped for breath. Fortis and Ystremski couldn't control their laughter.

* * * * *

Chapter Twenty-Two

Ward took the first watch while the rest of the men huddled down to get some sleep. The night was completely black, but he noticed a white glow on the horizon. It was a steady light, not the flickering of a flame, but there was no sound. He puzzled over it for the entirety of his watch but couldn't decide what it was.

When Gomez relieved him, Ward pointed out the light. Gomez agreed it was unusual and said he would keep an eye on it. Ward curled up under the self-propelled gun and tried to sleep, but his mind turned over the strange light.

Just as he thought of an idea what it might be, Ward dropped off into a heavy slumber.

At first light, Ward woke to find the rest of the Space Marines up and ready to go.

"I wracked my brain until I fell asleep, and I think it's a space port," he told the group. "It makes sense that the Maltaani would establish a logistics hub to support their troops."

"It could be a mine," interjected Donk. "Is there anything on this rock worth digging up?"

"I don't know. Maybe. Whatever it is, we should recon it. We'll patrol that way until we make contact and then figure out how to proceed. Questions?"

Nobody spoke.

"Gear up, ladies, we move out in five."

They made rapid progress across the rocky desert. There wasn't much cover, so Ward had Gomez take point a hundred meters in front of the trucks. Ward drove the self-propelled gun and Welch handled the truck, while Donk and Jocko patrolled fifty meters to their flank. They would enter an area of low rolling hills, Gomez would signal for a halt, then scramble to the top of the next hill to take a look. If it was clear he would wave the formation into motion.

After six hours of steady movement, Gomez spent a long time observing the far side of a distant rise before he jogged back to the trucks.

"There's a big white building over there," he told the gathered Space Marines. "It has a tall antenna-looking thing on top. There's a fence around it with lights on top and some vehicles parked inside. I watched for a while, but I didn't see any movement."

"It's not a space port?"

"I don't think so, but we're not close enough to get a good look."

Ward and Gomez returned to the observation point to recon the mystery building while the others waited with the vehicles.

Gomez's description was spot on. The white building had a tall antenna on top and the facility was surrounded by a wire fence. The vehicles parked inside the fence had four wheels and looked like Terran golf carts. After a few minutes, Ward waved Gomez down and they huddled up.

"I don't see anything happening there, but we need to get a look from different angles. Let's work our way around this side and see what it looks like from the far edge of this rise."

Gomez led Ward along the base of the rise until it started to become level with the surrounding desert. They crept up on all fours and peeked over the top. Ward saw two large garage doors on the back wall, but still no personnel and no other vehicles. They watched and waited, but there was no activity.

Ward wanted to continue, to get a look at the fourth wall, but there was no suitable cover that would allow them to get close enough for a clear view.

"Let's head back the other way and see what it looks like from over there," he whispered.

They stayed low and worked their way around until they'd gone far enough to get a look at the other side. When Ward chanced a look over the top he saw a blank wall. He slid back down to Gomez.

"Blank wall, Gomez. No windows, no doors, nothing. The place looks deserted. Any idea what it could be?"

"I don't think it's a space port," said Gomez. "There are no support vehicles, and I didn't see anything that looked like a landing pad. Maybe it's a navigation beacon or a communications relay station."

"That would explain the antenna. The fence keeps out curious Space Marines and other assorted riff-raff and they house a security force inside and give them golf carts to drive around."

"Are we going to attack?"

"I don't think so. Not without more information. Let's get back to the others and tell them what we've found."

The platoon regrouped, and Ward scratched the layout of the compound into the dirt. He described what he and Gomez had observed.

"It looks like a simple set up to me," said Donk. "What's the problem?"

"Who does it belong to? I didn't see any signs or writing. For all we know it's a top-secret Fleet facility."

"Ring the doorbell. If a Maltaani answers, shoot him in the face."

The group chuckled.

"I didn't see a doorbell, so here's what we're going to do. Gomez and Welch will set up an observation post along this ridge here. The rest of us will back the vehicles off another klick and find a low spot to conceal them. Welch, when you're done setting up the OP, come back here so we can all find it. We'll take it in three-hour shifts tonight and reassess in the morning."

Ward, Jocko, and Donk found a depression and shoveled dirt on top of the truck to disguise the straight lines. They depressed the gun as low as it would go, but Ward balked at piling dirt on it. They settled for piling pieces of ammunition crates along the barrel to give it some texture. When they were finished, Ward walked out fifty meters and inspected their handiwork. The result wasn't great, but it was the best they could do under the circumstances. It would be dark soon and then the vehicles would be indistinguishable in the blackness of the desert.

* * *

The Maltaani artillery barrage commenced before first light. Shells landed at random all over the Space Marine position and the troops on the perimeter watched and waited for the expected attack. As soon as it was light enough to see, Liz made a run for the field hospital.

After an hour of harassing fire, Fortis looked at Ystremski.

"What do you think's going on? Why aren't they attacking?"

"I don't know, LT. Maybe they saw us setting up the tripwires last night and decided to shift around to attack another section of the perimeter."

"Maybe we finally killed enough of them to convince them that they can't win."

"Wishful thinking is a dangerous hobby."

"Speaking of dangerous hobbies, yesterday you said you might have some ideas about taking the fight to the enemy. Did you come up with anything good?"

An artillery round exploded close enough to shower them with dirt and send a cloud of dust billowing over their position.

"Fucking artillery," growled Ystremski.

"I guess it wouldn't help to move to another hole, would it?"

"This hole is as good as any. Besides, the lads might frown at their officers and NCOs running for cover."

"Good point."

"Anyway, back to your question. Red, er, Corporal O'Reilly, the platoon leader who found the water tankers, came up with an amusing idea. If we dig up one of the empty tankers and get it running, we could pour fuel into the empty tank. Then tonight, we use an FGU to heat up the tank to vaporize the fuel. Rig the accelerator and steering to run at the Maltaani, and when they engage it, it will explode."

Fortis snorted. "You think that would work?"

"I have no idea, but it's fun to think about. Maybe we could use it as a diversion to sneak up on their lines and launch some hand grenades at them. At this point, I think we need to do something besides butcher them when they attack."

"A diversion isn't a bad idea. I wish we could follow it up with something more serious than a grenade raid."

"If wishes were horses," started Ystremski.

"We'd eat meat tonight," they finished together. It was an old saying from the International Space Marine Corps training ground, recited by drill instructors who overheard trainees wishing for something. Wishing was not a winning strategy and ran counter to the DINLI ethos, and those caught wishing paid for their mistake with sweat.

Another near miss made them duck into their hole.

"I would drop and start doing pushups but getting killed by an arty round isn't on my agenda today."

"Too bad, LT. You'd be a legend."

"I'm already a legend." Fortis patted the pocket where he kept his notebook. "It says so right here in my report."

The duo decided to split up and tour different parts of the Space Marine position. Fortis wanted to look in on the wounded at the field hospital, and check the progress of the water tanker excavation. Ystremski agreed to make a circuit of the perimeter.

"I'm worried that we're getting too thin," he told the lieutenant. "The reserve force took a beating yesterday, too."

"If you think we need to fall back, we'll fall back. I hate the idea of concentrating our position under that artillery fire, but we can't stay spread out and repel the mass attacks."

"If we dig deep enough, the arty won't be a problem. I'd rather die from a shell exploding on my head anyway."

"All right, Gunny. I'll see you when I see you."

"Keep your damn fool head down, sir."

"Yes, Mom."

When Fortis arrived at the field hospital, he stopped and stared at the stack of body bags lined up outside. When he'd discussed casualty numbers with Ystremski, it was in abstract terms, but the sight of all those dead bodies was a sharp reminder that the dead were more than just numbers.

Liz spotted him and waved him over.

"How are things going here, Liz? Is there anything you need?"

"Nothing we can get here," she replied with a sad smile.

She led him on a tour through the rows of wounded, and Fortis made it a point to exchange a word or touch with the conscious. To a man, they were anxious to rejoin their platoons. It pleased Fortis to see morale was still high.

"Where's Thibodeaux?"

"Who?"

"Thibodeaux. He demanded a hug and returned to the line when I was here for my arm. He was brought back yesterday."

Liz's face fell. "I'm sorry, Abner. He died this morning."

"Died? How?"

"We patched him up and he demanded to be released again, so we let him go. A few hours later, a shell landed near him and took off a foot. They got him back here, but we couldn't stop the bleeding."

Fortis frowned and shook his head.

"He was a good man and a brave Space Marine."

"The best."

Pops approached.

"Ach, Lieutenant Fortis. I'm glad you've come back to let us have a look at your arm."

Fortis held up the bandage. "I figured I would come and get the best medical care on the planet."

Pops chuckled and pointed Fortis to a treatment area. The doctor hummed under his breath as he cut away the old bandage and exposed the puncture wound. It was puckered and reddish purple, but there was no pus or other sign of infection.

"Hmm. The wound looks clean. How does it feel?"

"Most of the time I don't feel it. If I bump it, it throbs, but otherwise it feels good."

Pops nodded as he examined Fortis's arm. "I think you are out of danger. I'll wrap this up to keep it covered, but only for another day or two."

Pops coated the wound with antibiotic cream and wrapped it with fresh gauze. Fortis and Pops locked eyes, and the older man winked. "Good as new."

His next stop was the Maltaani prisoner. Ystremski had put Space Marines from Foxtrot Company in charge of him—it?— and Fortis was curious to see a live Maltaani close up. When he got close to where Ystremski told him he could find the prisoner, he heard loud voices and laughter.

"Fuck you!"

"Fuck you, too!"

The Space Marines had their prisoner confined in a small cavity they'd carved into the side of the crater. Several of them stood around and laughed as Corporal Harrigan flipped his middle finger at the captive and shouted.

"Fuck You!"

"Fuck you too!" the Maltaani shouted back, and the Space Marines laughed.

"What the hell's going on here?" demanded Fortis.

"A little cultural exchange, sir," Harrigan said with a grin. "We're teaching our language to Fuck You Too."

"Fuck You Too?"

"That's his name. Ask him." He stepped close to the prisoner. "What's your name?"

"Fuck You Too."

Fortis glanced around at the other Space Marines. "You've got to be kidding me. Why did you do this?"

"It just kind of happened, sir. Some of the lads came by and shouted at him, so he started to shout back."

Fortis looked closely at the prisoner. The Maltaani looked eerily human, though his facial features were defined by sharp angles across his cheekbones and jawline. His eyes were narrower than a human's and lacked sclerae, or whites. Instead, his green-gray irises covered his eye. It wasn't obvious from his seated position, but Fortis imagined his arms and legs were elongated like he'd seen on other Maltaani.

"Has he said anything else?"

"That's all we've taught him so far."

The prisoner stared back at Fortis, and the lieutenant sensed intelligence in his eyes. He felt a peculiar emotion building, and he forced himself to blink and drag his eyes away.

"Corporal Harrington, come here." Fortis motioned for the Space Marine to follow him as he stepped well out of earshot.

"I don't want the sentries, or anyone else, to interact with the prisoner. No more 'Fuck You Too,' no more language lessons, nothing."

"Sorry, LT."

"No apology is necessary. We don't know anything about the Maltaani, so we need to be careful. For all we know, they speak Terran languages, and he knows exactly what you're saying. If someone said the wrong thing about our defenses or the Fleet in front of him, who's to say he wouldn't understand and try to escape with the information."

Harrington nodded. "I understand. It won't happen again."

Fortis slapped him on the shoulder. "You guys are doing a great job out here. I'm proud of every one of you. Please pass this down to your relief and make sure they understand my instructions. If anyone has any questions, tell them to ask."

"Roger that, sir."

Fortis headed to the tanker truck excavation and found O'Reilly and his men hard at work. There were two trucks completely exposed and one partially buried. When the red-haired Space Marine saw the lieutenant standing on the edge of the hole, he set down his makeshift shovel and scrambled out of the hole.

"Morning, LT."

"Hey, O'Reilly. How's it going? Looks like you boys have been busy."

"Yes, sir. We dug out the empty trucks and got them upright. We covered up three of the others; we don't want the Maltaani to get lucky with an artillery round. Gunny Ystremski told us to dig the ramp in case you wanted them taken out of here, so that's what we're doing now."

"He told me you had an idea for one of the empties. A rolling bomb?"

"I come from a family of firefighters back on Terra Earth, and my dad always warned me about vaporized fossil fuels. The stuff in the fuel tanks is synthesized, but it's combustible and gives off strong vapors, so I think it will work the same way."

"It burned the Maltaani bodies pretty well."

Two artillery shells landed nearby in close succession. Fortis ducked, and O'Reilly slid back into the hole.

"I gotta get back to it, sir. Arty is bad for my complexion."

"Keep at it, you guys are doing good work," Fortis called, loud enough for the others to hear, too.

His next stop was Sergeant Coughlin and the pulse rifle ammunition project, but he spotted Sergeant Freivald hunched over a pile of drone components and detoured. Freivald didn't look up until Fortis spoke.

"What's up, Freivald?"

"Trying to get this—ah, Lieutenant." The drone technician stood up when he recognized Fortis. "Sorry about that, sir. I've almost got it."

"Almost got what?"

"As I suspected, the techs on *Atlas* stripped the sensors off this thing but left everything else intact, including the transceiver. Some of the components were damaged in the crash, but I wired it back together and I think it's going to work. I just need a little more time and less artillery."

"Outstanding work, Freivald. You think you can reach *Atlas* with that?"

"For sure, sir. The Sun God built a charger for the battery pack, so I've got plenty of power."

"Who? The Sun God?"

"That's what the guys have been calling Coughlin since he started using solar to recharge pulse rifle magazines."

"The Sun God. I like it."

"When I get this thing working, what message do you want me to send to Fleet? Do you want me to demand a refund for this fucked up vacation?"

Fortis laughed. "They won't give us a refund, but if you complain they might send us on another one. Tell them to send fresh fruit and ammo. Lima bean DINLI is pretty awful."

It was Freivald's turn to laugh. "I'm with you there, sir."

Fortis didn't have the heart to remind Freivald about the Maltaani jamming. If he got the transceiver working, it would be a boost to morale but not much else. Still, Fleet had to send reinforcements at some point, so a working transceiver would come in handy.

Fortis approached Coughlin's set-u, and he saw several Space Marines exchanging armloads of magazines and heading back to their positions.

"How's things, Sun God?"

Coughlin shook his head. "Not you too, LT. The guys started calling me that when they found out the LBA solar panels was my idea."

Fortis gestured to the solar chargers arrayed around them. "And now look. You're the master of all you survey. Is there anything I can do to help you?"

"Not unless you've got three hots and a cot I can have, I'm good to go. I'm getting a little sick of pig squares and sleeping on the ground."

"It's only been three days. You headquarters Marines are pathetic."

"Have you looked around lately? This place sucks."

"It won't be much longer. The Fleet flew over us with drones last night, so they know where we're at."

"You think they're coming, sir?"

"Yeah, of course. They're not going to leave without us."

As Fortis went in search of Gunny Ystremski, he wondered how much he believed what he had told Coughlin.

Where is the Fleet?

* * * * *

Chapter Twenty-Three

Anders waited in the drone operations center while the flight crew recovered the infrared drone. Staff Sergeant Thein expertly guided the capture boom, pulling the drone into the hangar, and sealed the doors behind it.

"Major, give us fifteen minutes to equalize the hangar pressure and plug up the umbilical, and the imagery will be available at your console."

Anders recognized Thein's comment was a polite way of telling him to go away, and he gave a sheepish grin.

"I'm sorry, Thein, I don't mean to hover, but there's a lot riding on this data."

"I understand, sir. It's just that my guys get nervous when officers fidget and look over their shoulder, and nervous techs make mistakes. I'd hate to see the data get wiped instead of downloaded because of a missed keystroke or a misaligned umbilical, you know?"

"Point taken, Thein. I'll head back up to the intel center. Please give me a buzz when the data is available?"

"Sure thing, Major. You'll be the first to know."

Anders had his console logged in when Thein called, and he immediately accessed the drone footage. He sped the recording up to five times normal speed and his face cracked into a wide grin. There was no mistaking what he saw. Four brilliant hotspots outlined a rough square where he estimated Ninth Division had deployed.

He captured several images and saved them into a file which he addressed to Admiral Kinshaw's account with a note: *Sir, I'm on my way to see you.*

He rushed to the door and nearly ran headlong into Major Niskala standing in the passageway outside.

"We got them, Kiti!"

"Really? I heard the drone was back."

"C'mon, I'm on my way to tell the admiral. Four hot spots around the original drop zone. It's them, it has to be. There's no other logical explanation."

"Do you think he'll authorize the mech wave?" she asked as they raced down the passageway.

"I can't say for sure, but I don't know why he wouldn't."

Anders paused at the door to the FOC to catch his breath and compose himself. He traded smiles with Niskala.

"Ready?"

The FOC was blanketed in a grim silence when the majors entered. Anders led the way through the darkened space to Kinshaw's flag console.

"Excuse me, Admiral. The IR mission returned, and preliminary analysis of the data shows four distinct hotspots around the drop zone."

The admiral looked up with an uncomprehending look on his face.

"The IR drone, sir. It's back. I sent you a file with some of the images to confirm. They got our message."

Kinshaw didn't respond.

"Sir, we know where they're at. We can coordinate support for them."

"We can drop in the mechs," added Niskala.

Kinshaw blinked, and his eyes finally focused on Anders and Niskala.

"What are you two babbling about?"

"The infrared surveillance mission returned, Admiral. We have confirmation that the Space Marines on Balfan-48 received our message and marked their position for the drone."

A tall, barrel-chested Fleet captain with a bushy mustache and eyebrows to match stepped forward between the Space Marines and the admiral.

"Can't you see this isn't a good time," he scolded them. "It's probably better that you leave the FOC and make an appointment to see the admiral later."

"Captain, I'm Major Anders, Second Battalion Intelligence. Admiral Kinshaw ordered—"

The captain held up his hand in a "stop" gesture.

"Major, didn't you hear me? This is not the time. Leave the FOC and make an appointment to see the admiral. Is that clear?"

Major Niskala jostled forward and pushed Anders aside.

"Captain, we need to talk to the admiral *now!*"

The confrontation drew the attention of everyone in the FOC, and several Fleet personnel surrounded the Space Marines. The captain loomed over Anders and Niskala, and his neck flushed a dark shade of red that bled into his face.

"Major Anders, this is your final warning. Take your companion and leave this space right now, or I'll have you confined to your quarters until further notice."

Defeated, Anders grabbed Niskala by the sleeve and dragged her toward the door. She didn't put up much resistance, but he sensed an explosion was imminent and hustled her out of the FOC.

Once they were in the passageway with the door shut, Niskala lashed out.

"Son of a bitch!"

She punctuated her outburst with a kick at the door.

"What do you think is going on?" she demanded.

Anders threw up his hands. "I have no idea. The admiral ordered the IR mission, but something must have happened."

"We *have* to talk to him. We have to get authority to drop the mechs."

"I understand, Kiti, but what do you want me to do, put a gun to his head?"

Niskala leaned against the bulkhead, deflated.

"I'm going up to the intel center to find out what's going on. You need to find a quiet place and cool off. I thought you were going to slug that captain."

"I probably should have."

Anders waited a few seconds.

"Are you okay?"

She straightened. "Yeah. I'll be in the drop ship hangars. Call me when you hear something."

"Will do."

Anders watched her until she disappeared around the corner at the end of the passageway. He shared her sense of desperation to get support to Ninth Division, but they were at the mercy of the admiral and his staff. A confrontation wouldn't serve their cause well, and he was anxious to find out what had happened to turn the tide of decision-making against them.

* * *

The sporadic artillery became a constant rain of shells, but it was area fire and not aimed at specific points on the line or within the perimeter. The Space Marines hunkered down in their holes and braced themselves for the attack to come, but firing stopped as suddenly as it started, and no attack materialized.

"What do you think they're doing, LT?" a nearby Marine asked Fortis.

"Maybe they're trying to make us question our life's decisions," he answered, and the Marine guffawed.

Fortis took advantage of the lull in the bombardment and jogged over to Foxtrot Company. After he greeted the men, he dug out a pig square and settled down to eat. When he reached into his pack, he discovered he was down to one hydration pack.

Should have refilled at the tanker.

Ystremski sat down next to him and dug out his own pig square.

"Sir, how was your tour?"

"As well as can be expected." The lieutenant related the details of what he'd found. When he told him about Thibodeaux, Ystremski shook his head.

"Damn. I liked that kid."

When Fortis got to the part about Fuck You Too, the gunny groaned and rolled his eyes.

"Leave it to me, sir, I'll straighten them out."

"There's no need, Gunny. I took Harrington aside and explained what I wanted, and he promised to pass it down to his relief. They'll be okay. How does the perimeter look?"

"I saw a lot of empty holes and bloody bandages on Marines who should probably be in the field hospital and not on the line. We're mighty thin in places."

"Is it time to pull back to the crater?"

"The problem with falling back to the crater is that once we're there, there's no getting back out. The artillery will be able to concentrate their fire. We can dig deep and hunker down, but time won't be on our side. There won't be much room to organize a counterattack, but I don't know that we have the strength to do much more than go out in a blaze of glory. There's just too many of those fuckers."

Ystremski's assessment shocked Fortis. He'd spoken frankly to Liz about their situation the day prior, but it was unexpected to hear from a seasoned veteran like the gunny.

"So, we have to retreat."

"Hmm, not exactly. I mean, eventually we will. What we have to prepare for is a sudden break in the perimeter. Our guys are some of the fiercest and bravest men from Terra Earth, but in the confusion of battle, they can be routed. If we hold what we have, at some point the Maltaani will send enough troops to break through the line and roll up the flanks. The reserve force has held them off so far, but we've taken too many casualties."

"How do we prepare for a rout?"

"Give the lads a rally point, somewhere to fall back to and organize a defense. With your permission, I'll order the reserve force to dig fighting steps into the rim of the crater and some holes to duck into when the artillery starts. We can hold out a long time, even if they decide to shoot artillery at us until we starve. Unless the Maltaani have something we haven't seen yet, I think we can last a month at least, or until the water runs out."

"Long enough for the Fleet to arrive."

"It would be nice to know when they're coming back."

They chewed in silence for a moment and then Ystremski gestured at Fortis's arm.

"How's the arm? Did you get it looked at?"

"Yeah, Pops himself changed the bandage. No obvious infection, and it feels pretty good." Fortis flexed his hand. "It only hurts when I cry."

The two men chuckled, and Ystremski stood up.

"When you get finished sitting around, there's something I want to show you."

* * *

Ystremski deflected the lieutenant's questions as he led Fortis to the perimeter where he'd been attacked by the Maltaani dog.

"You'll to have to wait, sir, but I promise you'll like it."

The Marines of Bravo Company emerged from their holes and gathered around Fortis and Ystremski. Corporal Branch stepped forward and held out his hand.

"Lieutenant Fortis, the boys made you this token to commemorate your fight with the Maltaani dog."

Fortis accepted the proffered token and saw it was a necklace. Two long fangs dangled from it, flanked by two enormous claws. The necklace itself was a frayed and knotted bootlace. It was a crude piece of handiwork, and Fortis had to blink away the sudden pressure in his eyes.

"It's magnificent!" He slipped the necklace over his head and beamed broadly at the assembled Marines. "I don't know what to say but thank you."

Branch waved to some other Marines, and they came forward carrying a tall totem. Mounted on top was the head of the Maltaani dog and the ragged pelt was spread over a crosspiece mounted below the head.

"After yesterday's action, we caught those bastards eyeballing us and thought they were going to attack, so we decided to use some old-fashioned hoodoo to strike terror in their hearts."

Fortis nodded his head in approval. "If that doesn't scare them, nothing will." He touched his necklace. "I can't thank you enough for this gift."

A distant explosion announced the resumption of the Maltaani artillery harassment and Bravo Company broke up and returned to their positions.

"I've been a Space Marine for a long time, and I've never seen anything like that necklace," Ystremski said as they jogged back to their own holes.

"I feel a little guilty accepting it."

"Don't be. I think the lads are a little ashamed about the whole Campanile situation, and that's their way of apologizing for taking orders from that maniac."

Fortis stopped. "They don't need to apologize."

Ystremski turned and jogged back. "They think they do, sir. Space Marines aren't a bunch of mindless automatons who blindly follow orders. Campanile endangered his entire company when he ordered them to maintain their position. A bunch of those guys were ready to follow his orders, and if you hadn't ordered them to fall back there would have been a helluva lot more than three guys chopped to pieces and fed to those damn dogs."

Three shells in quick succession sent them sprinting the last fifty meters to their holes. As he ran, Fortis tucked the dog fang necklace inside his LBA.

He didn't want to lose it.

* * * * *

Chapter Twenty-Four

After his informal attempts to discover the reason for Kinshaw's change of heart were unsuccessful, Anders was forced to call Commander Burlee, the Fleet assistant intelligence officer.

"Kinshaw's younger brother was the XO on a Fleet Cruiser on a scouting mission that was destroyed by the Maltaani a couple days ago. We just got the word via flashing light a few hours ago."

Flashing light was an antiquated Fleet communications path which used pulses of light to transmit data. It was slow and unreliable compared to modern comm techniques, but it couldn't be jammed.

"Damn it. What a shame."

"Yeah, it is. Kinshaw personally ordered the mission, and he's pretty distraught."

"Yeah, that's understandable. Well, at least I know why he's been unapproachable. Do you think there's any chance of me getting in on a briefing sometime soon? I've got the latest IR mission data from Balfan-48, and I think he needs to see it."

"Hmm. I don't know. The Chief Staff Officer is filtering everything right now to give the admiral some space. You can send it to me, and I'll pass it up the chain, but honestly, Balfan-48 is old news."

"What do you mean, 'old news?' Ninth Division is still down there, and we're still in orbit."

"I guess you haven't heard. The Fleet is withdrawing."

"Withdrawing? What about Ninth Division?"

A heavy silence descended over the line.

"I'm sorry, Major."

Anders hung up and sat in shocked silence. The Fleet was about to abandon five thousand Space Marines.

I've got to see the admiral.

* * *

The FOC was buzzing with activity, and the atmosphere was thick with tension when Major Anders entered the space. He waded through harried staffers and arrived at the vacant flag console.

"Where's Admiral Kinshaw?" he asked a worried-looking petty officer.

"I don't know, sir. Maybe try the flag mess?"

The flag mess was a private dining room where embarked admirals and generals took their meals. It was both a privilege of rank and a symbol of the rigid caste system that existed aboard Fleet vessels. The cost of maintaining such a facility was ostensibly explained as the place where visiting Terra Earth dignitaries would be served while aboard, but Anders had witnessed more battles to preserve flag messes at budget time than he'd ever seen dignitaries aboard Fleet vessels.

Anders cracked the flag mess door and saw Admiral Kinshaw huddled at the table with a steaming mug cupped in both hands. The admiral looked up and frowned when he saw the Space Marine.

"What do you want, Major? I'm a little busy right now."

"Sir, I heard we're breaking orbit and heading for deep space."

Kinshaw nodded. "That's correct. We received word that UNT Fleet Cruisers *Turner* and *Crutchley* were destroyed by a Maltaani fleet two days ago in a position one days' travel from Balfan-48. That means the Maltaani fleet could be here within hours."

"What about Ninth Division? Do you want to send another messenger drone?"

"No."

"Then how are we going to coordinate an evacuation?"

Kinshaw didn't respond.

"We're not leaving them there, are we?"

"We're making a tactical withdrawal, Major."

"It's an accepted tactic to abandon five thousand Space Marines on a hostile planet?"

Anders regretted his words as soon as he spoke them.

Admiral Kinshaw slapped his hand down on the table and shot to his feet. Coffee splashed across the table, and his mug shattered on the deck.

"Five thousand Space Marines landed on Balfan-48, but we don't know what's become of them. There are fourteen thousand other personnel in this Fleet, not to mention seventeen ships of incalculable value to the United Nations of Terra. An enemy fleet of unknown strength and composition will be here at any time, and we can't defend ourselves because our sensors are being jammed.

"That's a whole lot of unknowns, and you know *why* they're unknown? Because you and the other intel squirrels are too busy hiding your nuts to figure it out. So, Major, before you presume to question my decisions, *do your fucking job!*"

Anders opened and closed his mouth like a fish gasping for breath.

"If there's nothing else, Major, fuck off."

* * *

Niskala ran into Anders in the passageway that led to the intelligence shop.

"Nils, is it true? We're leaving them behind?"

His bloodless face and blank expression told her everything she needed to know.

"I don't believe it!"

"Kiti, I went to see the admiral, and he made it clear that it's not something that he wants to do but he has to."

"You're going along with this?"

"What choice do I have? He's the Fleet commander, remember? As hard as it is to accept, there are larger concerns than Ninth Division. The Maltaani destroyed two Fleet cruisers two days ago, and all indications are that they're headed this way."

"We have ships; we can fight back."

"And if we lose? What then, Kiti? Not only will Ninth Division be lost, but an entire fleet of warships will be destroyed, and fourteen thousand Fleet personnel will die as well."

"We don't know that. We could win."

Anders shook his head and sighed. "Kiti, I'm not an expert at Fleet warfare, but the Maltaani have a technological edge that we don't have an answer for. What happens when their fleet shows up, and we get jammed again? We'll be slaughtered."

Anger welled up in her chest and she struggled to control her voice. "I'd rather die on Balfan-48 than abandon Ninth Division." She spun on her heel and strode away.

"Kiti, come on. Kiti, please!"

* * *

Fifteen minutes later, Anders was typing on his console in the intel shop when the communicator buzzed.

"Major Anders, it's Major Niskala. Would you please come to the admiral's office?"

"Uh, okay. I'll be right there."

It took him less than a minute to arrive at the admiral's office. Kinshaw's aide was absent from his desk, so Anders rapped on the door and entered.

"Admiral, pardon the interruption, but, Major—"

Admiral Kinshaw was seated at his desk with his hands folded in front of him. Major Niskala was standing next to the door with a pulse pistol aimed at Anders. His heart fluttered and his fingertips tingled at the sight.

"What's going on here?"

"Pull a chair up and sit next to the admiral," Niskala ordered. "Keep your hands where I can see them."

"Kiti, I don't—"

"Shut up! Just do as I say."

"Do what she says, Major."

Anders noticed a bloody wound on Kinshaw's temple. He dragged a chair around the desk, sat down, and laced his fingers together in front of him.

Niskala gestured to the communicator on the desk with the pulse pistol.

"Admiral, pick up that handset, call the watch officer in the FOC, and authorize the launch of the mechanized battalion drop ships."

"Kiti, you can't be serious."

Niskala swung the barrel of the pistol over and pointed it at Anders. "You're here as a witness, so keep your mouth shut and be a witness, or I will shoot you in the face. Admiral—" she gestured at the communicator, "—make the call."

The admiral stared at Niskala for a long moment, and Anders thought he might refuse her order.

"Have it your way, Major." Kinshaw picked up the handset and punched in a number. "This is Admiral Kinshaw. Launch the mechanized battalion dropships." There was a momentary pause. "I know what I said, Commander, but the situation has changed. Launch the mechanized battalion dropships. Now." He hung up the handset. "Now what?"

"Now we wait."

The complete silence in the admiral's office unnerved Anders. Even though his workspace was far from any machinery or propulsion spaces, there was always some ambient noise. The admiral had a digital clock on his desk, and Anders imagined he could hear the colon flashing as each second ticked by.

When the communicator buzzed, Anders almost leapt out of his seat in surprise. Admiral Kinshaw didn't flinch.

Niskala gestured with her pistol. "Answer it."

"Hello. Yes, this is he. Okay, I'll tell her." He hung up and looked at Niskala. "The last dropship is standing by in the hangar."

"Very good. Thank you for your cooperation, Admiral."

Niskala holstered her pistol and slipped out the door. As soon as the door clicked shut, Kinshaw reached for the handset.

"Admiral, wait."

"Wait for what, Major? The security force will stop her before she gets to the hangar."

"Let her go."

"Let her go? Are you mad?"

"Please, hear me out, sir. This entire operation is fast becoming a debacle. Do you want to add a mutiny to the mix?"

"It wasn't my choice for her to stick a gun in my face."

"That's true, but only three of us know about that. What's the worst that could happen? An attempt to support Ninth Division goes terribly wrong and more Space Marines die, including Major Niskala? It was a long shot, but who could blame you for trying.

"Best case, Ninth Division prevails, and the mechs contribute to the victory. The mechs *you* ordered to drop. I witnessed the order.

"If Niskala survives, there's more than one way to punish her. A quiet word in the right ear, and she's relegated to the backwaters of the ISMC and her career is over.

"Alternately, Fleet convenes a court martial for her and the defense drags you through the mud. A smart defense lawyer will make you look like the worst kind of craven. 'Admiral Kinshaw turned tail and ran in the face of the enemy and left five thousand Space Marines to die. Major Niskala bravely chose to fight for her comrades.'

"Right or wrong, nobody will understand your decision to withdraw because nobody has faced this situation. The chain of command will want as much distance between you and them as possible, and the easy solution will be to blame it on a moment of weakness. Even if she's convicted, you'll be finished."

Admiral Kinshaw stared at Anders with his hand on the receiver. Finally, he withdrew his hand and leaned back in this seat. The major took a ragged breath and put his own hands in his lap to hide the shaking.

"You're a devious son of a bitch, Major, but my decision remains unchanged. I'm withdrawing the Fleet for the greater good."

* * * * *

Chapter Twenty-Five

Major Niskala kept a white-knuckled grip on her pistol the whole way to the dropship hangar. She expected *Atlas* security to stop her before she made it, but the only crewmembers she encountered stood aside as the grim-faced Space Marine strode through the passageways.

She stepped through the airlock hatch into the hangar and climbed aboard the dropship. Inside, she saw two battle mechs and a command mech chocked and chained to the deck. A large trailer loaded with supplies to support the mech company was hitched up to the command mech and filled the fourth spot. She slipped into the command mech and took her seat.

There were three mech companies in the landing force. Each company had a command platoon of two light battle mechs plus the command mech—First Platoon—and two platoons of five main battle mechs—Second and Third Platoons.

As the landing force commander, Niskala rode in the First Company command mech in their First Platoon, callsign 1-1. The platoon leader of Second Platoon was 1-2, and the platoon leader of Third Platoon was 1-3.

"We ready?" she asked Warrant Officer Seeton, the mech driver. Seeton gave her a thumbs up.

"The other nine drop ships are in the marshal stack orbit. As soon as they see us drop, they'll follow."

Niskala nodded and switched her headset to intercom.

"Pilot, this is the drop commander, we're ready for launch."

"Roger."

There was a bump when the dropship released from *Atlas* and Niskala strained against her restraints when they dropped free from the inertial gravity of the flagship. An unsecured object floated past her face, and she realized it was her mouthpiece. She snatched it out of the air and put it in her mouth. Seeton smiled and shook her head.

The dropship bounced and rattled as it skipped along the Balfan-48 atmosphere. Tiny thrusters *whooshed* as the autopilot adjusted their attitude to achieve the proper atmospheric entry angle. The ride smoothed out, and Niskala felt planetary gravity take over.

"Drop Commander, this is the pilot, we're in and dropping."

Before she could respond, Niskala heard the main engines roar to life. The dropship shuddered as the forces of Man and Nature battled for control of the craft, and she said a silent prayer in favor of Man.

"Twenty seconds," the pilot's voice said in her ear.

Niskala cinched her restraints tighter and braced for landing. The landings were bone-jarring, but mech drops weren't the violent bump-and-dump affairs the dropship pilots preferred to use to insert Space Marines. Mech landings meant the dropships had to touch down long enough for the cargo masters to release chocks and chains before the mechs charged down the ramp, ready for action.

"Ten seconds."

Wham!

The power flickered in the command mech when the engine roared to life. The cargo master stood on a platform where the mech drivers could see her. She put her hands by her sides, pointed her thumbs out, made the sign for "chocks removed" and then pointed at the ramp.

Ready to launch.

Seeton flashed the mech lights in acknowledgement, and the ramp opened. A hurricane of dust and dirt from the dropship engine wash cut visibility to zero as the command mech lurched down the ramp onto Balfan-48. The warrant officer piloted her vehicle forward until she was clear of the blinding dust and then stopped to wait for the battle mechs to join her.

In theory, the landing zone for a mech insert was large enough to accommodate all the dropships simultaneously. In practice, everyone knew dropships had the flight characteristics of a safe, and there was a significant risk of an errant landing. The best thing to do was clear the LZ as quickly as possible, but a single mech, especially a lightly armed command mech towing a logistics trailer, was a vulnerable target.

Niskala had a moment of self-doubt while they waited. In the dark, without communications and no way to distinguish friend from foe, she realized the odds were stacked heavily against them.

She heard the dropship engines whine and the mech was buffeted as the dropship clawed its way back into the dark sky.

"1-2 and 1-3 are waiting, Major," reported Warrant Officer Seeton. "What are your orders?"

Niskala looked at the heads-up tactical display in front of her. Only the last known positions of Ninth Division were drawn in; without sensor data or communications, actual friendlies and hostiles could not be displayed. She chose the dropship LZ because the IR data Anders gave her showed the area to be clear of enemy soldiers, but that information was a day old.

"Turn right and head for the Space Marine perimeter. Approach no closer than one hundred meters."

"Roger."

Coordinating the movements of three mech companies in the dark with no communications would have been impossible. Before they dropped, the other company commanders agreed to conform their movements to Major Niskala in the lead mech. Seeton turned on the light bar mounted on the back of her machine for the other mechs to follow and steered toward the Space Marine lines.

* * *

The first indication the Space Marines on Balfan-48 got that dropships were inbound was the roar of engines in the dark sky above.

"Are those dropships?" Fortis called to Ystremski as they sprinted for the perimeter.

"That's what it sounded like to me."

"I hope they're ours."

They dove alongside the Space Marines manning that section of the perimeter and watched vehicle lights move around the desert.

A dropship roared and landed somewhere in the desert. More engines howled overhead and then suddenly cut out. Seconds later, there was a thunderous explosion and a fireball rose high in the air.

"Holy shit!"

"The engines must have flamed out," Ystremski said. "Poor bastards streamed in and I think they clobbered another dropship."

"What do we do?"

"We stay the hell out of the way and hope none of them land short."

Three more drop ships touched down and blasted off without mishap. A formation of mechs approached the Space Marines and stopped with their engines running.

Another dropship shrieked low overhead and the sounds of a violent collision reached the horrified Space Marines. More flames flared in the distance, and Fortis imagined he could hear screams.

"Too much horizontal momentum," the gunny explained. "Came in sideways, buried a skid, and tumbled."

To the right, Fortis heard gunfire and saw muzzle flashes from the Maltaani lines as a confused firefight erupted. Cannons boomed and a long stream of tracers ripped the darkness. A mech exploded in a shower of brilliant white sparks and the unmistakable sound of Maltaani artillery joined the cacophony of battle.

The last drop ship clawed its way back into the sky, and the sounds of fighting faded as the mechs withdrew from the Maltaani lines. The night grew quiet except for the throaty rumble of mech engines.

"What do you think we should do?" Fortis asked Ystremski.

"I was gonna ask you the same question," the gunny replied. "How sure are you that those mechs are ours?"

"We just watched them engage the Maltaani. Who else could they be?"

"I've taken my share of not-so-friendly fire from Space Marines who got turned around in the dark to know that everyone shooting at the enemy isn't friends. We should be cautious, that's all."

"I'll go out and make contact." Fortis rose to his feet and Ystremski grabbed his arm.

"Not you, LT. I'll take a couple of the boys and see what I can find out."

* * *

"What the hell's going on?" demanded Niskala. "Who are they shooting at?"

The major and Warrant Seeton stood in the hatches in the command mech roof and watched the fireworks from the fighting in the distance.

"It looks like they got lost in the dark and ran into the Maltaani, ma'am."

"Any idea how many we lost?"

"I saw two explosions, plus the dropships. Ten, maybe twelve."

"Damn it!" Niskala slapped the mech roof in frustration. "If Kinshaw wasn't such an ass, we could have dropped during daylight and avoided this."

"Major, look!"

Niskala looked in the direction Seeton pointed and watched as a loose handful of dirt-covered Space Marines materialized along the edge of their headlights. They held their pulse rifles at the low ready, but there was no mistaking their readiness for action. The apparent leader of the group held up one hand and approached.

"Who are you?"

"Major Niskala, International Space Marine Corps. Who are you?"

Their relief was obvious.

"Gunny Ystremski, ISMC Ninth Division."

"Can you take me to General Gupta?"

"The general is dead."

"Who's in command?"

"I think you are, Major."

The gunny climbed inside the command mech to brief Niskala on the situation.

"Your display looks about right. We've got about nineteen hundred Space Marines in a position surrounding the crater where the command headquarters was."

"*Nineteen hundred?* That's it?"

Ystremski nodded grimly. "As soon as we got deployed, the general called a meeting with the officers and senior NCOs. The Maltaani fired a nuke and killed the command element, the aviation element, and a bunch of others. After that, the Maltaani attacked, and they've been back every day. We butcher them, but they don't seem too worried about casualties."

"How many of them are there?"

"We don't know, ma'am. So many that they attack head on, although today they settled for shooting artillery at us all day."

"Who's been in command this whole time? You?"

"No. Second Lieutenant Fortis has been in command. He wanted to come out and greet you, but I wouldn't let him. He got bit by a dog yesterday, and I've been trying to protect him from himself ever since."

"A dog?"

"The Maltaani have dogs. Charming brutes."

"Give me some time to get the mechs organized and then you can take me to meet Lieutenant Fortis."

* * * * *

Chapter Twenty-Six

Fortis paced behind the Marine earthworks after Ystremski went out to meet the mechs. He hadn't heard any gunfire, so he assumed everything was going well.

One of the men who'd gone out with Ystremski came back with a report.

"They're our mechs. Three companies, thirty-nine in all."

"Excellent."

"The mech commander's a major named Niskala. She'll be here as soon as she gets the mechs organized. They don't have any comms either, and they're spread out all over the place."

Twenty minutes later, a mech rumbled toward the Space Marine perimeter. The driver extinguished the headlights and navigated by small orange lights on the front corners. Fortis recognized Ystremski guiding it forward. The Space Marine stepped aside and the mechanical monster rolled into the perimeter and lurched to a stop.

A wave of relief overcame Fortis, and he struggled not to hug Ystremski. Instead, he greeted the gunny with a broad smile and warm handshake.

"Damn, sir, I was only gone an hour."

"I was worried I would have to find another corporal to take your place."

The hatch opened and a major in clean, creased utilities climbed out.

"Lieutenant Fortis, I'm Major Niskala."

Fortis gave a half-salute before he accepted her extended hand.

"Welcome to Balfan-48, Major."

Niskala, Fortis, and Ystremski sat together in the command mech.

"I have twenty-five mechs remaining. Three command mechs, six light battle mechs, and sixteen main battle mechs."

"I'm sorry, Major. That was a costly drop."

"It would have—" She stopped and looked at Ystremski and then back to Fortis. "Lieutenant, can we talk privately?"

"Ma'am, Gunny Ystremski is the most trustworthy Marine I've ever met, and he's saved my life several times. I'm going to share anything you tell me about our situation with him anyway, so it will save time if you tell us both."

Niskala's eyes flicked between the two men.

"Okay, but what I'm about to tell you cannot leave this mech. Is that clear?"

The duo nodded.

"Fleet is planning to withdraw from this sector any time now."

"What?"

"It's true. The Maltaani jamming has shut down Fleet operations, and there's a Maltaani fleet out there somewhere. They can't shoot what they can't detect."

"What about us?"

Niskala didn't respond, and Fortis's eyes widened at the realization of what she wasn't saying.

"They're going to leave us here," he croaked.

"Bastards!" exclaimed Ystremski.

"Wait a second. Why would they drop you in if they're leaving us behind?"

The major winced. "I didn't give them a choice. I put a gun to Admiral Kinshaw's head and forced him to order our drop."

"Holy shit!"

Fortis stared in disbelief, and Ystremski threw his head back and laughed.

"It's true. He wouldn't authorize the drop for three days because of the jamming. When I heard the Fleet was leaving, I knew we were out of time, so I acted."

"Major, that's the ballsiest thing I've heard in a long time," Ystremski said.

"I'll be sure to mention that at my court martial."

The trio turned their attention to the tactical situation.

"The Maltaani have us surrounded clockwise from about eight o'clock around to five o'clock. They attack at first light, usually from about the eleven o'clock direction. Their attacks are pretty much head on. They brought up some artillery and ran a feint yesterday that almost broke through our lines, but our reserve force responded and drove them back."

"What do you know about their defenses?"

"Nothing. A seven-man recon patrol went out two nights ago to locate and destroy their artillery, but they haven't returned. They attack with five or six times as many soldiers as we have Space Marines, so going on the offensive hasn't been an option. Without comms or terrain to conceal troop movements, we've been kind of stuck. I expected Fleet support, too."

"Well, Lieutenant, the offensive starts tomorrow. I'll spread eight companies of Space Marines across my sixteen main battle mechs, and at first light we'll roll up their right flank, here." Major Niskala pointed at the nine o'clock position. "The light mechs will swing wide left, around their rear, and conduct a hit-and-run raid to cut off their retreat."

Fortis and Ystremski exchanged glances.

"Ma'am, we don't know anything about their positions. Maybe we should do some reconnaissance first, probe them for weak spots? With your mechs integrated into our defenses, we'd be damn near impregnable."

"For a day or two, until they figure out how to defeat them," Niskala snapped back. "Lieutenant, you've lost half your force in four days, and you told me the enemy still has overwhelming numbers. What have you been doing to counter their numbers besides hunker down? How much longer to you think you can hold out?"

Hot blood rushed to Fortis's face, but he kept his mouth shut.

"The Fleet is not coming to the rescue. Waiting and hoping to be rescued is not a winning strategy. If we don't seize the initiative and generate some offensive momentum, then we all might as well dig our own graves."

Ystremski cut in. "Major, we've been on our heels since we hit this rock, but eight companies is over half our strength. Let's say the attack doesn't go as planned and we take heavy casualties. What then?"

"Gunny, it's time to stop thinking about failure and fretting about worst case scenarios. It's time to attack. I'm in command and my mechs can't attack without infantry support. I'm ordering you to provide that support or I will find someone who will. DINLI."

* * *

After Major Niskala explained what she wanted from the Space Marine infantry, Fortis and Ystremski set off to notify the companies of Second Regiment who would join the attack.

"That fucking major is crazy, LT," Ystremski muttered.

"She's in command, Gunny."

"She's gonna get us all killed!"

Fortis put a hand on Ystremski's arm and they stopped. "Weren't you the one who told me the lads were getting restless? 'It would be good for morale if we fought back.' Remember that?"

"Yes sir, I do, but I also remember telling you it's too early for suicide."

"This isn't suicide. It's a heavy blow aimed at an enemy who has kicked our asses for four days. We have the advantage for the first time. The Maltaani don't have mechs or we would have seen them by now. Frankly, I'm a little restless too, and if Fleet doesn't care enough to help us, then what difference does any of this make?"

"She really wounded your pride, didn't she?"

Fortis balled his fists but kept his hands at his side. He was grateful that the darkness hid the tears of anger that leaked down his cheeks.

"No, Gunny, she didn't. I don't have any ego when it comes to following orders from superior officers. DINLI, remember?"

"Fuck," Ystremski scoffed. "It's not like we've been sitting on our asses since we got here. When did you start blindly following the order of crazy people?"

"Gunny, just stop. We're wasting time and this discussion is going nowhere."

"You're right, LT. DINLI. Why don't you go cool off and do some officer stuff while I get Second Regiment ready for the meat grinder?"

Fortis hesitated. It annoyed him to realize Ystremski was right. Niskala *had* stung his pride and his blind obedience to her orders was the result.

"Okay, Gunny, we'll do it your way. Get them ready, and I'll meet you at the jump-off point."

* * *

As Second Regiment filed out of their fighting positions on the perimeter to form up with the mechs, the rest of the Space Marines began their quiet withdrawal to the new positions the reserve force had dug along the rim of the crater. It was a gamble to have the entire division in motion at once, but, so far, the Maltaani hadn't attacked in the dark. If the Space Marines waited until daybreak, they might be caught unprepared to meet an assault.

Major Niskala was everywhere in the assault formation, moving troops and aligning vehicles as though their jump-off positions were critical to the success of the attack. Fortis caught up with her near her command mech.

"Major, is there anything I can do to help you out?"

"Not right now. The mechs are ready and the infantry seem well trained. I need to align two more companies, and we'll be ready to go."

"Ma'am, you said you brought supplies. Does that include medical supplies? Our field hospital could use them."

"There are medical supplies in the trailers. I'll have the command mechs drop them inside the perimeter before the attack jumps off. Take anything you want except for rations and spare parts."

"I'll see to it. Thank you."

"Where are you going to be in all this, Fortis?"

"I honestly haven't given it a lot of thought."

"If we had comms, I'd offer you a seat in one of the command mechs, but since we don't, I think you'll be more valuable on the ground with the lead company. Do you agree?"

"Yes, ma'am. I completely agree."

"Good. I've got more to do, so carry on, and I'll see you out there."

Despite the major's micromanaging, morale among the Space Marines of Second Regiment was high. Fortis saw smiles everywhere by the dim lights of the mechs, and their excitement was palpable. The lieutenant shared their excitement, but the sight of the body bags stacked near the field hospital was seared into his memory.

How many of them won't come back?

He shook his head to banish the thought. Their profession was hazardous and death was a constant companion. Fortis had seen death in many forms during his first year of service, but never at the scale he'd seen on Balfan-48. He felt some trepidation at his role in the coming assault. The young officer wasn't afraid of dying, he was afraid of failing and the consequences of that failure.

"Abner, how's it going?"

Liz Sherer had slipped up unnoticed and stood at Fortis's elbow.

"So far, so good. The lads are moving with purpose, and Major Niskala seems happy. The rest of the division has begun to contract the perimeter. It's taken a lot of hard work to make this happen."

"Hmm."

"Major Niskala said we can have all the supplies they brought with them. You and Doc will be happy; you've been working miracles with first aid kits this entire time. After we step off, please make sure that stuff gets to the right place."

"'We?' What do you mean, 'we?'

"I'm going in with the attack."

"You can't go. You're in command here."

"I'm leaving Gunny Ystremski in charge here."

"This is crazy. Why are you going?"

"Major Niskala is in command now. She ordered me to assist her with the attack and lead the infantry, and that's what I'm going to do."

"Have you lost your mind?"

"No, I haven't. I've been reminded of my duty, which is to follow orders and do my utmost to support my superior officers. The battle plan is solid, and I'm confident of victory."

Their voices rose, and the more Liz questioned him, the deeper Fortis dug in. Gunny Ystremski appeared out of the darkness.

"LT, Liz, could you keep it down, please? The troops are starting to notice."

"Have you heard, Gunny? He's leading the infantry."

"That's where ISMC officers belong, Liz. Out front, leading the way."

Liz threw her hand up in frustration. "You, too?"

"No, not me. The Space Marine with the most combat experience in the entire division has been ordered to remain in the rear with the gear."

Ystremski's voice dripped with sarcasm.

"Gunny, I need someone here who can lead the defense in case the Maltaani counterattack while we're gone. That's you." Fortis struggled to keep his anger out of his voice. "Now, I have to make final preparations for the attack. Gunny, make sure Liz and Doc get the medical supplies out of the mech trailers."

He strode away into the dark before they could argue with him.

* * * * *

Chapter Twenty-Seven

Finally satisfied with the formation, Major Niskala mounted her command mech. Fortis breathed a deep sigh of relief. At last, they would be on their way.

One company of Space Marines was deployed forward as skirmishers in a loose line abreast. One hundred meters behind them, three main battle mechs and two additional infantry companies made up the first wave. Fifty meters behind them, five more mechs and two more companies made up the second wave. The eight remaining mechs and three Space Marine companies followed fifty meters behind the second wave.

Her battle plan was simple. The skirmishers would uncover enemy positions and the main body would engage. If the first wave met too much resistance, the second and third waves would add their weight to the attack. The lack of communications necessitated a straightforward approach, so the infantry would guide on the lead mech of their respective wave.

While the main attack focused on the expected Maltaani positions, the light battle mechs would swing wide around the flank to seek out and disrupt any Maltaani forces they encountered. Niskala put Warrant Officer King in command of the six-mech force. The silver-haired mech commander winked at Fortis when her role was explained.

I hope they don't disappear like Ward and his men.

Major Niskala's command mech would advance with the first wave, and Fortis would proceed alongside on foot with the first wave companies. He tightened the shoulder straps of his pack for the tenth time and gripped his pulse rifle until his hands hurt. He couldn't allow the Space Marines to see his nerves, but his stomach churned, and his pulse pounded in his ears. His mouth became so dry that when Niskala signaled for the advance, his voice came out as a croak.

"Space Marines, forward!"

The light battle mechs took off for their end-run, and Fortis soon lost sight of them in the predawn darkness.

Space Marines cheered as the main battle mech engines roared to life, and the metal behemoths lurched into motion. Sixteen battle mechs and almost a thousand Space Marines stepped off to take the fight to the enemy. The excitement was contagious, and Fortis smiled and cheered with the men as the feeling surged through him. They'd proven their mettle as defenders, and now, backed up by the irresistible force of the mechs, they would teach the Maltaani a lesson about the power of the ISMC.

The sky lightened, and Fortis could clearly make out the Marines marching alongside him. Those who had experience operating in close cooperation with mechs pulled the uninitiated away from the sides of the mechs. The armored behemoths could turn sharply without warning, as more than one hapless Space Marine had discovered. They gradually formed into narrow columns behind the mechs and used the hulls as moving cover in the featureless landscape.

Fortis thought about the fight to come. The Maltaani likely knew the mechs had arrived, but nobody knew how they would react. Would they run? Would they unleash some heretofore unseen weapon? He knew the Maltaani had artillery and some heavy caliber crew-served weapons, but were they capable of effectively employing them against mechs?

Fortis felt an unfamiliar twinge of doubt as more troops and mechs became visible in the early dawn. His unanswered questions grew more important with every step, and he had a corresponding stab of guilt for not examining Major Niskala's attack plan more closely.

Gunny Ystremski's voice nagged at him. *She really wounded your pride, didn't she?*

Truthfully, she had, but not his personal pride. Instead, she had injured the pride he felt in the Space Marines of Ninth Division for their fighting prowess demonstrated during the days before the mechs arrived. In his opinion, the selfless valor and grim determination he witnessed was the stuff of legend. To have a ranking officer call it all into question angered him. Fortis was anxious for the men to show her that they were capable of more than huddling in fox-holes and waiting for the attack that would overwhelm their defenses.

Fortis almost bumped into the back of the command mech, and it surprised him to discover the formation had stopped.

Major Niskala was shouting at him from the turret. "Fortis! Get in here."

A side hatch swung open, and a crewmember beckoned him to climb inside.

"Were you sleepwalking?" demanded Niskala.

"No, ma'am. I was mentally rehearsing preplanned responses in case of attack, and I guess my mind wandered for a second. My apologies."

"Never mind that. Just pay attention. Look." She pointed to a monitor displaying a multicolored infrared image. "That's the IR camera, the only sensor that's working on this crate. Those hot spots are the skirmishers."

Fortis saw a row of reddish orange shadows lying flat on the ground.

"For some reason they've all taken cover, but there's been no firing. I can't quite make them out yet and we don't have time to wait for it to get lighter. I want you to move forward and find out what's going on."

"Me? I mean, yes, ma'am. I'll grab a squad and investigate."

Niskala shook her head. "Get your shit wired tight, Fortis, and get it done, quick. We're sitting ducks here."

Fortis scrambled out of the mech and gestured at a group of nearby Space Marines who had taken a knee when the mech stopped.

"I'm going forward to find out what's going on with the skirmish line; I need you to back me up. Let's go."

An eerie silence fell over the Space Marines as they slowly advanced. The sound of the mech engines faded until the only thing Fortis could hear were the scuffs of his boots over the rocky soil. He finally caught sight of the skirmishers prone on the ground and he waved the squad down.

"Stay here, and stay alert," he whispered. "I'll go up and see what's going on."

As he crept forward, he sensed someone behind him and stopped. One of the Space Marines had followed him. When Fortis scowled the other Marine, a private, grinned.

"Can't let you officers have all the fun, LT."

Fortis nodded and started forward again. None of the skirmishers moved or made a sound. His senses were on high alert and his nerves screamed at him, *Danger!*

He got close enough to make out details and realized the Space Marines weren't lying prone. They were dead.

Fortis immediately dropped flat and the private mirrored him. Neither man spoke for a long moment as they searched the area.

"What now, sir?"

"Cover me. I'm going to crawl up and see if I can figure out how those men died."

"Let me go, sir. I'll be there and back in no time and then we can get the fuck out of here."

The private scrambled away before Fortis could protest. He inspected several of the bodies before he gathered several shiny pieces of metal and scampered back to the waiting officer.

"They're all dead, LT, but they weren't shot. It looks like somebody chopped them up. I found these."

Fortis examined the pieces of metal and he realized they were metallic fabric.

"These are infrared blankets," he told his companion. A tickle of fear ran down his spine. *The owners might still be close.* "They're not ours. Let's get out of here."

The pair jumped to their feet and sprinted back to the relative safety of the squad. Fortis waved them back to the main formation, where he reported to Major Niskala.

"What's going on, Fortis?"

"They're dead, ma'am. Cut to pieces, and we found these on the bodies. I think they're Maltaani thermal blankets, to shield them from infrared sensors."

"Keep the men back, Fortis. We'll conduct reconnaissance by fire."

She dropped into the command mech and the vehicle lurched into motion. The other mechs in the first wave followed. When they were clear, Fortis waved the infantry forward.

The mechs opened up with automatic pulse guns on the area beyond the dead skirmishers. The air crackled as brilliant blue and white bolts of energy ripped through the air. Dirt and rocks filled the air until a giant cloud engulfed the entire horizon. The guns ceased after the sustained pounding and silence blanketed the area. There was no Maltaani response and Fortis was certain that nothing could have lived through the maelstrom.

Fortis and the infantry advanced at a half-crouch as the mechs continued forward. The machines stopped at the line of fallen Space Marines and the hatch on the command mech popped open.

"Fortis, have your men clear the bodies so we can move up."

"Yes, ma'am."

As he turned to give the order, Fortis heard the unmistakable sound of Maltaani artillery.

"Incoming!"

The Space Marines scattered in search of what little cover they could find as the first rounds landed among the mechs. Fortis dove behind the command mech and watched the chaos unfold.

The ground next to one main battle mech exploded and the heavy track clanked and rattled as it rolled off the wheels. Two more rounds landed close by, and a third scored a direct hit on the turret. The body of the mech bulged as the round exploded inside and thick black smoke erupted from the hole created by the shell. An escape hatch on the undercarriage banged open and the mech's crewmembers tumbled out.

The artillery barrage engulfed the first wave in a thundering rain of death. The surviving infantry scattered and ran for their lives as any thoughts of an orderly withdrawal vanished. Fortis was immobilized behind the command mech and watched in shock as the shells ripped into the mob of panicked infantry.

A shell exploded against the hull of a second main battle mech. The force of the impact knocked the main gun askew and the mech veered erratically across the battlefield and fired its automatic pulse gun in all directions before it finally collided with the first burning mech. Top and bottom hatches opened and stunned crewmembers staggered out. More shells landed among them. When the dirt cleared Fortis saw they were gone.

The command mech engine roared and the vehicle spun around while the surviving main battle mech reversed. The crew fired their main battery and automatic pulse guns in impotent anger at their invisible enemy as they withdrew. Fortis sprinted back to where the second wave waited and threw himself down among the other Space Marines. The command mech skidded to a stop nearby.

"Fortis! What the hell happened? Why did you run?"

Fortis stared at her in disbelief. "We were caught in the open by an artillery barrage, Major. Just like the mechs."

"Well, get them up and organized. We're going back in, and this time we're not stopping."

* * *

Gunny Ystremski flexed his fists and muttered curses to himself as he paced along the rim of the crater.

"What's wrong, Gunny? Everything went according to plan, didn't it?"

Ystremski turned and saw Liz standing on a set of steps cut into the crater edge.

"Yeah, it did. Exactly as we planned."

"Then why are you upset?"

"Because I don't have anything to worry about, except for the thousand Space Marines who are following that idiot major."

He turned his face toward the horizon and held up a finger for silence.

"Did you hear that?"

Liz cupped her ears and listened. She detected an ominous rumble, barely audible in the morning air.

"Maltaani artillery," Ystremski said. "A lot of Maltaani artillery." He pointed in the direction of the field hospital. "You should go get ready. The lads are catching hell. You're about to get busy."

* * * * *

Chapter Twenty-Eight

Donk shook Ward awake.

"Ward, you gotta get up. We've got trouble."

Ward was instantly awake and alert. He saw the other Space Marines gathered around him in the early morning light. "What is it?"

"About thirty guys came running around the building and went out the gate. Definitely Maltaani."

"Where were they headed?"

"I lost sight of them; they headed that way." Donk pointed at the horizon. "They were moving fast."

"You think they're headed to our perimeter?"

"No idea. You want me to chase them down and ask?"

The group chuckled. Ward heard a *crack* and Donk's head exploded all over him in a spray of bone and gore.

The other Space Marines dove for cover as more rounds snapped and sizzled overhead. Ward glimpsed a mass of troops silhouetted at the top of the rise, and he recognized the weirdly human shape of the Maltaani.

"How many?" he shouted as the trio returned fire.

"Thirty, maybe more," Jocko called back. "Too many to fight from here."

"Leapfrog back to the trucks! Move and cover!"

Ward rose up on one knee and sprayed the Maltaani as Jocko fell back twenty meters and began to lay down covering fire. Gomez followed and ran past Jocko for another twenty meters before he turned and began to fire.

As soon as Ward heard Gomez open up, he dashed past his comrades. He slammed a fresh magazine into his pulse rifle as he ran, then turned to cover the others. As soon as he fired, Jocko turned and ran past at a crouch.

The covering fire slowed the Maltaani pursuit, and Ward heard an engine roar to life as they neared Welch and the vehicles.

"They must have seen us!" he shouted to Welch as he grabbed a shell from the truck and clambered into the gun turret. "Pass me some ammo!"

He slammed the first round into the breech, squeezed the safety, and yanked the lanyard.

KABOOM!

The first round roared across the desert and exploded thirty meters behind the Maltaani troops, but they threw themselves flat. Jocko and Gomez used the lull to sprint for the vehicles. Ward depressed the barrel elevation handwheel and looked down the barrel.

Perfect.

Eject, reload, safety, lanyard.

KABOOM!

The shell exploded in the middle of the enemy troops. Bodies flew in all directions and survivors scrambled for safety.

Maltaani ricochets buzzed around the gun like angry bees. Ward saw a group of Maltaani advancing on their right flank.

"Over there!" he shouted and pointed. Jocko and Gomez immediately pivoted and poured fire on the new threat. "Welch, I need—"

Welch lay spread-eagle on his back, his left arm gone above the elbow, and blood covering his LBA where the leg sections attached at the groin.

Ward pushed the image of the dead Marine out of his mind as he jumped down from the gun, grabbed a shell from the back of the truck, and hoisted it up into the turret. He grabbed two more rounds and climbed back into the turret.

"Hey, man, we need to get the fuck out of here," called Gomez. "There's too many of them."

Eject, reload, safety, lanyard.

KABOOM!

The Maltaani had regrouped to resume their attack and the new round sent them running.

"Welch is dead."

"What?" Gomez looked around the side of the gun and saw the medic. "Aw, shit." He fired a long burst at the flanking enemy. "This is fucked."

"What are you two bullshitting about?" demanded Jocko. "We've got beaucoup bad guys to kill."

"Welch is gone, bro."

"Aw, shit."

"What now, Ward?"

"Let's hit that building, go out in a blaze of glory."

"Are you nuts?" Jocko sniped two Maltaani that exposed themselves as they tried to move to cover.

"It's important enough to have all these troops guarding the place, which means it's important enough to hit. Do you have something better to do?"

The air overhead snapped and crackled with incoming fire.

"Gomez, drive this thing. Jocko, grab the ammo truck and stay right up our ass. We'll head straight over the ridge and blast the building as soon as possible. Move!"

Ward fired his pulse rifle from the open turret as Gomez powered the self-propelled gun up the rise and Jocko fired through the open truck window. The Maltaani ran and hid at the approach of the vehicles though neither Space Marine scored any hits.

When the gun roared over the top of the rise, Ward saw more Maltaani running for a gate on the right side of the compound. He pounded on the roof to get Gomez's attention.

"Go left! Go left!"

The gun lurched left, and Ward was gratified to see Jocko was still right behind them with the ammo truck.

They pulled around to the side of the building with the garage doors and Ward hammered on the roof again.

"This is good. Point us at the building and shut it down."

They had left their pursuers far behind and the Maltaani in the compound looked confused at the appearance of one of their own artillery pieces. They didn't open fire right away and the Space Marines took full advantage of the lull in the action. Ward slammed a round into the gun.

"As soon as I fire, open up on those guys. I've got three rounds up here, so after you hear the third shot, somebody pass me some more."

Ward lined up the barrel with the building, squeezed the safety, and pulled the lanyard.

KABOOM!

Jocko and Gomez immediately laid down a murderous blanket of fire on the Maltaani soldiers gathered inside the fence. The artillery round shrieked over their heads and punched a neat hole in the side of the building. There was a muffled *boom* when it exploded inside.

Eject, reload, safety, lanyard.

KABOOM!

Enemy rounds rattled off the turret as their pursuers finally caught up with the Space Marines and the troops inside the compound returned fire. Jocko and Gomez struggled to keep up their own rate of fire as the Maltaani crossfire pinned them down.

Ward focused on working the gun.

Eject, reload, safety, lanyard.

KABOOM!

"Ammo!" he screamed down to his teammates. Ward picked up his pulse rifle and hosed down the troops on the flank until he emptied his magazine and then looked around for the ammo.

Gomez was propped up against the truck with a gaping hole where his jaw used to be. Blood spilled across his chest, but the wounded Space Marine still aimed and fired his rifle at the enemy. Ward jumped down next to his comrade and dug out his med kit.

"Hold still, Gomez, let me get a bandage on that."

Gomez made a gurgling noise, blood spraying from his throat, and he was dead.

"Fuck!"

Ward slammed a fresh magazine into his rifle and searched for targets. Jocko scrambled around the gun and stopped short when he saw Gomez.

"Oh shit! We need to get the hell out of here, Ward." He turned and mowed down a Maltaani soldier who had ventured too close. "We gotta go now!"

A burst of enemy fire stitched the ground around them, and Ward felt a deep burning sensation in his left hip. Jocko yelped, spun around, and sat down heavily. He rolled onto his side and Ward saw three neat holes in a line across his back.

A rocket whooshed by overhead and detonated against the ammo truck. The explosion stunned Ward and a whirlwind of stone splinters and shrapnel tore into his exposed skin. The temptation to lie back and stop fighting was strong, but he knew that meant sure death.

He used his rifle as a crutch and struggled to his feet. Jocko was facedown three meters from where he'd been sitting. Ward staggered over to his body. Remarkably, Jocko heaved himself to his hands and knees, but when Ward saw his face he almost screamed.

Jocko's left eye was an empty, ragged socket, and the explosion had peeled his nose away from his face so it hung across his cheek by a few shreds of flesh. His right eye was swollen to a narrow slit in his burned and shattered face.

"Come on, Jocko." Ward grabbed at his arm to help him up.

"I'm blind, Ward," whined Jocko. "It hurts so goddamned much!"

"I know." The pair leaned on each other for support as they shambled to the ammo truck, which had begun to burn. "Let's end this."

Ward boosted Jocko into the cab of the truck and gave him his rifle. "Point and shoot out the window, Jocko. Can't miss, the fuckers are everywhere."

A Maltaani round punched Ward in the middle of the back and drove him face-first into the truck door. He went down on one knee as searing pain shot through his body. Jocko blindly hosed down the area and Ward watched the Maltaani somersault backward as the energy bolts found their marks.

Slowly, painfully, Ward dragged himself to his feet and staggered to the other side of the truck. A strange sense of calm came over him. The agony of his wounds faded into an all-over warmth. A Maltaani round took off two fingers. He knew should feel pain, but he viewed the injury with a numb, detached air.

Jocko continued to spray the area with his rifle. He didn't score any additional hits, but he forced the enemy to stay covered and advance slowly, which gave the two Space Marines a few valuable seconds of breathing room. Ward crawled into the cab and slammed the door shut. Flames lapped at the back of the cab and roasted the two fighters.

"Fuh-fuh-fucking hot," moaned Jocko. "Are we on fire?"

For some reason Ward found Jocko's question hilarious and he guffawed. After a second, Jocko choked and coughed. The pair laughed as the truck engine roared to life, and Ward steered it at the white building.

"We're burning now!" he shouted, but Jocko didn't respond. He looked at his friend and saw him slumped against the door, dead.

Ward focused on the white building, thirty meters away. Thick black smoke poured from the holes he had punched in the walls with the gun. Every few seconds orange flames lapped out.

The Maltaani defenders pounded away at them with every weapon they could bring to bear. The truck shuddered under the volley of thousands of rounds. The windshield shattered and collapsed into Ward's lap and a stream of bullets pieced his chest.

The ammo truck jerked to a stop, hung up on the remains of the fence. The edges of Ward's vision faded to black and the world began to shrink and draw back.

A brilliant flash of lightning seared his eyes and a thunderclap deafened him as the building exploded. Ward was dead before the shockwave flipped the truck into the air and killed everything within a five-hundred-meter-radius.

* * * * *

Chapter Twenty-Nine

Major Niskala had a quick conference with the five main battle mech commanders of the second wave along with the one surviving mech from the first wave and Fortis.

"They fired when we stopped to clear the bodies. I think they have the entire area pre-sighted. So, we need to push forward without stopping. I want to move as quick as possible, but the infantry has to keep up." She gestured at Fortis as if the first failure had been due to the infantry, and he felt the eyes of all the mech commanders on him. He wanted to protest, but this was no time to argue. He merely nodded instead.

They'll find out soon enough when they get a taste of that artillery.

"Our number one priority is those guns. Find them and destroy them. Any questions?" No one spoke up. "Mount up!"

The six mechs formed two vees of three mechs each, with Niskala's command mech tucked between them. When they began to roll, the two infantry companies of the second wave, plus the survivors of the first wave, trotted behind. As the force approached the burning mechs, Fortis steeled his nerves against the image of the mechs grinding over the bodies of dead Space Marines.

DINLI.

The formation moved beyond the area of the first engagement and the lead mechs fired their main guns at distant targets. Fortis braced himself for the inevitable response, but the Maltaani didn't immediately return fire. For a brief second, he wondered if the Maltaani had withdrawn to new positions, but a series of rapid explosions in front of the mechs answered that question.

The infantry flinched and began to recoil, but Fortis urged them forward.

"Let's go! Stay with the mechs!"

The duel between the mechs and Maltaani artillery grew in intensity as the enemy emplacements came into view. Fortis caught a glimpse of tracked vehicles through the dust and smoke: self-propelled guns. His ears rang from the sustained gunfire, so he never heard the rifle fire that revealed Maltaani infantry positions on the left flank. Space Marines were flung to the ground like ragdolls as the murderous volley ripped through their ranks. They quickly sought cover and returned fire.

Meanwhile, Major Niskala and the mechs continued forward, seemingly oblivious to the fate of their infantry support. He wanted to run and stop the mechs, but they were already fifty meters ahead and pulling away, fast. The Maltaani rifle fire was rapid and deadly, and in no time dead and dying Space Marines littered the ground. Time and again, a Space Marine would jump to his feet to dash for cover only to fall under the guns of the Maltaani.

An engine roared nearby. Fortis rolled over and saw a pair of mechs from third wave charge toward the Maltaani positions. Their automatic pulse cannons spat blue-white lightning at the enemy and the volume of incoming fire dropped immediately.

"Space Marines, follow me!"

Fortis jumped to his feet and charged behind the mechs, toward the flank. The other Space Marines joined him in twos and threes as they realized their only choices were fight or die. The artillery fire was concentrated on Major Niskala and the second wave, although the occasional round still landed among the Marines. The Marines fired from the hip at the enemy as they followed the mechs into the forwardmost Maltaani positions.

WHAM! WHAM!

One of the mechs shuddered from the impacts and began to smoke. The top hatch popped open. A crewman struggled to escape, but flames belched around her, and she sank back into the turret.

WHAM! WHAM!

A second mech swerved wildly as another salvo tore off the turret and threw it high in the air. Space Marines scrambled to escape the flying debris as the vehicle ground to a halt and burned furiously.

Fortis saw a group of Maltaani crouched over a crew-served weapon. They pivoted the gun to take aim at the other third wave mechs that had moved up.

"Fire there! Fire there!" he shouted at nearby Space Marines. White and blue sparks flew as pulse rifle rounds ricocheted off the weapon and the Space Marines mowed down the crew. Another crew with a second weapon appeared, and Fortis and his men shot them to pieces before they could get a round off.

The battle became a savage, confused kaleidoscope of noise and death as the two infantry forces collided. A Maltaani soldier charged a Space Marine, sword raised. Instead of shooting his attacker, the Marine parried the stroke and drew his kukri, and the two squared off. Another nearby Maltaani shot the Space Marine, and he was shot down in turn by three Space Marines who had come to the aid of their comrade.

A random artillery round landed in the middle of the fighting, killing Maltaani and Humans alike. Fortis watched in amazement as a

Space Marine fielded a Maltaani grenade and threw it back, where it exploded in the Maltaani ranks.

Small knots of Maltaani soldiers shot and slashed their way into the Space Marine lines, their progress marked by the bodies of friend and foe alike.

Additional mechs arrived and threw their weight into the fight. The additional pressure forced the Maltaani to withdraw. They defended like they attacked, stubbornly and without regard for casualties, so the Space Marine progress slowed. They held their ground, and the firing dwindled away as the attack stalled.

"Fortis, what the fuck are you doing? Why did you stop?"

The command mech had pulled up behind Fortis, but he'd been so focused on the fight that he hadn't heard it approach.

"They flanked us, Major. You kept rolling and we had to take them on."

"You should have stopped us, Lieutenant."

Fortis's temper started to boil over and he struggled to keep control.

"Major Niskala, you were fifty meters ahead of us when they attacked our flank. Take a close look—" he pointed at the battlefield, "—there's a lot of dead Space Marines out there because the mech support left us behind. If the third wave hadn't come up, there would be a lot more of them dead."

She surveyed the area. "Why aren't you pursuing them?"

The infantry had broken off their counterattack as the enemy withdrew, and were regrouping near the third wave troops.

"Ma'am, they have us outnumbered and we've seen this tactic before. They want us to advance so they can encircle us. They've probably got the area pre-sighted for the artillery."

Three more second wave mechs approached. One of them had a deep gouge across the bonnet and the body was blackened where flames had scoured the paint. Dense black smoke belched from the exhaust of a second as the engine rumbled ominously. Smoke and dust blanketed the area, and the burning mechs added an acrid tinge to the air. Wounded Space Marines trickled back from the fighting, aided by uninjured comrades or leaning on their pulse rifles.

"Get your men organized, Fortis. One more push, and we'll finish them!"

Fortis stared back at the major.

"Major, didn't you hear me? We've taken a lot of casualties. Just because the Maltaani have fallen back doesn't mean we're winning. They *want* us to attack."

"We can't stop now, Fortis. They're on the run. Now, get your men organized for the attack or I'll find someone who will."

She disappeared into the command mech and the hatch slammed shut. The vehicle spun around and drove to where the third wave mechs were waiting.

"What are your orders, sir?" asked one of the Space Marines nearby.

Fortis scowled as he shot a look at the cluster of mechs.

"Form up!" he ordered. "Send the wounded back to the crater and stand by to advance."

A brilliant light flashed on the horizon, followed a split second later by a deep BOOM. Everyone turned and stared as the light faded. Fortis heard the crackle of static in his helmet earpiece.

"What the hell was that?"

"Was that a nuke?"

The lieutenant looked at the Space Marines gathered around him. "I don't know what that was, but we have orders. DINLI."

* * *

A handful of Space Marines joined Ystremski on the rim of the crater and listened to the distant battle. Their mood was subdued, and there was none of the usual banter. They knew their comrades were fighting and dying within earshot of their position but there was nothing they could do to support them.

A bright flash on the horizon caught their attention.

"What the hell was that?"

"Did they get nuked?"

The gunny shook his head. "I don't know what that was, but it wasn't a nuke. That's the wrong direction." He looked around and spotted one of the command mech drivers. "Take a platoon and scout that direction, see if you can find out what the hell is going on."

* * * * *

Chapter Thirty

Major Anders was stretched out in his stateroom, deep in thought. Kiti Niskala's mutiny had shaken him, and the deflection and deception he'd discussed with Admiral Kinshaw had left him sleepless with a bilious stomach. He replayed the conversation over and over in his head, but he arrived at the same conclusion every time.

Ninth Division is fucked.

His communicator buzzed, and he fumbled with the handset.

"Major Anders."

"Major, this is Chief Knight in the FOC. The Maltaani jamming has lifted."

Ander sat upright. "What?"

"The jamming, sir. It's gone. Just now."

Anders dropped his handset, jumped up, and ran out the door. Seconds later, he burst into the FOC and went straight to the admiral's console. As usual, the admiral was at the epicenter of a swarm of staff officers scurrying in all directions as if the entire Fleet depended on the papers and folders they clutched in their hands. Anders bulled his way through the crowd to the flag console.

Kinshaw looked up.

"It looks like Chief Knight found you."

"Yes, sir. What happened?"

Kinshaw shrugged. "Beats me. You're the intel squirrel, why don't you tell me?" He dismissed his own remark with a wave of his hand. "We don't know what happened, Major. The Fleet control circuits came up first, and then all our sensors started working again. The comms folks are checking the network, but it looks like we've got full connectivity."

"Any word from Ninth Division?"

"Just this." The admiral handed Anders a piece of paper. "What the hell does 'send fresh fruit and ammo' mean? They've sent it four times now. Is that some kind of Space Marine code?"

"I have no idea, sir."

"I guess we'll find out soon enough. We have connectivity with the surveillance satellite constellation, so we'll have pictures any minute."

"What about the Maltaani fleet?"

"Nothing yet. As soon as I get confirmation that the rest of the Fleet is fully operational, I'm going to send out more scouts."

"Surveillance birds are up, Admiral," announced a lieutenant from a nearby console. "Ninth Division landing zone on Screen Two."

The center screen on the bulkhead flickered to life and an overhead view of the battlefield appeared.

"What's that?" demanded Kinshaw.

The lieutenant poked at her keyboard and the image sharpened.

"It's a crater, sir. Maybe from a meteorite. It looks like the Space Marines have taken cover in it."

"That can't be all of them. Zoom out," ordered Anders."

The image zoomed out. On the far edge of the display, a mass of movement was visible.

"There. On the left. Pan over and zoom."

Scorch marks stained the ground and black smoke billowed into the sky from burning vehicles. Bodies littered the ground, visual testimony to the ferocity of the fighting. As they watched, a group of mechs formed a fighting wedge as the infantry fell in behind.

"Are those Space Marines?"

The display zoomed in and then zoomed in again, but the image blurred.

"Sorry, Admiral. The pixel rate on this system isn't high enough for extreme zoom. I've got another bird on station in twelve minutes—"

"Never mind that. Those are our mechs. Pan up and let's see what they're up against."

The view changed again and several FOC personnel gasped. The small knot of Space Marines and their mechs was dwarfed by a large formation of enemy troops massed several kilometers away. Anders saw vehicles interspersed among the infantry, and he noted a number of prepared artillery emplacements.

"They're going to get wiped out," said the lieutenant.

"We have to help them!" insisted Anders.

Admiral Kinshaw stared at the screen for a long second before he swiveled his seat and faced the staff gathered in the FOC.

"We don't have pilots to deploy hovercopters." He pointed to a Fleet captain standing next to Anders. "Ops, get the FADCs on the ground ASAP. We'll launch strike drones after they report readiness. And find that Maltaani fleet!"

Forward Area Drone Controllers, abbreviated to FADCs and pronounced "fad-seize," were an elite group of Fleet personnel trained to provide strike drone support to ground forces. FADCs could insert into a combat zone on short notice and provide immediate air cover via heavily armed strike drones. Military planners and military budgeteers had clashed over manned close air support for ground operations—the never-ending battle between requirements and funding. The FADC program had grown up in the cracks as a stopgap measure until a long-term solution could be found. The FADCs had deployed with Ninth Division as a proof of concept.

The scrum of staff members around the admiral exploded in all directions as they scrambled to follow his orders. The Staff Operations Officer issued a stream of instructions to the cluster of officers who trailed him out of the space and soon only Anders remained next to Kinshaw.

"It's a good thing you're doing, Admiral," Anders said softly.

Kinshaw cocked an eyebrow at the major. "I don't always need a gun pointed at my head to make the right decision." He pointed to Screen Two, where ant-sized Space Marines were advancing on the swarm of waiting Maltaani. "I lost four drop ships landing Niskala and her mechs. If we don't get those boys some air support, and soon, all of that might be for nothing."

* * *

The recon team returned with a load of wounded Space Marines they discovered wandering in the desert.

"There are a lot of casualties out there trying to get back here," the mech driver reported to Gunny Ystremski as the litter bearers offloaded the injured at the field hospital. "We never got close to the fighting, but the wounded I talked to told me the mech assault was taking heavy fire. There's a couple of them who are still conscious if you want to hear their story."

"Any sign of Lieutenant Fortis?"

The mech driver shook his head. "I don't know who he is, but we didn't pick up any officers."

"Okay, thanks."

"Gunny, if it's all the same to you, I'd like to take both command mechs out and collect as many casualties as we can find. There are a lot of guys out there who aren't going to make it back here on their own."

"Yeah, okay, do it. Take as many men as you need."

Ystremski walked through the Space Marines in the triage area until he found one propped up on one elbow. A bloody bandage covered most of his head and his right hand was wrapped in a heavy wad of gauze.

"You okay, Marine?"

The wounded man nodded but didn't speak.

"Can you tell me what's going on out there?"

"That fuckin' major... We were supposed to stay with the mechs, but they left us behind and the Maltaani hit us in the flank. Artillery everywhere." He motioned to his head with his injured hand. "That's what got me."

"Are we holding them off?"

"I don't know. They were all over us for a while there, and then I got hit. They might all be dead, for all I know."

Liz appeared with two orderlies.

"Sorry, Gunny, but I need to get this man into the operating room as soon as possible."

Ystremski touched the wounded Space Marine on the leg for good luck as he was carried away.

"Any word from Abner?" she asked in a low voice.

"None. The fighting has been heavy, but I don't have any news about the lieutenant." He got a thick feeling in his throat. "No news is good news, I think. He'll be okay."

"God, I hope you're right."

* * * *

Chapter Thirty-One

The remaining four companies of infantry formed up, and Fortis was shocked to see how thin their ranks were. He knew they'd taken casualties, but even with the walking wounded who refused to evacuate, the Space Marines were under half strength. He felt a guilty sense of relief that they were Second Regiment troops; he didn't recognize any of their faces, which made it easier to lead them into battle. Despite what he'd told Liz that night in their foxholes, the emotional insulation provided by DINLI was not enough when the death was widescale.

"Fortis!"

He turned around and saw Niskala waving from her turret. He jogged over.

"Yes, ma'am?"

"Comms are working. Tune up the mech command net." She gave him the numbers.

"How did that happen?"

"How should I know? Maybe that nuke did it. Perhaps now you'll be able to follow my lead."

Fortis put the mech command net in one ear and the Second Regiment command net in the other. He would have to switch back and forth to talk, but the voices reassured him. The restoration of comms was a force multiplier, and he felt a surge of optimism. If the infantry and mechs could coordinate their movements, they might avoid Maltaani flanking maneuvers like the one that derailed their last assault.

"Fortis, can you hear me?"

He looked around to wave acknowledgement before he remembered the transmit button.

"Yes, ma'am, I hear you loud and clear."

"Good. We're moving out. Vee formation, three mechs in trail the left side of the formation to protect the flanks. We're not stopping until we punch through to their artillery. Stay with us, Fortis. That's an order!"

Fortis switched to the infantry net and repeated Niskala's orders. The Space Marines fell in behind the mechs and the formation moved out.

Smoke from the burning mechs destroyed by the last assault drifted across the battlefield and obscured the vision of the infantry as they approached.

"Be alert, Fortis. Infrared sensors show Maltaani soldiers massing two hundred meters straight ahead."

"Roger."

Fortis barely got the word out of his mouth before the main battle mechs opened up on the distant enemy. The horizon disappeared in a cloud of dust and smoke. The mechs continued to fire as they rolled forward. The three flanking mechs scoured the desert with their automatic pulse guns to uncover any Maltaani concealed in ambush positions. The infantry tucked in behind the mechs and the human assault rolled forward.

The lack of response by the Maltaani unnerved Fortis. The Space Marines had experienced the Maltaani tactic of falling back before unleashing a mass attack several times, and he couldn't shake the feeling that they planned to do it again. Still, the nearby mechs added power to the infantry formations that they hadn't had before, so he felt a surge of confidence.

The mech command net crackled with a loud burst of static, and Fortis heard snatches of a broken transmission.

"...fire...turn right...damage..."

He didn't see any of the main battle mechs take fire. The Maltaani ability to jam their communications made Fortis wonder if it was a spoof transmission sent by the enemy to confuse the Space Marines.

Niskala's voice broke in on the mech command net.

"Scout One, this is Mech Lead. Say again, over."

Silence.

"Scout One, this is Mech Lead. Your last transmission was garbled. Say again, over."

"This...One...falling back..."

A pair of vehicles raced into view through the dust and dirt on the left flank and the flanking mechs fired in unison. All three pulse cannon bolts went high. Fortis recognized the targets as light battle mechs. Before he could shout for a cease-fire, the main battle mechs fired again and one of the smaller mechs exploded in a shower of white sparks. The other mech veered wildly as a panicked voice cried out over the net.

"Hold your fire! Friendlies! Friendlies!"

The light battle mech began to smoke, and by the time it reached the Space Marine lines, a loud screeching noise from the engine compartment drowned out the noise of its tracks. It skidded to a halt ten meters from Fortis, the hatches banged open, and crewmembers scrambled to get clear of the stricken machine.

Fortis raced forward and dragged one of the burned and battered mech crew to safety. As he splashed a hydration pack on her soot-stained face, he saw she was a private.

"Private, what happened?"

Her eyelids fluttered as she hovered on the edge of unconsciousness and he splashed more water and wiped it away.

"You're safe now, Private. Take it easy."

The wounded Space Marine strained to sit up and coughed up dark red blood that spilled over her chin and stained her uniform.

"There's a couple thousand of them out there." Her voice grew weak. She choked and more blood leaked from her mouth. "On their way." Her body spasmed as she died.

Fortis scanned the horizon, but all he could see was the hazy dust cloud raised by the mechs.

"Fortis, what's the delay?" Niskala demanded over the mech command net. "Why have you stopped?"

"One of the light command mechs returned from the end-run and reported thousands of Maltaani massing to attack the flank, Major."

"All the more reason for you to close up, Lieutenant. Get your men moving; we're driving them back. We have their artillery in sight."

Before Fortis could respond, he heard the familiar sound of artillery rounds landing behind him.

Boom! Boom! Boom!

Dirt and rocks flew high in the air as the Maltaani guns overshot the infantry and plowed up the desert behind them.

"Move out!" he ordered over the Second Regiment command circuit. "Close up on the battle mechs."

The Space Marines, who had halted and taken a knee when the light mechs approached, hurried forward to escape the shelling. Fortis kept an eye on the flanks as he advanced, but the troops reported by the dead private didn't materialize. The artillery barrage targeting behind the troops lifted, and an eerie calm descended over the battlefield.

Where are the Maltaani?

Without warning, the artillery barrage resumed, concentrated on the battle mechs advancing on the flank. The ground shook as dozens of shells rained down, and shrapnel whizzed by overhead. One of the mechs exploded with an ear-shattering *crack!* and white sparks showered the surrounding area. A pair of explosions bracketed a second mech and the vehicle clanked to a stop as the tracks unspooled and stopped the vehicle dead. The mech command net was overwhelmed with angry shouts and cries of anguish.

Suddenly, Fortis spotted a shadowy mass of Maltaani soldiers moving behind the smoke of the shelling.

"Contact left!"

Volleys of pulse rifle fire tore into the swarming Maltaani as the last flanking mech hosed them down with a stream of automatic rounds. The main body of mechs pivoted and charged into the Maltaani assault. Fortis saw the enemy break and scatter in all directions.

"Follow me!"

He jumped to his feet and charged into the fray. The remaining Space Marines followed. Fortis gritted his teeth and fired from the hip as he waded into panicked enemy soldiers. He butt-stroked Maltaani when they came within range and shot at others as they ran away. A Maltaani approached the lieutenant with his hands stretched overhead in a gesture of surrender and he went down under a burst of pulse rifle fire that stitched a patch across his chest. Fortis saw an unfamiliar private smiling at him.

"Kill 'em all, sir."

Several rounds snapped by Fortis and ripped into the private. His smile became a shattered mass of blood and bone as a Maltaani bullet carved a vee through his forehead, and he went down hard. A pair of unarmed Maltaani soldiers ran past Fortis, and he shot them dead without hesitation.

The Space Marines scrambled forward behind the phalanx of main battle mechs and mopped up the shredded remains of the Maltaani troops. Fortis looked up and realized he was staring down the barrels of a self-propelled artillery emplacement. The Maltaani flank attack had been another ruse, but it wasn't meant to encircle the infantry, it was intended to lure the Space Marine mechs into a point-blank slugfest.

The Maltaani battery fired and the world around Fortis disappeared in a blizzard of dirt and sand. A fist slammed into his chest and threw him onto his back. He fought to catch his breath through the pain radiating throughout his body. He choked on clouds of sand and dust as he rolled over and struggled to his hands and knees. Fortis's eyes burned and tears poured down his face as tears tried to flush the irritants away. He felt rather than saw vicious fighting swirl around him, punctuated by the thunder of big guns and the *crack-whiz* of Maltaani rounds snapping overhead.

Fortis was yanked to his feet and shoved to the rear by an anonymous Space Marine.

"The mechs are bugging out, LT. We gotta get the fuck outta here!"

The lieutenant recognized his rescuer as the private who had investigated the dead skirmishers with him before the battle began. He looked around and saw a group of three main battle mechs retreating from the Maltaani artillery. Space Marines struggled to keep up with the machines and maintain an orderly withdrawal. Fortis was gratified to see their movements were still deliberate and not a rout.

"Niskala? Where's the major?" Fortis croaked.

"Fucked if I know, sir. The last time I saw the command mech, it was upside down and on fire."

Fortis keyed his mic as he staggered rearward.

"Second Regiment, this is Lieutenant Fortis. Fall back to the crater. I say again, fall back to the crater."

* * * * *

Chapter Thirty-Two

Master Chief John "Duke" Earle led his team of FADCs from the ready room to the hangar where the Jumper Delivery Vehicle, or JDV, waited. He looked at the ungainly craft and winced.

The JDV was a former rocket body Fleet engineers modified to carry personnel and equipment from orbit to a planetary surface. They removed the powerful rocket engines and fuel tanks and replaced them with retractable flight surfaces, a single centerline bench seat, and a storage room for five hundred kilos of gear.

The theory behind the JDV was simple: After the team of FADCs mounted the JDV, the rocket would be released into space from *Atlas*. A small solid fuel motor would fire and propel the vehicle toward the surface at a precalculated speed and angle of entry. When the JDV entered the atmosphere, a set of retrorockets would slow the JDV down. The wings and tail would deploy, the landing gear would extend, and the JDV would glide to a smooth landing. All of this would be controlled by a triple-redundant autopilot that required no manual intervention.

The problem was that it was all still theory. Fleet engineers had evaluated the JDV in a wind tunnel and conducted two successful unmanned test drops from the mesosphere over Terra Earth before *Atlas* and Ninth Division deployed, but they hadn't conducted any test flights with humans aboard, nor had they dropped the JDV from a nominal low earth orbit. In fact, the auto pilot had only been bench tested once. The plan was to test the JDV on deployment during Space Marine exercises.

Some test.

The G-suit encased Duke's body in an uncomfortable hug, and the straps of his emergency chute chafed his balls.

If it doesn't hurt, you're not doing it right.

Duke traded nods with the launch operators as he mounted the short ladder and took his place in the front of the crew compartment. As the "pilot," Duke sat at the control station in front, and the remaining FADCs climbed in behind him like the crew of a bobsled back on Terra Earth. The official term for the seating configuration was "centerline stack," but FADCs referred to it as "nut to butt." He plugged up the comms umbilical and waited until the rest of his team was in place.

"Count off. One."

"Two."

"Three."

"Four."

Duke flashed a thumbs up. "All four, all secure. Close the hatch."

Launch operators lowered the hatch, and Duke and his team were plunged into darkness. There were no viewports or windows, only the tiny screen on the control station fed by a single exterior camera. In theory, if the autopilot failed, and Duke was forced to take manual control, he could use the display to bring the JDV down safely.

In theory.

Duke shifted his body to ease the strain of the chute straps on his groin. He made a mental note to recommend leaving the chutes off the equipment list for future JDV operations. Wearing the chutes was reflexive for flight ops, but, at the velocities that the JDV traveled, a parachute would be useless.

Duke heard a *clunk* and the JDV jerked as the launch gantry picked it up from the hangar deck. There was a long silence before he heard the launch commander on the circuit.

"All systems are green. Stand by to launch in five, four, three, two, one, launch."

For a split second, Duke thought the launch had failed. There was no sensation or sound to indicate they were free of the flagship, only a slight surge against their restraints as the induced gravity subsided.

WHOOSH!

The solid fuel motor fired, and Duke was pressed back against the man behind him. The G-suit squeezed his lower body while Duke panted and strained his abdomen to avoid passing out from the G force of the sudden acceleration. The rocket burn only lasted a few seconds, but it felt like an hour.

The JDV shook and rattled as it punched through the atmosphere of Balfan-48. Duke began to sweat as the interior heat built up. He briefly wondered if he had hitched a one-way ride to hell in a sauna.

"F-f-fuckin' baked potato," Controller First Class Prater spat over the team circuit, and the rest of the men chuckled through gritted teeth. Duke started to admonish Prater but changed his mind; if they were going to roast to death, they might as well do it with smiles on their faces.

There was a slight rumble as the retrorockets fired and the stack of bodies pressed forward against Duke. In his mind's eye, Duke imagined the JDV descending on a smooth glide path, but the forces that acted on his body and the attitude indicator told him the JDV was pointed straight down and descending at a high rate of speed.

What the hell?

Fear stabbed him in the chest when he realized the flight control surfaces had not deployed. Just as he reached for the autopilot override switch, he heard the motors whine and a *thud* as the wings locked into place.

Duke grunted as the nose of the JDV pulled up out of the vertical dive and the resulting G forces crushed him onto the bench. Despite the pressure of his G-suit, his vision grayed out, and his skin burned as though he had a full body sunburn.

His next conscious thought was that the attitude indicator showed a slight downward pitch as the JDV glided in a relatively slow descent toward the preselected landing zone.

"I think I crapped my pants when I went to sleep," Prater quipped. "Who's driving this heap?"

Duke grimaced at the stabbing pain behind his eyes as his G-suit relented, and his toes tingled as blood returned to his lower extremities.

"Count off. One."

"Two."

"Three."

"Four."

"All four, all secure. Stand by for touchdown. As soon as we stop, Prater and Ramirez set security while Ngo and I unload. Don't shoot unless we're shot at, and, even then, make sure you're not shooting back at Space Marines. They've been fighting for five days and don't know we're coming, so they might be a little trigger-happy."

* * *

Gunny Ystremski stared as the silver rocket made a wide circle and touched down on the desert floor where the dropships had inserted the mechs. When the craft touched down, the nose gear collapsed into a crater and flipped over, tail first, in a cloud of dust. Ystremski sprinted for the crash site.

"What the hell is that thing, a bomb?" shouted one of the Space Marines who followed the gunny to the wreckage.

"No idea," answered Ystremski. "Not a bomb. Not with wheels. Some kind of logistics drop maybe."

The rocket came to rest on its side. It looked like it had wings at one point, and the rocket body was dented and burned. Ystremski watched in amazement as a hatch on top opened and four humans tumbled out.

"Who the hell are you?" he asked as the Space Marines helped the newcomers to their feet.

A tall man with a tight crewcut sprinkled with gray stepped forward and extended his hand. "I'm Duke. This is Prater, Ramirez, and Ngo. Admiral Kinshaw sent us. We're FADCs."

"Who?"

"Forward Area Drone Controllers. We're your close air support."

"We're experimental," quipped Prater, and Duke elbowed him.

"Some experiment." Ystremski gestured to the crumpled rocket. "I hope this isn't the strike drone."

Duke looked at his watch. "No, but they'll be overhead in sixteen minutes. If you and your men can give us a hand, I'll show you what we've got."

Duke and Ystremski talked as the Space Marines hauled the FADC gear to the crater and helped them unpack and set up the drone control station.

"This screen is linked to the surveillance constellation. The resolution isn't great, but here's what you're up against."

Ystremski whistled when he saw the Maltaani troop dispositions and what remained of the Space Marine force that had set out on mission hours earlier. As he watched, the surviving Space Marines crawled across the screen as they fought a rearguard action to withdraw toward the crater. His heart sank when he remembered that Lieutenant Fortis was somewhere in all that carnage.

"We have to help them."

"In two minutes, we will," Duke replied. He looked at his crew. "What's our status?"

"Satellite link is solid," answered Ngo.

"Drone control network is up and tested satisfactory. Two flights of two will be on station in two minutes," snapped Prater.

"Standing by to assume tactical control," said Ramirez.

Duke turned to Ystremski. "We have four flights of two drones each. The first two flights are armed with a mix of high explosives and napalm. We can order up whatever ordnance we need after that."

"Nukes?"

"No nukes. I can dial up some thermobaric weapons; those'll work just fine against a large number of hostiles in the open if we can get some distance between them and the friendlies."

"I love it when you talk dirty, Duke."

"Give it a rest, Prater."

The petty officer shrugged and smiled. "Your drones are here."

"I have assumed tactical control of two flights of strike drones. Flight One is in low orbit, Flight Two is high. Standing by for orders," announced Ramirez.

Duke tapped a stylus on his screen and entered a command on his keyboard then looked at Ystremski.

"I've designated target coordinates and payloads for the tactical controller, Ramirez. Now the fun begins."

* * * * *

Chapter Thirty-Three

Lieutenant Fortis directed the fighting withdrawal as the Space Marines and the three remaining mechs retreated toward the crater. The Maltaani pushed forward with steady pressure, but they didn't attempt to overwhelm the humans. The artillery fire was random and sporadic, and most of the shells landed in empty desert. Maltaani rifle fire found an occasional target and the Space Marines did their best to triage on the move and carry their wounded comrades toward the relative safety of the crater. The mechs spread out to cover the infantry with bursts of automatic pulse guns, but they didn't stop to engage in duels with the advancing enemy.

Fortis tried to raise Gunny Ystremski on every frequency he could dial up, but the only response he got was static. The indestructible case on his communicator was cracked and the wiring was exposed, so he tore it off in disgust and threw it away.

Lowest bidder crap.

Instead, Fortis sent runners ahead to alert the Space Marines at the crater of the approaching threat and to request assistance with the wounded.

Thus far, the retreat had been orderly. After the initial shock of the order wore off, the Space Marines accepted their defeat and acknowledged that their priority now was to get as many troops back to the crater as possible. More than one had expressed disgust at their withdrawal, but Fortis's response was always the same.

DINLI.

The whine of turbojet engines surprised Fortis, and he searched the sky for the source. A pair of aircraft flashed by overhead, and the lieutenant glimpsed a squarish body with twin engines mounted on the back of the fuselage. Heavy ordnance was mounted under stubby wings and an automatic cannon protruded from the nose. The drones zoomed over the Maltaani troops and both aircraft released weapons before making a steep climb into sky over Balfan-48.

BOOM! BOOM! BOOM! BOOM!

The ground shook as the bombs found their targets and a mushroom cloud of dirt and sand blossomed over the Maltaani troops. The Space Marines paused their retreat and watched as the drones circled and swooped low over the enemy.

WHOOSH!

A wall of fire erupted along the front. Fortis felt the hot breeze on his face as the incendiary weapons absorbed the surrounding air to feed their fiery detonations. Oily black smoke belched skyward, and the Maltaani rifle fire died away. All around Fortis, Space Marines whooped with excitement at the sight of the hellish inferno, and he felt a surge of hope with the arrival of the unexpected reinforcements.

The drones made three bombing passes and emptied their wings over the Maltaani to devastating effect. Fortis thought they would depart, but they made a tight turn and commenced on a shallow gun run.

BRRRRRRT!

The sound of the heavy machineguns ripped through the sky as thousands of rounds plowed the ground around the Maltaani troops. Just as the aircraft pulled up from the gun run, twin streaks of lightning raced skyward and chased the drones until they exploded in brilliant orange balls of unspent fuel.

* * *

"The FADCs are operational and in control of two flights of drones, Admiral," reported the FOC watch commander. "Screen Two."

The now-familiar overhead view of the Balfan-48 battlefield appeared. The troop positions had changed in the thirty minutes since the admiral ordered the FADC insertion. The Space Marines appeared to be withdrawing toward the crater, and the Maltaani forces arrayed against them were not pressing the humans as closely as they had been.

"Here they come."

The drones approached from the right and passed over the Maltaani. A second later, violent explosions blew gaping holes in the middle of the enemy troops. When the dust cleared, Major Anders saw bodies and vehicles scattered in all directions. The drones circled around and made another bombing run, and more gaps appeared in the Maltaani ranks.

The drones reappeared from the right and the ground erupted in flames as napalm canisters tumbled across the surface and spewed their fiery contents. The camera view was obscured by thick black smoke, but the napalm created an impassable barrier between the Space Marines and their pursuers.

"Last run is guns only," announced the watch commander. "Next flight overhead in three minutes."

The drones passed over the enemy lines for the final time and turned to climb out of the engagement zone. Two bright flashes appeared behind the craft and they disappeared in twin explosions.

There was a long moment of silence and Anders looked at Admiral Kinshaw.

"Shit."

* * *

"What the hell happened?"

Ramirez threw up his hands. "I don't know, Duke. I was about to transfer control back to *Atlas* when they flat lined."

"That looked like shoulder-fired anti-air to me," said Ystremski.

"No time to worry about it now. Where is the next flight?"

"Overhead. Same tasking?"

Duke looked at Ystremski. "Any suggestions?"

"Concentrate on their artillery if you can. The infantry is easy enough to kill, but those damn guns are murder."

"You heard the man, Ramirez. Artillery is on the menu, but skip the gun run. Too damn slow. Prater, let *Atlas* know not to expect the first flight to return. Tell them we want Flight Three with standard weapon mix, Flight Four all thermobaric. We're going to murder those bastards."

* * *

Fortis caught sight of the JDV wreckage as he approached the crater and veered off to investigate. Two more drones zoomed by overhead and moments later he heard distant explosions.

When he got to the wrecked JDV, he found Coughlin and several other familiar faces among the Space Marines gathered around it.

"What is this thing, Coughlin?"

"Some kind of rocket, sir. The drone controllers came on it."

"Who?"

"Fleet drone controllers. From *Atlas*. They got here a little while ago."

"Where are they now?"

"Over in the crater, sir. Gunny Ystremski took them over there and got them set up. They're putting on some show, aren't they?"

"Yeah, they sure are. Thanks, Coughlin."

Fortis turned to go, but the armorer stopped him and pointed at his chest.

"Hey, LT, what happened to your LBA?"

Fortis looked down and saw a fist-sized piece of shrapnel protruding from his chest protector. He had a vague recollection of being hit when the Maltaani tried to encircle the Space Marines, but he hadn't realized how close he'd come to death.

"Bad day at the office." He pawed at the shrapnel, but it was embedded too deep.

"Come see me later, I'll get you a new set of armor," said Coughlin.

Fortis nodded and set off to find Ystremski and the drone controllers. The drones whizzed by again, and bright orange napalm erupted on the horizon.

Burn the bastards. Burn them all.

* * *

"Admiral, the FADCs reported the loss of Flight One was due to unidentified surface-to-air weapons, probably shoulder fired. They're going to cease gunnery and stick to fast-moving bomb runs."

"Very well." Kinshaw studied the overhead view. "It looks like the Maltaani have fallen back, for now."

"Yes, sir. The Space Marines have broken contact, so the drones will concentrate on Maltaani artillery."

"What's the status of Flights Three and Four?"

"Flight Three is standing by to launch with standard HE/napalm load. The load toads are hanging a full rack of thermobaric weapons on Flight Four per FADC request. They should be finished within the hour."

268 | P.A. PIATT

"It's going to be dark soon, sir. Are the FADCs capable of night operations?"

"Sir, they're equipped with a no-strike fence, but they haven't reported if it's set up."

"What kind of fence?"

"A no-strike fence. It's designed to prevent friendly fire incidents."

* * *

"Hey, Duke, *Atlas* asked me about the fence. Are we going to set it up?"

"Yeah, I think so." He looked at Ystremski. "What do you think, Gunny?"

"We gotta build a fence?"

"We deployed with an electronic no-strike fence," Duke replied. "It's a chain of transponders we plant around the perimeter to create an electronic map for the drone targeting system. When the fence is operational, the system won't allow aim points that would jeopardize friendly forces inside the fence boundary."

"This isn't another one of those experimental projects, is it?"

Duke chuckled. "The fence has been thoroughly tested in live-fire exercises. We haven't tested it in combat, but I trust it."

"Okay, let's do it. Do you need our help?"

"We could use a hand with the sensors. We brought thirty, so it won't take long. Prater, inform *Atlas* that the fence is in progress. What's the status of Flight Three?"

"They just told me they're going to wait for bomb damage assessment from One and Two before they launch Three and Four. I think they're still mad about Flight One."

Just then, they heard the heavy rumble of mech engines.

"Sounds like Second Regiment is back." Gunny Ystremski got up and headed for the steps leading out of the crater. "Keep blasting those pricks and set up the fence. I'm going to find out what happened out there."

* * * * *

Chapter Thirty-Four

Fortis trudged the last hundred meters to the crater behind the three surviving main battle mechs. All three mechs were scorched and dented from ricochets and near misses, but their throaty engines and heavy armor reassured him nonetheless.

"Welcome back, Lieutenant."

Fortis turned and saw Gunny Ystremski approaching. He held out his hand to shake, but the day-long running fight had taken a toll on his body, and he almost collapsed when he was overcome by the sudden urge to hug the older man.

"Whoa, take it easy," protested Ystremski as he struggled to keep the young officer upright. "Let's find you somewhere to sit down. Are you hit?"

Fortis laughed and pointed to the shrapnel embedded in his LBA. "Bad day at the office."

The gunny let Fortis slump to the ground and took a knee next to him. "What the hell happened out there?"

"The mechs moved too fast, and we got separated. The Maltaani hit us in the flank before we could close up, and it got pretty hairy. If it wasn't for those drones—"

"The drones are a gift from *Atlas*."

"*Atlas*? I thought Fleet left."

"I guess they changed their minds because they sent the controllers down to help us out. They're set up in the crater with the rest of the division."

"Here, help me up." Fortis groaned as Ystremski hauled him to his feet. "I need to look in on the wounded and send out patrols to look for stragglers."

"It's all been taken care of, LT. The command mechs have been hauling back casualties all afternoon, and Doc and Liz are treating the injured as fast as they come in. The rest of Second Regiment, the guys that weren't killed or wounded, are in their new holes on the rim of the crater. Right now, you need to eat, hydrate, and rest for a few minutes. You've earned it."

"What about the Maltaani?"

"The drones are hunting down their artillery with thermobaric weapons right now. The enemy shot down a couple, but there are still six left to support us. Some of the lads are setting up a sensor field so the drones don't accidently engage us, and I think they plan on bombing the Maltaani all night."

Ystremski pointed to the other side of the crater. "Foxtrot Company is dug in over there. They've got a hole prepped and waiting for you."

Fortis nodded wearily. "Okay, you're right. I could use a break."

"I'll be around if you need me, LT."

"Hey, Gunny."

Ystremski waited, wordless.

"Look...I...uh..."

The gunny nodded. "Go get some rest. We'll talk later."

Before Fortis could speak, Ystremski strode off in the direction of the field hospital.

* * *

The FOC watch commander scowled as she listened to the communicator handset at her console. "Keep me posted," she said curtly before she hung up.

"Admiral, the strike drone hangar reports the launch/recovery rail is inoperative at this time. One of the Flight Two drones was improperly aligned when they recovered it and it twisted the cradle."

"Damn! How long to repair it?"

"Unknown at this time. They have to cut the cradle off and weld it back on straight, but they can't do it with a drone on the rail."

"What's the status of Flight Three?"

"Still in the hangar, sir," replied the air coordinator. "Flight Two returned before Three was launched and the hanger crew decided to recover Two first. That's when someone got in a hurry and tried to bring Two in before it was aligned."

Kinshaw scratched his wiry crewcut and took a deep breath. No amount of shouting would solve this dilemma, so he kept his voice even.

"Notify the FADCs that we'll get the next flight to them as soon as possible." He looked up at Screen Two, which showed the darkened surface of Balfan-48. "We should have some breathing room. If the reports are accurate, the Maltaani won't attack at night."

* * *

Gunny Ystremski searched the field hospital until he found Liz Sherer.

"Abner's back, and he's okay," he said softly.

The reporter took one of his hands in hers and squeezed. "Oh, thank God. I've been terrified I would find him on a litter in triage." She glanced around at the tent full of wounded Space Marines.

"I gotta go check on things, Liz. I just thought you'd want to know."

The gunny continued through the encroaching darkness to the drone control station, where he was greeted by a grim-faced Duke.

"We've got trouble. *Atlas* reported a casualty to the drone deck gear, and they can't launch any more until they get it fixed."

"How long?"

"They don't know."

The gunny looked up at the sky. "At least it's getting dark."

"Yeah. Hey, take a look over there. Ramirez, show him the fence."

Ystremski peered at the drone controller's screen and saw a gray shape overlaid on an overhead view of the crater.

"That's the no-strike zone we created with the fence," Ramirez explained. "The system won't let me select an aimpoint inside that area, and depending on what weapon I have selected, I can't designate an aimpoint inside a pre-programmed minimum range outside the boundary. I can override it, but with the area of uncertainty around an aimpoint, it's not recommended."

"And this works? It's been tested?"

"I tested it myself on the range back home. I set up a fence and tried to call down all kinds of weapons in and around me and none came through. So yeah, it works."

The gunny looked at Duke. "What's the word from the flagship? Besides the broken drone launcher, have they told you what their plan is?"

"I don't know. Truthfully, I don't think they know. They don't have many options left. How long would it take to evacuate the wounded? A day? We might be able to hold off the Maltaani for the first wave of dropships, but as soon as they see healthy Space Marines climb aboard, they'll attack with everything they have."

Ystremski rubbed his whiskered chin. "So we stay until we win. Or die."

* * *

After he left the drone controllers, Gunny Ystremski made a circuit of the crater rim. He spent a lot of time talking with Space Marines of Second Regiment, and it pleased him to see their morale wasn't as low as he'd feared. There was a general feeling of contempt toward Major Niskala and her command of the mech assault, but the sight of the command mechs racing back and forth, loaded with the wounded, tempered their anger. Ystremski sensed they had a strange but well-deserved kind of pride for having been dragged through the meatgrinder and survived; he was regaled by their tales of heroism and derring-do.

Next, he circulated through the mech crews encamped on the desert floor next to their behemoths. Ystremski wasn't surprised to find them isolated and their morale poor. Of the thirty-nine mechs that had dropped from *Atlas*, there were only three main battle mechs and two command mechs left. They were reluctant to talk at first, but the gunny finally convinced them that he wasn't looking to make accusations or assign blame. They had fought like hell, but they'd been poorly led against overwhelming odds and the resulting carnage wasn't their fault.

Ystremski sent a couple of them to locate some DINLI among the infantry dug in nearby, and it wasn't long before the two groups intermingled and traded stories about the battle. He left the area and completed his inspection of the crater, confident that the mech crews would recover their *esprit de corps* and be battle-ready when needed.

The gunny made it to his hole with Foxtrot Company as total darkness settled, and he smiled when he heard Lieutenant Fortis snoring from the next hole over. As Ystremski tried to get comfortable, Fortis coughed and snorted himself awake.

"You okay over there, LT?" Ystremski whispered.

Fortis cleared his throat and spat. "Yeah, I'm good. Snored myself awake, I guess."

Ystremski chuckled. "It sounded like you were making love to a grizzly bear."

Fortis sat up. "Do you know what our status is?"

"We are right at a thousand able-bodied Space Marines on the perimeter and another four hundred wounded, most of whom can fight if we put a rifle in their hands. There are three main battle mechs and two command mechs standing by. We don't have any drone support right now because something is broken on the flagship, but Duke tells me they're working on it."

"Who's Duke?"

"He's the master chief in charge of the drone controllers."

"We're pretty thin."

"Indeed."

They sat in silence for a few minutes before Fortis spoke.

"The mech attack was a debacle."

Gunny Ystremski remained silent.

"When I saw Major Niskala land with those mechs it made me happy, you know? It wasn't until we moved out that I realized how bad her plan was, but by then it was too late. I should have listened to you."

Ystremski fought the urge to respond with an I-told-you-so remark.

"We were all happy to see those mechs."

"Yeah, but I was happy for selfish reasons. The pressure was off because I wasn't in command anymore, and I was ready to go along with just about anything. I was scared. She showed up, and I ducked instead of standing up. It was cowardly."

"There's no shame in being scared. It's what you do when you're scared that makes the difference. Maybe you fucked up, but what the hell? You're a second lieutenant, you're supposed to fuck things up."

"Still—"

"Still nothing. You're supposed to be a platoon commander, not a division commander. I have holes in my socks that have been in the ISMC longer than you. We only got to the point where Niskala and the mechs showed up because of your leadership, and we're gonna finish this fight with you in command."

Ystremski waited, but Fortis said nothing.

"Now, if it's all the same to you, sir, I'm tired, and I don't have time to hold your hand while you feel sorry for yourself. We've got a battle to win tomorrow. DINLI."

"DINLI," Fortis echoed softly.

"Damn right."

* * *

"Admiral? Admiral, sorry to bother you."

The FOC watch commander's voice was insistent, so Admiral Kinshaw sat up straight in his chair where he'd been dozing.

"What is it?"

"Screen Two, sir."

Kinshaw saw an infrared image of the now-familiar Space Marine perimeter and he blinked to focus. A large red blob, the bulk of the Maltaani force, was advancing toward them under cover of darkness.

"Alert the FADCs. What's the status of the launch rail?"

"We talked to the drone controllers as soon as we saw the movement. The hangar techs gave me an estimate of two hours to complete repairs."

"Call them back and tell them they have an hour. We have to get those birds overhead now!"

* * * * *

Chapter Thirty-Five

"Gunny Ystemski! Gunny!"

A familiar voice shouted across the dark crater and Ystremski sat up out of a dead sleep.

"Over here. Is that you, Prater?"

"Gunny, *Atlas* reports the Maltaani are massing to attack. The IR sensors picked them up and sent the image down to us."

In the next hole over, Fortis jumped to his feet.

"Do we have drones?"

"Negative. Not for two hours."

"Space Marines, on your feet!" Ystremski bellowed over the dark crater. The command was passed around the crater and a thousand Space Marines woke up and stood to their posts. He grabbed one of the nearby Foxtrot Company men.

"Do you know Corporal O'Reilly? Bright red hair, digging up the water tankers?"

"Yeah, Gunny, I know him."

"Go tell him I said to pull the fire truck up by the mechs and get it ready to go."

The Space Marine disappeared into the darkness.

"Fire truck?" Fortis asked as he and Ystremski set off for the FADC tent.

"While you were gone yesterday, O'Reilly and his guys got one of the empty tankers running. They drained the fuel tanks into the water tank and rigged it to run straight. Then they stuck a shitload of grenades in the cab for good measure. Come on, let's go watch the fun. This ought to be good."

Fortis and Ystremski picked their way across the crater, climbed up to the rim, and strained their eyes against the darkness. To their left, flames from an FGU was lapping at the water tanker to which O'Reilly had added several hundred liters of fuel.

"You think it'll work, Gunny?"

"It's a good idea. If he rigged the steering and acceleration right, it should head straight for the Maltaani. If they don't engage it too early, the fire should give us plenty of light to shoot by."

"Here's hoping it doesn't circle back at us."

Ystremski snorted. "You're a font of positivity, sir."

The tanker engine roared, and Space Marines cheered as the truck rumbled toward the approaching Maltaani. Fortis couldn't see it, but he tracked its progress across the desert floor by the noise.

It wasn't long before they heard Maltaani gunfire, and the Space Marines laughed in anticipation. The tanker exploded and sent a boiling orange-red fireball three hundred meters into the sky, which illuminated the desert for a half-klick in all directions. Thousands of Maltaani soldiers were exposed by the sudden light.

"Fire!" shouted Fortis, and pulse rifle fire poured into the enemy formation. Burning fuel showered the area and the grenades stuffed into the truck cab cooked off and added deadly sprays of shrapnel to the maelstrom. The command mechs contributed a volley of illumination shells to the hellish light of the burning tanker, and the main battle mechs blasted the Maltaani ranks with high-power pulses of blue-white energy.

Enemy soldiers milled around in confusion in the face of the sudden Space Marine barrage, and the Space Marines took full advantage of the opportunity to slaughter them. Fortis emptied two magazines into the enemy horde before the flames died down, and the illumination shells burned out. In the last few seconds of dim light, he saw the lead ranks of the enemy withdraw.

"Cease fire! Cease fire!"

A deathly silence settled over the crater, and the Space Marines cupped ringing ears to try to detect the sounds of the next Maltaani assault. Fortis laughed and slammed the gunny on the shoulder.

"That was great! We need a dozen of those trucks."

"I'd rather have drones. LT, why don't you go see what intel *Atlas* is sending to the FADCs. It would be good to know what direction they're coming from next."

"Yeah, okay. Maybe there's an update on the drone launcher, too. I'll be right back."

Fortis joined Duke under the tarp that covered the FADC equipment.

"Here's the latest image, LT. It looks like they're holding at a klick or so, but it doesn't look like they're shifting left or right."

"Can you see their artillery?"

Duke shook his head. "We don't have the processing power for that level of resolution from IR data. I'll see what we can get from the flagship, but it won't be more than rough bearing and range. Nothing we can use for targeting."

"Any update on the drones?"

"Nothing new. They got the new cradle welded on and now they have to test it. This night attack has added some urgency to their situation."

"And ours."

Duke chuckled. "And ours. Just a reminder, LT, when we get the drones back, it will be Flight Three up first. They're loaded with a standard mix of HE and napalm. Flight Four is loaded with all thermobaric weapons. They can change the weapon load if you want, but they can't switch weapons until they're finished with the launch rail."

* * *

All eyes in the FOC were on Screen Two. The Maltaani force had advanced to within two klicks of the Space Marine position, but the defenders hadn't engaged the attackers yet.

"What are they waiting for? They know the Maltaani are coming, right?"

"I notified the FADCs myself," replied the watch commander.

Suddenly, a small heat source separated from the Space Marine position and made a beeline for the enemy. Before Kinshaw could say anything, it vanished in a superheated plume that whited out the screen.

"What the fuck?"

In a few seconds, the heat bloom shrank to an intense spot of heat surrounded by smaller hot spots scattered across the desert. More bright spots appeared over the Maltaani and the edge of the Space Marine perimeter began to glow red.

"It looks like illumination rounds," remarked the watch commander. "The Space Marines are firing."

After a sustained fusillade of pulse rifle fire, bolstered by rapid firing mechs, the Maltaani force retreated from the crater. The blob paused about five klicks from the Space Marines.

"What's the status on the drones? We need them ASAP!"

"The hangar reported a satisfactory weight test on the weld, Admiral. They are repositioning drones now and estimate they will be ready to launch in ten minutes. Twenty-five minutes until they're overhead and available for tasking."

"Very well. Notify the FADCs and the hangar crew that we're sending Flights Three and Four as soon as possible before we refuel and rearm Flight Two."

* * *

"Hey Duke, *Atlas* said they're launching Flight Three in ten minutes, so we should have control in twenty-five."

"Outstanding." Duke turned to Fortis. "You think the Maltaani will hold off that long?"

Fortis shrugged. "I have no idea. That was the first night attack we've seen. We're a long way from daylight."

"Oh shit." Ramirez exclaimed.

"Oh shit, what?"

"They're coming."

The three men huddled over the controller's screen and examined the latest IR imagery. The Maltaani were indeed closing on the crater from the same direction they had attacked before.

"Can you zoom out and see any other Maltaani around us?" Fortis asked.

"You think this is a feint, LT?"

"No, but we're going to need as many men as we can on the line, and to do that I'll need to strip other sections of the perimeter."

Ramirez panned out and shook his head. "Nothing, sir. Not for five klicks, at least."

"Good. Duke, when the drones arrive, do your thing. We'll be the noisy ones killing the Maltaani."

"Stay inside the fence and you'll be as safe as a babe in his mother's arms."

Fortis jogged back to the perimeter and called the command mechs.

"This is Fortis. We need another salvo of illumination rounds, same place as last time."

"You got it, sir. Be advised, we've got enough rounds for one more illumination salvo. After that, we're down to flares and Willie Pete."

"Roger that."

Willie Pete was the nickname for the white phosphorus rounds Space Marines commonly used to flush out bug holes and create enormous clouds of choking smoke. Although it was an incendiary weapon, the United Nations of Terra discouraged its use except in emergencies.

"Here they come!" he shouted as he mounted the steps cut into the side of the crater. "Same vector!"

"LT, over here."

Fortis veered toward Ystremski's voice and found the gunny crouched in a fighting hole on the rim of the crater.

"We're going to need as many men as we can get over here," he told Ystremski. In the distance, he heard the command mechs fire. "The Maltaani are attacking in force."

"How many are coming?"

The illumination rounds soared overhead and threw glaring white light over the seething crush of attacking Maltaani.

"All of them."

* * *

"Admiral, the Maltaani are attacking," announced the FOC watch commander.

The mass of heat signatures was advancing again and the rim of the crater began to heat up as the Space Marines engaged.

"How much longer on the drones?" the admiral demanded.

"The hangar crew is loading the first onto the rail at this time."

"Launch the drones as soon as they're ready and alert the FADCs," replied Kinshaw. He despised conditional orders, but when the drones were ready he wanted them launched without the usual delay as the hangar called for authorization. Even a few seconds could make all the difference to the men on the ground.

* * * * *

Chapter Thirty-Six

The Space Marines unleashed a blizzard of fire on the attacking enemy, and scores of their soldiers went down. The Maltaani advanced at a run, firing from the hip as they raced for the crater. Rounds snapped overhead and dug divots in the Space Marine earthworks, but the fire was more distraction than threat.

Reinforcements from the far side of the perimeter filled in the fighting holes around Fortis and Ystremski and the volume of pulse rifle firing doubled. Automatic pulse cannons blasted holes in the Maltaani ranks and Willie Pete rounds from the command mechs sprayed the attackers with white-hot death.

The Maltaani assault halted fifty meters from the crater, and they threw themselves down onto the ground.

"They've had enough!" an excited Space Marine shouted from a nearby hole.

"Incoming!" bellowed Ystremski as he dove for the bottom of his hole and dragged Fortis with him.

Maltaani artillery rounds rained down onto the Space Marine positions. Shrapnel whizzed overhead as dirt and dust covered the defenders. Near misses picked Fortis up and slammed him back down into the hole, and he had a sudden panicked thought that he would be tossed out of the hole and shredded.

Eerie yellow light blanketed the crater as Maltaani illumination rounds drifted high in the sky above and hundreds of rounds pounded the edge of the crater. A five-meter section of the rim collapsed.

A dozen Space Marines survived the tumble to the bottom, only to die when a pair of rounds exploded in their midst.

"As soon as the barrage lifts, they're gonna charge!" screamed Ystremski over the din of the artillery. The gunny's voice was distant and muffled, and it took Fortis a long moment to process what he was saying.

The Maltaani artillery fire died away, and the gunny jumped to his feet, yanking the lieutenant up with him.

"Fire!"

All around them, stunned Space Marines emerged from their hiding places. Many of them stared numbly at the onrushing Maltaani until the first mech rounds exploded among the attackers. By the time the Space Marines recovered and began to fire, the Maltaani were on them.

* * *

"Duke, I have control of Flight Three, standing by for tasking," announced Ramirez.

The FADC leader picked several spots along the perimeter with his stylus and designated them as aim points. "Dump all your HE here," he commanded.

"Can't do it. Aimpoints are too close to the fence."

"That's why they charged!" Without hesitation, Duke entered a series of keystrokes.

"Fence is overridden. Dump your HE there."

Ramirez transmitted the aimpoints to the drones circling overhead and watched as the symbols flew across his screen.

"I hope those guys know how to duck."

* * *

Charging Maltaani overran the Space Marine lines in several places and tumbled into the crater.

A Space Marine used an FGU to hose down some enemy soldiers who crowded toward one of the breaches and the stench of burning flesh swept over the battlefield.

The Maltaani illumination rounds winked out and darkness blanketed the area. Suddenly, a salvo of shells exploded in the midst of the enemy and showered nearby soldiers with burning white phosphorus. Still, the Maltaani pressed their attack and more of them gained the Space Marine perimeter.

BOOM! BOOM! BOOM! BOOM!

Thunderous explosions threw Fortis to the ground and the pressure waves stole his breath and caused his ears to equalize with a painful *pop*. He struggled to his feet and searched for his pulse rifle, but it was nowhere to be found. Dazed soldiers from both sides staggered around in near darkness and the choking cloud of dust and dirt.

Fortis found Ystremski on his hands and knees, hacking and coughing.

"Gunny, are you okay?"

Ystremski nodded as he spat, cleared his throat, and spat again.

"Fuckin' drone jockeys," he managed to gasp.

"Drones? I thought that was artillery."

"Too big. That was HE no more than about forty meters away. Had to be drones."

A screaming Maltaani soldier charged toward the two men and Ystremski shot him dead.

More of the enemy banded together as they recovered from the massive detonations, and Fortis realized there wasn't enough organized resistance to keep them out of the perimeter.

A wall of fire roared skyward as napalm canisters tumbled across the desert and Fortis caught a glimpse of a drone in the fiery light. Scalding heat washed over the Space Marines as the boiling flames consumed hundreds of Maltaani only meters away.

Two soldiers grappled in a horrific hand-to-hand fight even as flames lapped over them. They finally fell together into a smoking lump of burning meat and bile rose in Fortis's throat. Gunny Ystremski finished them off with a burst from his pulse rifle and then dragged the LT away from the flames.

"You might want to start shooting," he growled as he blasted Maltaani soldiers one after another. "There's still a helluva lot of them."

Fortis remembered that he'd lost his rifle and he cast around for another among the dead and dying littering the ground. He found one, cleared the action, and fired at the growing mass of Maltaani threatening to resume their assault. The ground trembled as more HE ordnance exploded among the attackers somewhere behind the wall of fire.

As the napalm flames died down, Fortis saw the sky had begun to lighten as daylight approached. The Maltaani didn't attack; they took whatever cover they could find and kept up a steady rate of fire at the Space Marines regrouping on the rim of the crater. Rockets whooshed skyward in search of the drones, but the sky was empty.

Fortis and Ystremski dove into nearby holes as the Maltaani artillery resumed shelling the Space Marine positions. The fire was scattered and uncoordinated, and some rounds whistled overhead to explode inside the crater while others landed short, among their own troops.

"We gotta check on the lads, LT," shouted Ystremski above the cannonade. "Those fuckers broke through all over the place."

Fortis nodded. "You go that way, I'll go this way. Watch your ass!"

The lieutenant dodged shell bursts and bodies as he scrambled along the rim of the crater by the early morning light. He stopped at every hole and checked on the occupants. Morale was still high, but he saw relief in a lot of faces when the Space Marines saw his rank. He knew they'd fight as long as they knew somebody was in command and there was a reason for the fight.

Fortis came across a pair of wounded Space Marines struggling to get back to their holes, and he helped them find safety with their comrades. A few meters further on, he discovered the rim of the crater had collapsed after several direct hits by Maltaani artillery. Dead Maltaani littered the ground where they had breached the Space Marine perimeter, and when Fortis peered down into the crater, he saw more dead enemy soldiers mixed in with dead Marines.

A massive explosion shook the ground like an earthquake. A shock wave buffeted Fortis a split second before a mountainous cloud of fire erupted behind the Maltaani lines.

Thermobaric weapons!

Two more explosions threw boiling fire skyward and the Maltaani artillery fire suddenly ceased. The ground trembled and shifted as the crater rim collapsed under Fortis's feet, tumbling him downward in an avalanche of dirt and rocks.

* * *

"We've lost contact with the FADCs," announced the FOC watch commander. "They reported a heavy attack and then the circuit went dead."

"What's the status of the drones?" demanded Admiral Kinshaw.

"Flight Two is rearmed and ready for launch, all thermobaric weapons per ground controller request. Flight Three is about to enter the recovery pattern to be refueled and rearmed. I have no status on Flight Four. The FADCs had control when the circuit went out."

"Hmm. Can we control drone attacks from here?"

"In theory, yes sir."

"'In theory?' What the hell does that mean?"

"Some features of the attack drone program are still under technical development and evaluation," interjected Major Anders, who observed the exchange. "Before now, remote commanders haven't had stick and rudder control of autonomous aerial vehicles because of communications lag. Flight plans are loaded pre-flight via umbilical in the hangar, just like the commands we used for the surveillance drones. Once the drone is launched, we have two options: complete the mission as programmed, or abort and recall.

"There is a great deal of resistance to pre-programmed drone strikes, especially in tactical situations. Real-time remote control of tactical drone strikes hasn't been tested outside the laboratory and was one of the program goals on this deployment."

"It's still a theory."

"Yes, sir. There's no reason it won't work in real-world conditions, but right now, it's theoretical."

"This is no time for theories." The admiral swiveled toward the screens above his console. "What's the tactical situation?"

"The Maltaani mounted a major attack during the last two hours of darkness," reported the watch commander. "Based on our IR sensors, they committed all their forces to the attack and breached the Space Marine perimeter in at least three places. The FADCs overrode the no-strike fence and delivered HE, napalm, and thermobaric ordnance within the danger area, causing the attack to stall. It's just now first light, so we'll have better imagery available in a few minutes."

Kinshaw turned back to Anders. "Major, any recommendations?"

"Program Flight Two to conduct strikes in the middle and rear of the Maltaani positions, well away from the crater. Best case scenario, we kill a bunch of Maltaani. Worst case scenario, we bomb the empty desert. Either way, we keep their heads down without hazarding our own men.

"Meanwhile, we rearm Flight Three, try to get control of Flight Four, and reestablish comms with the FADCs or anyone else on the surface."

"Enemy fleet detected! Disposition on Screen One."

The entire FOC went quiet at the sensor supervisor's voice. All eyes went to Screen One, and Anders got a tight feeling in his chest. A hostile fleet symbol had appeared at the far edge of the display, where it remained stationary.

"What are they doing?" demanded the admiral.

"Sir, intel has reassessed the hostile with all-source collecting and they assess it is a single craft, designated Hostile One."

"One vessel?"

"That's what they reported, sir." The hostile fleet symbol winked out and a single hostile symbol appeared.

"Some kind of scout ship, probably," said the FOC watch commander.

"Based on their current course and speed, it appears the craft will enter an orbit directly opposite ours," the sensor operator added.

"What the hell are they doing?"

* * * * *

Chapter Thirty-Seven

G unny Ystremski patrolled his section of the Space Marine perimeter. Considering the ferocity of the Maltaani attack, the situation could have been a lot worse. He found two gaps in the line where enemy soldiers had penetrated the defenses, and the crater below was littered with dead Maltaani.

"A few of them got past us, Gunny, but we wiped them out before they got too far," a private from Third Regiment told him. "They're easy to kill when they're down there."

Ystremski climbed into the crater for a quick look at the damage. A series of heavy explosions caused a small landslide behind him and a big cloud of dust rose above the rim further down the line. He almost tripped over a dead body, and when he looked at it, the gunny saw it was a heavily bandaged Space Marine. A few meters away, another Space Marine lay on his back, bare from the waist up with bloodstained bandages wrapped around his chest. Reddish-gray intestines bulged from a ragged gash across his abdomen and his hands were slashed and bloody.

Ystremski saw there were more dead Space Marines scattered on the crater floor like a macabre breadcrumb trail leading toward the field hospital.

What the hell?

When he came across the first dead Maltaani, he broke into a run. He dodged more Maltaani and human bodies as he got closer.

At the field hospital, Ystremski saw many of the makeshift tents had collapsed and several others smoldered where they'd burst into flames.

"What happened here?" he demanded from the nearest Space Marine.

"Maltaani attacked," the trooper answered. "They came out of nowhere and started killing the wounded, throwing grenades and shit."

"Are they all dead?"

"Yeah, they're dead, but they got a lot of ours first. Fuckin' savages."

Litter bearers pulled the living from the wrecked hospital and lined up the dead. He spotted Liz tending to a wounded Space Marine, and saw her arm was wrapped in a bloody sling.

"Liz, are you okay?"

She shook her head, and he noticed clean streaks on her cheeks where tears had washed away the grime. He reached out to steady her, and she collapsed into his arms.

"We didn't know who they were at first," she sobbed. "They came out of the darkness, and it happened so fast. All those boys…"

Ystremski pushed her away and held her at arm's length.

"Liz, I'm sorry, but I don't have time for this right now."

He left her standing amid the rubble and went in search of Duke and the FADCs. He found two deep shell holes where their tent had been. He recognized a body in the distinctive Fleet coveralls half-buried under a nearby pile of dirt.

"Hey, Gunny."

Ystremski searched for the voice and found Ramirez slumped on the ground with a bloody shirt wrapped around his head. His uniform was scorched and shredded, proof of a near miss by an artillery shell.

"What happened?" asked Ystremski as he knelt by the injured man.

"I tasked Flight Four, then we got shelled," Ramirez wheezed. "Blew us all to hell."

"Let me take a look here," the gunny said. He unzipped Ramirez's coveralls and saw several holes stitched across his chest. When the drone controller inhaled, bloody bubbles appeared as the wounds leaked.

"Goddamn, I hurt," Ramirez moaned.

"Yeah." Ystremski looked around, but he didn't see any corpsmen. "Look, Ramirez, stay here and be still, I'm going to get some help, okay?"

Ramirez didn't answer. The gunny saw his unseeing eyes focused on the sky above.

"Damn it."

Ystremski gently closed the dead man's eyes and stood up. It was now full daylight, and he knew the Maltaani would resume their attack at any time. Fortis needed to know that the Space Marines had lost their drone support. He turned to go in search of the lieutenant and saw Controller First Class Prater standing nearby with a portable computer clutched to his chest.

"Prater, are you okay?"

The FADC team member nodded and gestured toward Ramirez. "Is he dead?"

"Yeah. Sorry."

"Duke's over there," Prater said and pointed to the half-buried body. "I don't know where Ngo is."

"Why don't you let me help you to the field hospital?"

"Nah, that's no good. I just came from there."

"Hmm. Me, too. Look, I gotta go tell the LT that we don't have drone support. I don't suppose you saw him around, did you?"

Prater stared at the gunny, puzzled. "What do you mean, no drones?" He held up the computer. "I can't control them, but if I can get a signal, I can talk to *Atlas*. They can control them."

* * *

Lieutenant Fortis landed in the bottom of the crater and was promptly buried under a huge pile of dirt and rocks. He struggled to extricate himself, but it took him a long second to realize he was upside down. He could kick his legs, but his torso was stuck fast. The harder he struggled, the tighter the dirt squeezed him, and he had to fight to draw a breath.

Hands grabbed his legs and pulled. Fortis screamed as the pressure on his chest threatened to crack his ribs.

"Hang on, buddy," a muffled voice shouted. Fortis heard the sounds of frantic digging and the pressure eased. It wasn't long before his rescuers again pulled on his legs and dragged him free.

Fortis ended up on his hands and knees as he retched and coughed up the dirt that filled his nose and mouth. Someone pressed a hydration pack into his hands and he sat back and rinsed out his mouth.

"Damn, LT, we thought you were stuck for good," one of the Space Marines gathered around him said.

The lieutenant nodded weakly and squirted more water across his face. "Me, too," he croaked.

For some reason they all thought this was funny and the group broke into laughter.

"The gunny was just up on the rim looking for you, sir. Said something about the drones."

"Shit." Fortis groaned as they helped him to his feet. "Where is he?"

"Hey, Gunny! Gunny!"

Ystremski appeared on the crater rim and the Space Marines waved at him.

"We found the lieutenant."

Ystremski scrambled down and joined Fortis on the crater floor.

"You okay, LT?"

"Yeah, I'm okay. Doing a little landscaping."

"While you've been playing in the dirt, I've been assessing our situation."

Ystremski briefed Fortis on everything he'd learned. When he finished, he gestured at the collapsed crater wall. "And now this. I don't know if we can dig new holes in this. I just climbed down through it, and it's as soft as a sand dune."

Fortis hawked and spat the last of the dirt from his mouth. "Do we have comms with the flagship?"

"That weird little guy, the funny one?"

"Prater?"

"Yeah, that's his name. He was pounding away on his keyboard when I left him. Updating the Fleet, he said."

"That's it then."

"What's what?"

"Our plan. If the Maltaani want this God forsaken hole so badly, let's give it to them."

* * *

"They want to do *what?*"

Major Anders stifled a laugh at the admiral's reaction to the latest message from the Space Marines. It was an audacious plan, even absurd, but the long odds against them only grew longer as time went on.

"They want to lure the Maltaani down into the crater and use it as the aimpoint for drone strikes," repeated the FOC watch commander. "The crater rim has collapsed and made their position untenable."

"How are they going to control the strikes? They reported their control terminals were destroyed."

"If we coordinate a time on top, we can pre-program the strikes before launch, sir."

Admiral Kinshaw stood up and started to pace in front of the FOC.

"And if they can't get clear of the crater in time?"

"Abort and recall. We have until just before weapon release plus a little time for comms delays. Thirty seconds, maybe."

"There's no room for error."

Anders spoke up, "Admiral, we'll have two flights of drones available very soon. Flight Two is ready to launch and the hangar crew is refueling Three right now. If we launch Two and Three with, say, ten minutes between attack times and Two is aborted, we'll still have Three. It's not much, but it's better than nothing."

"Do we have an estimate of remaining Maltaani troop strength?"

The watch commander tapped her keyboard and a data table appeared on Screen Three.

"Based on early imagery from this morning, about five thousand," she said. "All infantry."

"Still so many. What about our guys?"

"Six hundred, give or take. They also have three main battle mechs and two command mechs, all of which are low on fuel and ammo."

"Any update on the drones of Flight Four?"

"No contact since we lost comms with the FADCs, sir. Missing, presumed lost."

"Call the Space Marines and let them know what we can do to help. If they want to abandon the only defensible piece of real estate on this whole damn planet, that's on them."

* * *

"That's no good," said Fortis when Prater read him the reply. "Tell them to launch a flight now and drop everything they have between us and the Maltaani as soon as possible. We need to keep them from attacking before we're ready. If they see us pull back, they'll attack right away. In the meantime, we'll evacuate the field hospital to the far side of the crater and get the mechs moved into position."

Space Marines scattered to carry out Fortis's orders while he and Ystremski watched.

The plan was simple. Once the Maltaani recovered from the latest drone strike, Fortis expected they would throw everything they had into another attack to get as close to the Space Marine positions as possible to avoid further strikes.

The main battle mechs would use the last of their ammunition to funnel the attack toward the undefended section of the crater rim that had collapsed. When their ammunition was exhausted or the

Maltaani got too close, the crews would bail out the escape hatches and race for safety.

Half of the infantry would be deployed in the holes behind the mechs to help push the Maltaani attack into the gap. They would hold as long as possible and then withdraw with the mech crews. The other half of the infantry would occupy firing positions inside the crater itself, reinforced by the rapid fire of the command mechs' automatic pulse cannons. Their job was to delay the Maltaani assault long enough for the first wave of defenders to leapfrog them and take positions along the far side of the rim. At that point, they would withdraw and climb the crater wall to join their comrades and pour fire down on the Maltaani until the drones delivered the coup de grace in forty-two minutes.

"You think this will work, LT?"

Fortis nodded. "Yeah, I think so. It's going to take some timing and some luck, but it has to work. The mathematics of this battle have favored the Maltaani since we got here, but it's taken them this long to figure that out. The last attack tells me they know we're outnumbered and we're one perimeter breach from being wiped out. If we continue to defend this hole, we all die here. If this plan doesn't work, we all die here, but we'll die trying."

"DINLI."

"Indeed."

* * * * *

Chapter Thirty-Eight

Twenty-five minutes later, the ground trembled as the drones delivered full loads of thermobaric weapons on the Maltaani. When the strikes began, the Space Marines jumped into action to execute Fortis's plan. A team of litter bearers hustled to move the wounded from the destroyed field hospital to the far side of the crater and up the steps cut into the rocky soil. Meanwhile, the main battle mechs moved into flanking positions above the rim between the Maltaani and Space Marines, while the command mechs took up station inside the crater.

When the smoke cleared, the main battle mechs opened up on the distant Maltaani forces. At first, there was no reaction, but as the Space Marines watched, the enemy surged forward. The infantry engaged at maximum pulse rifle range, and the attackers unconsciously shifted toward the gap in the lines.

From his position above the crater, Lieutenant Fortis could hear the tinny wail of the bugle urging the Maltaani forward. He nervously checked his watch as the main battle mechs fell silent and the crewmen climbed out the escape hatches to scramble for the rear.

Fifteen minutes.

Maltaani fire snapped overhead and dug furrows in the dirt, but they fired from the hip as they ran forward, so few rounds found their mark. The volume of fire from the Space Marines increased as the Maltaani approached, but it wasn't enough to blunt the attack.

The incoming fire became more accurate as the range decreased and wounded Marines began to leak back from the line.

Thirteen minutes.

"We've got to slow them down," Fortis told Ystremski. "If they get through now, they'll be out the other side before the drones get here."

Twin plumes of fire whooshed out and sprayed flaming death at the Maltaani on the right flank as two Space Marines with FGUs stood fast in their holes. The attackers shied away and steered for the gap in the lines. The combatants were only a few meters apart when the defenders abandoned their positions and threw themselves back down the sides of the crater.

As soon as the last of the Space Marines reached the bottom of the crater, the command mechs opened up on the Maltaani that appeared along the crater's rim. Scores of dead and wounded soldiers tumbled into the crater, and for a brief moment Fortis worried that they would veer around the crater instead of attacking straight through. The front ranks tried to pull up and fire down on the Space Marines, but the momentum of the troops behind them was unstoppable.

The Space Marines positioned throughout the crater poured pulse rifle fire into the Maltaani before they had a chance to reorganize their attack. Enemy soldiers atop the crater rim sniped at the Space Marines below. A Space Marine wearing an FGU jumped up to fall back from his position near the abandoned field hospital, but his backpack detonated in a fireball that consumed him and several other nearby Marines. Oily black smoke poured into the sky as the wreckage caught fire and quickly spread to the stack of body bags the Space Marines had been forced to leave behind.

Nine minutes.

The Space Marine withdrawal started to become a rout as the volume of incoming fire increased. The command mechs fell silent as they ran out of ammo, and the crews scrambled clear. Knots of Space Marines formed up and fought back, but the tide of battle ran too hard against them, and they fell under the Maltaani guns.

Wounded Marines crawled up the steps cut into the crater wall and staggered up the ramp O'Brien and his men had dug for the tankers while their comrades blasted and reloaded as fast as they could. The Maltaani advance slowed to a crawl as the surviving Space Marines gained the cover atop the crater and fired down on the exposed enemy.

"How much longer?" shouted Ystremski as he sighted and fired at the massed enemy soldiers.

"Four minutes!"

"Fuck!" Ystremski yanked a magazine from his pulse rifle and slammed another one home. "We're not gonna make it!" He squeezed off a short burst and several Maltaani went down.

"Three minutes, LT," shouted Prater. "The point of no return. Abort the mission?"

"Negative! Do not abort!"

"Look!"

A wounded Space Marine stumbled across the crater floor ten meters ahead of charging Maltaani. Blood streamed from a wound on his scalp, and his LBA was scorched and bloodied from where Maltaani gunners had found their marks. Fear and pain were etched on his face as he fought to stay ahead of his pursuers. He locked eyes with Fortis just before he stumbled and fell flat.

Fortis yanked a smoke grenade from his bandolier, pulled the pin, and threw it as far as he could. A dense purple haze billowed around the fallen Space Marine. Several other Space Marines followed his lead, and soon the entire end of the crater was obscured by thick, choking smoke.

The lieutenant jumped up and scrambled down the dirt steps into the crater.

"Where are you going?" screamed Ystremski as Fortis disappeared into the smoke, but he didn't stop to answer.

Fortis crouched low and ran for the spot where the wounded Space Marine had been lurching along when the smoke closed over him. He groped around in the heavy smoke until he found the injured man crawling along with wounds in both legs.

"C'mon buddy, let's go," Fortis said as he knelt by the fallen Marine and got him ready for a fireman's carry. He stumbled to his feet and started for the steps as Maltaani rounds snapped overhead and punched holes in the ground around him. The smokescreen began to thin as Fortis mounted the crater wall, and it took everything he had to climb all the way to the rim.

Several Space Marines greeted him at the top and took the wounded man from his shoulders.

"Stupid kid," Gunny Ystremski admonished. "What the hell was that?"

Before Fortis could answer, a giant fist punched him behind his right knee. He screamed in pain, his leg flew out from under him, and he tumbled backward into the crater.

* * *

"One minute until Flight Two is on top, Admiral," announced the FOC watch commander.

All eyes were glued to Screen Two where the near real-time tactical picture was displayed.

"It looks like their plan is working," said Anders.

Admiral Kinshaw grunted his agreement. "What's the status of Flight Three?"

"Flight Three is en route, estimated time on top eleven minutes."

"It's too late to abort, sir. I hope they're all clear of the crater."

* * *

Ystremski watched in horror as Fortis fell into the crater. He instantly jumped down the steps after him and landed next to the unconscious officer. Space Marines shouted warnings from above, but their voices were white noise compared to his instinct to save the lieutenant.

Blood spurted from the mangled mess where the Maltaani round had struck Fortis's right calf and Ystremski scrambled for his first aid kit. He tore away the damaged armor, wrapped his tourniquet just under Fortis's knee, and the blood stopped gushing from the wound. The gunny heaved the lieutenant onto his shoulder and started for the steps when shadows flashed by overhead. The drones.

"Holy shit!"

He dumped Fortis into the nearest depression and threw himself on top. The gunny looked up in time to see a Space Marine jump down in front of a trio of Maltaani soldiers two meters away and fire his weapon. The Maltaani disappeared in a blinding salvo of bluish-white pulse rifle bolts.

The world exploded.

* * *

The FOC watch cheered as the crater erupted in thunderous flames, and even Admiral Kinshaw raised his hands in triumph. The drone strike had been perfectly timed, and the bulk of the Maltaani army had been in the crater when the drone flight delivered its deadly payload.

"Silence!" ordered Kinshaw after a moment of celebration. "I need a bomb damage assessment ASAP. How much time until Flight Three is on top?"

"Six minutes, sir."

"Then I have five minutes to decide whether the follow-on strike is necessary. Do we still have comms with the FADCs?"

"Stand by, sir, let me try." After a long second, the watch commander spoke up. "Yes, sir, I've got good comms with the FADC."

"What's their status? Can he see what's happening in the crater?"

The watch commander relayed the admiral's demands and then listened intently. She scowled at the response.

"Negative on the BDA right now, sir."

"Are they still under attack?"

"No, sir."

"Instruct them to stay clear of the crater in case a follow-on strike is necessary."

* * *

Fortis didn't know where he was when he came to. His right leg throbbed with pain, his ears rang, and he could hardly move. When he heaved up at the pile of debris that covered him, it groaned, and Fortis realized it was a man. His memories flooded back.

Ystremski!

The lieutenant pushed and wriggled with all his strength and managed to worm his way out from underneath the gunnery sergeant. Ystremski came to as Fortis wriggled free and rolled over with a gravelly sigh.

"Medic!" croaked Fortis. He coughed up the dirt and dust that filled his mouth. "We need a medic!"

Fortis forgot the pain in his leg as he checked Ystremski for injuries. The back of his LBA was blackened and there were several holes across his buttocks and upper legs, but none of them were actively bleeding. He held Ystremski's head in his lap and looked around in desperation.

"Medic!"

Space Marines jumped down beside them and Fortis recognized them as litter bearers from the field hospital.

"Here, take care of Gunny Ystremski."

"We got him, LT," one of them said and Fortis relinquished his hold on the injured man. They lifted Ystremski onto a litter and scrambled up the steps.

"C'mon sir, let's get you out of here."

A white-hot lance of pain shot into Fortis's brain when the medic bumped his leg and he screamed in agony.

"Ah, shit. I'm sorry." The medic gestured up at the rim of the crater. "We need another litter!"

Fortis hovered on the edge of unconsciousness during the long climb up the crater wall. Every bump was fresh torment, and he chewed his lip bloody as he tried to stifle his cries. Finally, the litter bearers reached the top and deposited Fortis next to Ystremski, who was very much awake and arguing with Liz and Pops.

"I'm all right," he insisted while he struggled to get up from his litter.

"Sergeant, I'm afraid you are very much *not* all right," replied Pops as he held the wounded NCO down. "You have several shrapnel wounds across your back and parts of your LBA have fused to your skin."

"I feel fine, Pops. It doesn't hurt at all."

"The fire burned the nerve endings away. When your body begins to heal, you will most certainly feel pain. For now, we have to treat your wounds and prevent you from going into shock. Now, lie still. That's an order."

Pops turned his attention to Fortis.

"Lieutenant, what brings you here?"

"My leg hurts," Fortis replied. He propped himself up and looked around. "Did we win?"

"Ach, don't worry about such things." Pops examined his leg. "Hmm. Who put this tourniquet on?"

"I did," said Ystremski. "Right before the drone strike."

"Good."

Fortis allowed himself to fall into unconsciousness.

* * *

"Abort Flight Three!"

Kinshaw's order boomed across the FOC and the watch commander scrambled to obey. On Screen Two they could see the crater was a hellscape of bodies and wreckage scoured by thermobaric fire. The Space Marines were deployed in a loose perimeter on one end, and individual Maltaani survivors wandering away from the battlefield at the other.

"Separation detected from Hostile One," announced the sensor supervisor. "Trajectory estimates show payload impact on the surface in seventeen minutes."

"Visual please," ordered Kinshaw. Screen One switched from the tactical display to a grainy, long-range image captured by one of the intel satellites.

"That doesn't look like a weapon," said Anders. "It's a vessel of some kind, like a dropship."

"Reinforcements?"

"Unlikely, in my estimation. One drop ship can't carry enough reinforcements to make a difference unless they've got a nuke, and even nukes can't change what's happened here."

They lost sight of the drop ship as it penetrated the upper atmosphere and regained it in time to see it set down several kilometers away from the crater. The Maltaani troops hurried toward the craft.

"They're retreating."

The enormity of the admiral's words hung heavy over the FOC, and the elation from the drone strike was replaced by smiles and muted congratulations.

When the last of the Maltaani boarded the dropship, it blasted off in a cloud of dust. The intel satellites tracked it back into orbit.

"Admiral, do you want to engage?" asked the watch commander. "It's well within range."

Admiral Kinshaw stared at the display for a long second before he let out a long sigh.

"No. Do not engage. Let them go." He rubbed his face with both hands. "We won."

* * * * *

Chapter Thirty-Nine

Two days later, Lieutenant Fortis woke to see Liz Sherer napping in a chair next to his bed in the medical ward aboard *Atlas*. He grunted as he reached for a glass of water on the bedside table, and her eyes snapped open.

"Abner, here, let me get that."

She put the glass in his hands, and he sucked greedily on the straw until the water was gone. He ached all over, and his leg throbbed, but the water was a magical elixir that flooded into his body, and he instantly felt better.

"Do you want some more?"

"Ah, no, Liz, that was fantastic, thank you." He looked around the room. "How long have I been here? How long have you been here?"

"You've been here for two days. I've only been here a few hours."

"Huh. Don't you have a story to write?"

She nodded. "I do, but I don't know how to write it."

"What do you mean?"

"I don't know what to say. Over the last week, I've witnessed humans at their best and their worst. I saw Space Marines sacrifice themselves for their comrades without hesitation, and I watched them butcher the Maltaani with glee."

Fortis shrugged. "It's war. DINLI."

"How do I capture that? How can I make it believable to people who have never been there? Who would understand?"

Liz took a deep breath, and Fortis realized she was on the verge of tears. He felt his own eyes well up.

"Tell them the truth, Liz. Tell them about Parrello, and Carrasco, and the Jimmies. They need to hear about how the Maltaani treat their prisoners, too. The public needs to know what we fought and died for."

The door slid open, and an orderly entered with a gurney carrying Gunny Ystremski lying on his stomach.

"Hey, LT. Hiya, Liz. I'm not interrupting anything, am I?"

The orderly wheeled the gurney next to Fortis and Ystremski gave him a thumbs up.

"Thanks, pal. I appreciate the lift." He looked at Fortis. "Major Anders here yet?"

"Anders? Why would he be here?"

The door slid open again, and Admiral Kinshaw and Major Anders entered the room.

"Good, you're all here. It's time we talk about the Battle of Balfan-48," the admiral said.

Liz stood up. "I'll leave you military types to your meeting."

Kinshaw waved her back down into her chair. "Please stay, Ms. Sherer. You're a part of this, too."

The puzzled reporter sat down while Fortis and Ystremski traded glances.

"Thanks to the round-the-clock efforts of Major Anders and his intel team, we have recovered a great deal of Maltaani technology, including some very interesting bits of what appears to be a jamming station that was destroyed in the fighting. And, of course, we have a live prisoner to analyze, thanks to you."

"Fuck You Too," mumbled Ystremski.

Kinshaw smiled. "That's the one. Anyway, our mission here is complete. We'll begin the transit back to Terra Earth in fifteen hours. Then the real Battle of Balfan-48 will begin."

"Begging your pardon, Admiral, but the battle is over. We won, remember?" Ystremski pointed to the bandages that swathed his buttocks. "I have proof."

The admiral's tone unsettled Fortis, but he remained silent. His unease didn't go unnoticed by Kinshaw or Anders.

"The Battle of Balfan-48 isn't finished, Gunny. The shooting is over, but the real fight had just begun."

"I don't understand, sir."

The admiral gave a wry smile. "Now the battle turns to a matter of accountability. The ISMC just lost an entire division of Marines and three companies of mechs. Five thousand casualties. The public are going to want some answers. They'll want someone to blame."

Fortis thought for a second. "Blame the Maltaani, sir. They were the ones who shot at us."

"Ha! If it was only that easy. Unfortunately, it isn't."

Anders interjected. "The entire operation was an intelligence balls-up from the very beginning. The Maltaani were there the whole time. They spoofed our reconnaissance probes and jammed our communications, and we detected nothing. General Gupta landed his entire division in the middle of an enemy force estimated at twenty-five thousand and we didn't know they were there until it was too late."

The blood drained from Abner's face, and he felt faint.

Twenty-five thousand?

"The blame for a failure of that magnitude needs a place to land, Lieutenant."

Fortis thought for a second. "General Gupta."

Kinshaw nodded. "Where better than the shoulders of a man who can't defend himself? I can see the story now: In a moment of hubris, he led his division to slaughter."

"You just said it was an intelligence failure!"

"And it was." Admiral Kinshaw waved his hand toward Liz. "None of that will be released to the public. The information is classified, and the keepers of those secrets will keep it hidden for a long time. Someday, a graduate student at the International Defense Institute might do a deep-dive reconstruction project and uncover the truth. Meanwhile, the good name of an honorable man will be tarnished."

The unsettled feeling in Fortis's stomach turned to sour nausea and then bitter anger. "That's not fair, Admiral."

Kinshaw scoffed and traded a knowing look with Anders. "Fair? Life's not fair, son. Believe it or not, our mission out here isn't popular with everyone back home. There are some who would like nothing better than to see us fall on our asses. The ultimate responsibility rests with the person in command."

"I'm with Abner, Admiral. It's not fair that this all fall on General Gupta. What can we do?" Liz sat forward on the edge of her seat.

"That's what this meeting is about, Ms. Sherer. What *can* we do?"

"The general's decision was right!" Fortis blurted. "We *had* to engage the Maltaani, outnumbered or not."

The admiral stopped and stared at him for a long moment. "Say that again."

"The general made the right decision. Even if he made it for the wrong reasons."

"Explain yourself, Lieutenant."

"We were sent here to counter a Maltaani move in this sector. Our mission on Balfan-48 was to prevent the Maltaani from establishing a base of operations there."

Kinshaw nodded.

"Where are the Maltaani now, Admiral?"

Kinshaw shrugged. "They fucked off back through the gate, back to whatever slice of hell they came from."

"That's the point, sir. We won. We forced them to retreat. General Gupta forced them to retreat. Mission accomplished."

The admiral stroked his chin thoughtfully. "Go on."

"If General Gupta and his staff had known the Maltaani were there in force, do you think he would have ordered the landing?"

"Of course not."

"Which means we'd still be flying around in circles, working out a way to come to grips with a force that size, while the Maltaani established their base and improved their defenses."

"Hmm."

"General Gupta didn't lead us to slaughter, sir. He didn't act out of hubris. He evaluated the strategic situation and made the difficult decision to strike at the enemy, even if he had to sacrifice himself and the entire division. It took everything we had, but Ninth Division prevailed, with some timely and critical assistance from the Fleet. The Maltaani were forced to withdraw from this sector. He paid with his life for that decision, but General Gupta isn't a scapegoat. He's a hero."

Kinshaw stared at Fortis, and the lieutenant could almost hear the wheels turning.

"Admiral, we lost too many good Marines to chalk this whole thing up as a failure. When it was over, the enemy was in retreat and we held the field. By any historical measure, that's not a failure, that's a victory."

"Some would say a Pyrrhic victory."

"It was costly, but what choice did we have? If we had waited, the Maltaani would have a forward operating base within a few days of a jump gate to Terra Earth. We took on a larger Maltaani force and kicked their asses, and General Gupta led us."

Anders spoke up. "From an intelligence standpoint, Balfan-48 was a great victory. We began with little knowledge of the Maltaani, their technology, and their capabilities. We've seen their tactics up close, and we now have extensive insights that we can use to counter them."

Admiral Kinshaw rubbed his hands together. "You might be on to something here. If we seize the initiative and get ahead of the story, we can spin this any way we want."

"It's not spin, Admiral," Liz replied. "It's the truth. I was there. I saw too many good Space Marines killed to believe they died because of a mistake or an intelligence balls-up...or whatever." Her voice caught in her throat and dropped to a whisper. "They deserve better."

"Ms. Sherer, you're an important part of this effort. I can control the official story and the reports submitted to Fleet and the ISMC, but you have complete freedom to report whatever you like, including what we've discussed in this meeting here. Fleet regulations are quite specific in that regard."

"Admiral, ten days ago I would have jumped at the chance to report on a rash decision by a general that led to a military disaster. Now, I just want to tell the story about a lot of brave Space Marines who fought with skill and ferocity against overwhelming odds. *That's a story worth telling.*"

Admiral Kinshaw nodded in agreement. "Ms. Sherer, I can't tell you how gratified I am to hear you say that." He cleared his throat. "Now that we've got that out of the way, does anyone have anything to add? Gunny?"

Ystremski shook his head. "Not me, sir."

"Lieutenant Fortis?"

"No, sir."

"What the hell does 'Send fresh fruit and ammo' mean? We got your message but never figured out what it meant."

Fortis and Ystremski exchanged glances and started to laugh. "After the Maltaani nuked our supplies we only had pig squares and lima beans," Fortis began.

"You can't brew DINLI with pig squares, so we used lima beans." added Ystremski. "It has a distinctive flavor."

"It's awful," finished Liz.

Admiral Kinshaw groaned and wrinkled his nose. "Lima beans? Sheesh."

"That's why we needed the fruit, sir."

Kinshaw chuckled. "Fucking Space Marines are crazy." Kinshaw looked at Anders. "Major, anything to add?"

"A couple things, sir." Anders dug into his pocket. "Lieutenant, the medical staff told me you were wearing this when you came in." He held up the ragged Maltaani dog fang and claw necklace. "I have no idea what this is, but I'm sure there's one hell of a story behind it."

"Yes sir, it's all in—my notebook! Damnit, it was in my LBA."

"Your notebook is safe in my office. With your permission, I'd like to use it to reconstruct the battle."

Relief washed over Fortis. "That's why I keep it, sir. Be my guest."

"Then that's all I have, Admiral."

"Okay, now that we have all the formalities out of the way...Gunny Ystremski, I have forwarded my strongest personal recommendation to ISMC Personnel Command that your battlefield promotion to gunnery sergeant be made permanent. I don't have a lot of pull with those folks, but I did what I could. As for you, Mr. Fortis, as of today, you are a first lieutenant, ISMC. Congratulations."

Everyone beamed and Ystremski laughed aloud. "Third time's the charm, I guess."

Kinshaw nodded. "If there's nothing else, I've got a Fleet to get back to Terra Earth. Thanks for your time."

The door whooshed open, and the admiral strode out, followed by Major Anders. Liz stood up and rolled her head on her neck.

"That's my cue, boys. God, I need a shower and a nap. I'll come by and see you later."

When she was gone, Fortis and Ystremski traded smiles and then Fortis got a serious look on his face.

"Thank you for saving my life back there," he told Ystremski. "I would be dead if you hadn't thrown yourself on top of me."

"We'd both be dead if it wasn't for Lance Corporal Conrad."

"Who?"

"Conrad. When I was lugging you up the steps, there were some Maltaani up our ass. Conrad jumped down and blasted them right before the drone strike smoked the crater."

"I'll have to look him up. What company is he in?"

"He's in the best company a Space Marine could ask for."

It took Fortis a second to understand what Ystremski told him. "Damn."

"He was the last casualty from the Battle of Balfan-48. DINLI."

"DINLI, indeed."

# # # # #

About P.A. Piatt

P.A. Piatt was born and raised in western Pennsylvania. After his first attempt at college, he joined the Navy to see the world. He started writing as a hobby when he retired in 2005 and published his first novel in 2018.

His published works include the Abner Fortis, International Space Marine Corps mil-sf series, the Walter Bailey Misadventures urban fantasy trilogy, and other full-length novels in both science fiction and horror.

All of his novels and various published short stories can be found on Amazon. Visit his website at www.papiattauthor.com.

* * * * *

For More Information:

Meet the authors of CKP on the Factory Floor:

https://www.facebook.com/groups/461794864654198

* * * * *

Get the free Four Horsemen prelude story "Shattered Crucible"

and discover other titles by Theogony Books at:

http://chriskennedypublishing.com/

* * * * *

Did you like this book?
Please write a review!

* * * * *

The following is an

Excerpt from Book One of the Lunar Free State:

The Moon and Beyond

John E. Siers

Available from Theogony Books

eBook and Paperback

Excerpt from "The Moon and Beyond:"

"So, what have we got?" The chief had no patience for inter-agency squabbles.

The FBI man turned to him with a scowl. "We've got some abandoned buildings, a lot of abandoned stuff—none of which has anything to do with spaceships—and about a hundred and sixty scientists, maintenance people, and dependents left behind, all of whom claim they knew nothing at all about what was really going on until today. Oh, yeah, and we have some stripped computer hardware with all memory and processor sections removed. I mean physically taken out, not a chip left, nothing for the techies to work with. And not a scrap of paper around that will give us any more information…at least, not that we've found so far. My people are still looking."

"What about that underground complex on the other side of the hill?"

"That place is wiped out. It looks like somebody set off a *nuke* in there. The concrete walls are partly fused! The floor is still too hot to walk on. Our people say they aren't sure how you could even *do* something like that. They're working on it, but I doubt they're going to find anything."

"What about our man inside, the guy who set up the computer tap?"

"Not a trace, chief," one of the NSA men said. "Either he managed to keep his cover and stayed with them, or they're holding him prisoner, or else…" The agent shrugged.

"You think they terminated him?" The chief lifted an eyebrow. "A bunch of rocket scientists?"

"Wouldn't put it past them. Look at what Homeland Security ran into. Those motion-sensing chain guns are *nasty*, and the area between the inner and outer perimeter fence is mined! Of course, they posted warning signs, even marked the fire zones for the guns. Nobody would have gotten hurt if the troops had taken the signs seriously."

The Homeland Security colonel favored the NSA man with an icy look. "That's bullshit. How did we know they weren't bluffing? You'd feel pretty stupid if we'd played it safe and then found out there were no defenses, just a bunch of signs!"

"Forget it!" snarled the chief. "Their whole purpose was to delay us, and it worked. What about the Air Force?"

"It might as well have been a UFO sighting as far as they're concerned. Two of their F-25s went after that spaceship, or whatever it was we saw leaving. The damned thing went straight up, over eighty thousand meters per minute, they say. That's nearly Mach Two, in a *vertical climb*. No aircraft in *anybody's* arsenal can sustain a climb like that. Thirty seconds after they picked it up, it was well above their service ceiling and still accelerating. Ordinary ground radar couldn't find it, but NORAD *thinks* they might have caught a short glimpse with one of their satellite-watch systems, a hundred miles up and still going."

"So where did they go?"

"Well, chief, if we believe what those leftover scientists are telling us, I guess they went to the Moon."

* * * * *

Get "The Moon and Beyond" here:
https://www.amazon.com/dp/B097QMN7PJ.

Find out more about John E. Siers at:
https://chriskennedypublishing.com.

* * * * *

The following is an

Excerpt from Book One of Murphy's Lawless:

Shakes

Mike Massa

Available from Beyond Terra Press

eBook and Paperback

Excerpt from "Shakes:"

"My name is Volo of the House Zobulakos," the SpinDog announced haughtily. Harry watched as his slender ally found his feet and made a show of brushing imaginary dust from his shoulder where the lance had rested.

Volo was defiant even in the face of drawn weapons; Harry had to give him points for style.

"I am here representing the esteemed friend to all Sarmatchani, my father, Arko Primus Heraklis Zobulakos. This is a mission of great importance. What honorless prole names my brother a liar and interferes with the will of the Primus? Tell me, that I might inform your chief of this insolence."

Harry tensed as two of the newcomers surged forward in angry reaction to the word "honorless," but the tall man interposed his lance, barring their way.

"Father!" the shorter one objected, throwing back her hood, revealing a sharp featured young woman. She'd drawn her blade and balefully eyed the SpinDog. "Let me teach this arrogant weakling about honor!"

"Nay, Stella," the broad-shouldered man said grimly. "Even my daughter must cleave to the law. This is a clan matter. And as to the stripling's question...

"I, hight Yannis al-Caoimhip ex-huscarlo, Patrisero of the Herdbane, First among the Sarmatchani," he went on, fixing his eyes first on Volo and then each of the Terrans. "I name Stabilo of the Sky People a liar, a cheat, and a coward. I call his people to account. Blood or treasure. At dawn tomorrow either will suffice."

Harry didn't say a word but heard a deep sigh from Rodriguez. These were the allies he'd been sent to find, all right. Just like every other joint operation with indigs, it was SNAFU.

Murphy's Law was in still in effect.

* * * * *

Get "Shakes" now at: https://www.amazon.com/dp/B0861F23KH

Find out more about Myrphy's Lawless and Beyond Terra Press at: https://chriskennedypublishing.com/imprints-authors/beyond-terra-press/

* * * * *

Made in the USA
Monee, IL
07 January 2022

88158310R00184